THE TAURUS GUN

CHAPTER 1

How to Be Both Wrong and Right

ABOUT a month ago the army, in regimental strength, had filled Buckhorn's wide, dusty roadway as the last ragged, gaunt, and demoralized band of holdouts was herded like cattle the full length of Main Street to the loading chute at the railroad pen. While the engine puffed billows of white smoke, the Indians were loaded into cattle cars, which were then locked from the outside. The military band struck up "Goodbye Forever," the whistle let go a blast, and the train gathered momentum as it cleared town, heading east.

Prior to that time, cattlemen had been prevented by the Indians from expanding into the ryegrass country below the mountains, which was an area of considerable width and even greater east-to-west length. White men who tried to run cattle there had been shot out of their saddles for their attempts, and no amount of angry aggression by stockmen, vigilantes from Buckhorn, or even the sweeps in strength by soldier detachments had succeeded in dislodging the holdouts, who simply disappeared back into the dark timber and brushy canyons that went northward for more than two hundred miles.

Now the Indian wars were over. Toward the end, the Indians were trading ten to one in casualties. Finally, they could no longer afford to trade even one dead buck for ten of the enemy, because ten more whites appeared overnight;

whereas one dead Indian meant one less gun and there were no replacements.

The capitulation had come, as the cattlemen had known it would have to, when the last band of holdouts straggled out into the foothills with an old man riding a starved-looking horse. The old man rode with a white cloth bound to a broken lance.

Rancher Henry Burke had been with his riders, pushing cattle away from the foothills when he saw the ragged procession. He withdrew from gun range and sat his horse, chewing tobacco and watching. His range boss, Joe Holden, sat beside him, not as old as Burke, but just as weathered and wrinkled. Joe spat amber and said, "Well now, what do you know. No warning. No one sent ahead to palaver, just come out carryin' a white rag."

Burke did not reply until the last of the band had cleared the timber, then he turned and said, "Joe, ride to town. Tell the marshal. He'd better send for the soldiers. An' tell him not to breathe a word of this or for chrissake, every man in Buckhorn who owns a gun is goin' to come chargin' out here and we'll be buryin' dead In'ians until next winter."

Joe did not move. He sat chewing, watching the forlorn procession, and finally said, "Mr. Burke, maybe I'd better stay. You can't trust them. It may be one of their tricks. They seen us by now, sure as hell. There's broncos among them, carryin' rifles."

Burke turned irritably. "Joe, do like I said. Ride to town and get the marshal out here quick. And he's not to say a damned word to anyone. Now get!"

The rest was history. Although the army did not arrive until the Indians were two-thirds of the way to Buckhorn, Burke and his riders had placed themselves out front to watch for armed men. None appeared, not even after the horse soldiers arrived and took over from Burke's crew.

It was, according to a number of diehards at Buster Munzer's Antler Saloon, a hell of a climax. The army fetching them in and establishing a cordon around them, which was never lifted until the day the Indians were herded down to be loaded into the cattle cars and hauled off, probably to Indian Territory. No one in town was sure where they'd be taken, and no one actually cared.

Finally, the land was free of snipers, and horse thieves. That memorable day when the train had headed east, there was a celebration in Buckhorn that had probably never been equalled in the entire territory. There was not a single person who denounced the way the Indians had been driven the full length of Main Street, north to south, with both sides of the roadway lined with people three-deep, as silent as stones, and bitterly pleased at the final degradation of old Tenkiller's band.

There was abundant justification for the bitterness. The Marvin Massacre had occurred on the exact site where the town of Buckhorn now stood, and during the bloody, violent years between the massacre and the day of the great celebration, every permanent resident of the town had lost either kinsmen or friends to Indian marauders.

Perhaps as many as half the population of Buckhorn had not been in the territory at the time of the massacre, but the details of that affair were known to everyone. A man named Marvin had established a way station for travelers, hunters, trappers, freighters and detachments of soldiers sent out to survey the country. When the Sioux struck there had been, at least, according to the body count, forty-three people at the station. The war party had killed everyone: men, women, and children. Even dogs and pigs and cattle. They had not killed the horses. The Sioux had remained at the site for six days, waiting for more people to arrive. When none did, the Indians burned the buildings to the ground, rounded up the horses, and sped away, back up through the mountains. By the time the army arrived, the passes were closed by snow. By late the following spring, when it was possible to take up the trail, there was no trail left to follow.

To the day Tenkiller's people were hauled away, Buckhorn had had an ordinance against Indians being within the town limits. During the establishment of the town of Buckhorn, new inhabitants and those who had been in the area at the time of the Marvin Massacre got together on Sunday, when the stores and saloon were closed, and went up into the foothills Indian-hunting, the way pothunters went antelope or deer hunting.

No more than ten days after the Great Celebration there was a hint of what was to fill the vacuum created by the absence of redskin fanatics. George Dunhill had predicted as much to Abe Sutherland, who was the town marshal of Buckhorn, and in fact, the only officer of the law for about two hundred miles in any direction.

Abe was having a drink with Dunhill in the saloon when he told Dunhill he had returned from the foothills, where he had been summoned by Henry Burke. Those foothills adjoined Burke's deeded range for about nine miles. It seems that before Burke could push his cattle up there, Jeff Demis had brought in three riders to set up a camp, along with six hundred head of razorbacked cattle. Jeff usually ran livestock east of the Buckhorn road.

Burke was fit to be tied. Over the years he had not only coveted those foothills with their rich and abundant feed, he had from time to time tested the resolve of the holdouts by going up there alone or sending men up there. He had lost one man, shot dead; had been left afoot himself when the animal he had been riding was shot out from under him; and, as he had bitterly told Marshal Sutherland, he had been feeding those damned Indians for six or seven years—certainly not willingly, but because they would sneak down in the night, chouse a few head into the mountains, and that was the last anyone ever saw of them. Burke had, he'd said, put up with all that and more, and not once in all those years had Jeff Demis offered to ride over and help him get rid of the damned Indians, but now that the Indians were gone,

Jeff hadn't wasted a minute trying to claim the foothills. Henry Burke said he had no intention of putting up with that, no matter what it took to get Jeff the hell out of where Burke didn't think he had any right to be.

Dunhill listened to everything the marshal had to say, and reminded him of his earlier prediction that the absence of fighting holdouts was going to lay open all the land they had pre-empted.

Abe Sutherland was neither appeased nor enlightened. "George, if it makes you feel like some kind of wily old sage, go right ahead, but while you're doin' it, give me another prediction, one I can get my teeth into. Now, what the hell is going to happen?"

George Dunhill was a tall, lean man who wore red sleeve-garters and eyeglasses with lenses as thick as the bottom of a whiskey bottle. He was an Easterner, had only been in the territory about five years. Rumor had it that he had fled from a tyrannical wife, but since rumor and gossip in a place like Buckhorn were two sides of the same coin, a man like Marshal Sutherland allowed both to pass in one ear and out the other.

Dunhill had the local franchise for the stage company. On the side, he operated a drayage business. He was on the Buckhorn Town Council, and was a difficult man to beat at pedro and poker.

Now, as Dunhill peered from behind his eyeglasses at his companion, a slightly shorter man who was nearly twice as muscular and wide, he said, "Let 'em settle it, Abe."

The marshal scowled. "Henry Burke's not a man who'll make threats. I've known him since the first month I took office. Henry is a good man, honest as the day is long, but he runs his cattle outfit like all the old-timers do, an' that means he'll warn Jeff Demis off once, then he'll descend on him like a ton of bricks."

Dunhill raised his beer glass. "I know all that. As I just said, let them settle it."

Abe Sutherland gazed at his friend briefly, then he rapped the bar with his empty glass for a refill, and gave a rattling sigh. "You're a big help," he mumbled.

Dunhill's brows shot up. "What's wrong with letting them settle it? I know Jeff Demis, too. Of all the men I know, those two are the last pair I'd want to get between when they're snarling at each other. Abe, if it comes right down to it, there's not a damned thing you can do."

Abe watched the beer in his re-filled glass bubble. "That's not true," he exclaimed, and George Dunhill came back with an incisive, sharp retort.

"I'll put the facts right on the line for you," Dunhill said. "First off, those damned foothills are ten miles from town. The Second Coming could happen up there and neither you, nor I, nor anyone else down here in town would know anything about it for a week. If then. Secondly, Abe, and I know you don't believe this because I've watched you ignore it for years—you are the town marshal. *Town* marshal. Not a U.S. marshal. Your authority begins at one end of Buckhorn and ends at the other end of it."

Abe Sutherland was in the act of raising his glass. He held it in midair and turned his head, his pale eyes like rocks. He hung fire for a moment, then came back with a tightly controlled response. "George, you recollect last year when one of your damned coaches was robbed, and I rode myself to a shadow catching that son of a bitch and fetching him back?"

Dunhill did not say a word.

Abe put his glass down gently. "And last winter, when two In'ians snuck down and raided your horse corral, and I rode down two horses in eighteen inches of snow gettin' your damned horses back? If I'd stayed by the stove that time, you'd never have got those animals back." Abe leaned his powerful upper body on the bar, glowering. "Maybe my authority don't go beyond the town limits, but by gawd, my responsibility does. Someday maybe they'll incorporate this damned area—then you'll get a sheriff an' he'll have the authority to go anywhere he's got to go. But right now we don't have that kind of law; we got my kind of law." Abe drank half the beer and put the glass down again, as a fresh thought occurred to him. "An' since I've been the marshal here, you're the first person I've come up against that didn't like the way I keep the peace."

Several idlers along the bar were looking southward. Even the balding barman was looking down to where Dunhill and Abe were arguing, while he dried his glasses on a soggy old, soiled towel.

Dunhill emptied his beer glass, removed his spectacles and vigorously polished them on a red bandana, hooked them back over his ears, and gave thought to what he said next. "I didn't say I disapproved, Abe. All I said was that—"

Abe's face, with its square jaw, was reddening. He held up a hand, which stopped Dunhill in mid-sentence, pawed through his pockets for a five-cent piece, placed it beside his beer glass, turned on his heel, and walked out of the saloon, leaving Dunhill feeling embarrassed and looking chagrined as the barman came down and, without any expression at all, said, "You want a refill?" Before Dunhill could answer, the barman also said, "Let me tell you something. I been in the territory most of my life an' so help me Hannah, I've yet to see one of you Yankee Easterners come out here that you didn't want to change everything."

Several men lounging along the bar farther up nodded their heads in solemn agreement with the barman.

Dunhill did not get his refill. He did not ask for it, and the chances were excellent that he would not have gotten it if he had. Larry Spearman, the bartender, who rarely bought into other people's arguments, was also popular with his patrons.

Dunhill left the saloon, heading for his office down at the corral yard. He was right, and he knew it. But Abe had also been right. For a fact, Abe had brought back his stolen horses, and he had ridden down that highwayman. He had done both of those things without any authority except the kind that came from a man's convictions.

Dunhill dropped his lanky frame behind his desk, swung around to yank back the heavy door of his steel safe, clutched a bottle of old popskull, and took two long pulls from it before returning it to the safe. He had not intended to start an argument. He and Abe Sutherland had been friends for a long time. All he'd wanted to do was point out what the legal limitations were concerning town marshals.

He leaned back, gazing out the small roadway window, where a graying sky either meant rain was coming or it was getting along toward dusk. He did not care which it was because he was more concerned by the fact that Larry Spearman's suspicions of Easterners reflected the outlook and the attitude of everyone west of the Missouri River.

CHAPTER 2

The Razorbacks

HENRY BURKE was a turkey-necked, graying, shrewd man of about sixty. Through nothing short of twenty-hour days, summer and winter, he had built up a cow outfit large enough to warrant the employment of four permanent riders, including his range boss Joe Holden. Joe was half a head taller than Burke, just as shrewd, tough as a boiled owl, calculating, and almost sly, where Burke was about as subtle as a kicking mule. They both chewed the same brand of tobacco, Star, but that wasn't what had kept them together for seven years. Joe's absolute loyalty was. Even so, there were times when he got on Burke's nerves, irritated the hell out of him—like the day he had argued against riding to Buckhorn when they saw the holdouts straggling down from the back-country. On big issues, they were as alike as peas in a pod.

They stood leaning on the corral stringers out behind the big old log barn. Earlier, one of the riders had loped in to report that JD cattle were beginning to drift down to open range from the foothills. The Burke rider had gathered as many as he could, and had pushed them back, receiving no help from the three Demis riders who had watched him from half a mile off, sitting like statues on a little bald hill.

Burke was a man of temper. He'd had to have been to have created his cow outfit in the face of great odds. After the cowboy had led his horse to the barn to be cared for, Burke solemnly fished out his plug, offered it to his foreman first, then took it back and gnawed off a corner. He tongued the cud into place as he simultaneously pocketed the plug, then

9

he spat fiercely and said, "That's enough. By gawd, that's all we're goin' to take."

Joe chewed, indifferently eyed the using stock in the corral from perpetually narrowed eyes, and nodded his head. His voice was less angry than his employer's had been when he said, "Yeah. You knew it'd happen, Mr. Burke."

Burke did not deny this. Twenty years earlier, he wouldn't have waited this long. He'd have gone up there, busted Demis's damned cattle eastward in a run, and shot anyone who tried to stop him.

Joe spat to the side and cleared his throat. "How many men work for Demis?" he asked.

"Same as for me. Four, including a range boss."

"And he's got three up yonder."

Henry Burke turned his head slowly. He had known his foreman a long time. When Joe chewed slowly, squinted until a man couldn't see his eyes, and talked softly, he was hatching an idea. Burke had a fair idea about Joe's thought so he said, "It won't do a damned bit of good, Joe. We can ride over, maybe catch him at supper, and he'll stand there grinnin' with his two gold front teeth shining, and tell me to go to hell."

Joe continued to chew slowly and thoughtfully. "It's open range, for a fact," he murmured. "The law's likely take his side; say he's got as much right up there as you have, or anyone else has."

Burke shifted uncomfortably and shoved a scuffed boot toe over the bottom-most peeled log. He would have bet new money that he could predict what else his range boss was going to say. And he was right.

Joe withdrew his foot from the corral log he'd been leaning on, and turned to glance casually all around before he said, "What I was thinkin', Mr. Burke. . . . Three riders up yonder minding his cattle leaves just him and maybe one other man at his home place. . . . In our trade, accidents happen every day. That's fact."

Burke scowled. "Two accidents?"

"Maybe not. Not if we can isolate the other feller."

Burke wagged his head. As much as he loathed Jeff Demis, who was at best a conniving, unprincipled son of a bitch—he had a wife and two little kids. They'd be over there too, but even if they weren't. . . . "Naw," he said in a low growl.

Joe spat and shrugged his sloping shoulders. "It ain't going to get any better, Mr. Burke. You know better'n anyone how Demis's always been; he'll push someone, an' if they don't react, he'll keep pushing."

Burke knew that to be the truth. He'd had minor run-ins with Demis before. "I talked to Marshal Sutherland."

Joe snorted. "If I'd been in your boots, I'd never have done that because sure as hell there's goin' to be serious trouble, and now you've went and let Sutherland know. I'd have waylaid Demis somewhere far out and settled with him then and there."

Burke knew this was the truth, too. Over the years his foreman had settled small range disputes, which neither he nor Joe had ever mentioned to one another.

He turned and settled his back against the corral poles, gazing across the dusty yard without noticing anything. Joe watched his employer's profile, spat, and continued to squint far out in the opposite direction until Burke swore with feeling. "Gawdammit."

Joe turned and also leaned back as he faced the big, tree-shaded yard with its assortment of log structures. "One thing we got to do," he said quietly to Burke, "is go up there, because sure as hell them Demis riders won't make any effort to keep those JD cattle from grazing down across our grass. They proved that today."

Burke straightened up without a word, reset his old, greasy, sweat-stained hat, and went walking in the direction of the main house.

He had been a widower for eleven years, and the interior of his house reflected that fact. He lived in only three rooms: the kitchen, the parlor, and one bedroom. There were indications that at one time, long ago, a woman's hands had arranged furniture and dusted, scrubbed, swept floors, and kept the log house's four glass windows shiny clean. None of those things had been done since Henry had buried his wife in the little ranch cemetery out yonder with the wrought iron fence around it.

This evening, as Henry tumbled equal parts malt whiskey and water into a glass and went out onto the front porch to sit in the thickening dusk to sip it, he was not at all conscious of the boar's nest he lived in. There were times when he was aware of it, but not this evening.

For some indefinable reason, he felt old and reluctant, and the days' work had not been that hard. There were days, particularly when they all went over to the marking ground, when before sundown he'd feel maybe twice his age, but this evening there was no particular reason for it that he could understand—unless it was because lately he'd felt that now, with the holdouts finally crated up and shipped away, at long last he'd be able to slack off a mite, not have to wear a heavy damned gun all the time, even when he went out back to the wash-house, not have to ride with an eye in the back of his head.

He'd often thought, with nothing to really support the idea, that in a man's life there would be a time when he could ease up a little—sit back and keep things running right, but not have to work himself to a frazzle doing it.

He drained the glass, leaned over to put it atop the porch railing, and slouched back again. He had learned to live with the loneliness, but in order to do so, he had sacrificed the quick smile and the easy manner he'd once had.

And now this.

Joe was right about most of it; he'd tried reasoning with Jeff Demis several times. Demis had just sat his saddle, grinning like the cat that ate the canary, those two gold front teeth of his shining. Sometimes he'd even agree, then the very next day he'd be back hatching the same damned meanness.

Henry settled his head against the back of the chair, watching stars brighten as dusk passed and full night arrived. He made a little crooked grin as he said, "You sure know how to make a man fret." Then he arose, went indoors to make a meal and retire. His last thought was that by morning his rider who'd had to chouse back the JD cattle would have told the other riders, and when Burke appeared in the yard there would be four solemn, wondering sets of eyes put on him.

He was correct. After he'd made his breakfast of fried corn bread and tough beefsteak, buckled up for the day, and walked toward the barn, all four men stopped talking and waited.

He said, "Good morning."

They returned the greeting . . . and waited.

Burke pursed his lips and looked northward where the new day's light was beginning to slant down the sidehills. While standing like this he said, "Well, I expect you know about the JD cattle bein' on our range." He faced them. "This has been a good year, a nice wet spring, so there's plenty of grass. But if a man don't save a lot of dry grass for winter, he'll lose cattle, won't he? For years, I've been counting on someday bein' able to put cattle into those foothills, which would save a lot of the grass closer to the yard for wintering. I thought maybe we'd push a thousand head up there."

One of the riders fidgeted and looked at his companions. They ignored him to concentrate on Henry Burke.

Burke felt through his pockets for his plug as he said, "I expect Demis figures he's got a toehold up there, an' with his cattle scattered around, we can't very well drive up a thousand head or we'll have the damnedest mix-up you ever saw." He found the plug, picked lint off it, worried off a chew and pouched it into his cheek before continuing. The men were waiting. Every one of them had been with Henry Burke at least two years and some, like Joe Holden, much longer. They recognized Burke's way of painstakingly explaining things, then pausing before delivering his final statement. That was what the riders were waiting for now.

He turned and smiled without much humor. "I think we got to first sweep the country north and east clear of JD livestock before we make a gather and drive our own beef up there."

He led the way down through the barn and out back, where each man caught a using horse and led it back inside to be rigged out. There was very little conversation. It was easier to lead saddled animals to the log bunkhouse than it was to carry booted Winchesters and beltguns from the building to the barn. As they leaned to buckle holsters into place, Jack Waite grinned over his saddle seat. "Last time I done somethin' like this," Jack said, "we snuck up on 'em in the blankets an' had 'em gagged and trussed before you could roll a smoke."

Burke nodded. Basically this is what Joe had suggested last night. Burke had not made up his mind then. Now as they swung astride, Burke leaned to expectorate heartily, then looked around; five heavily armed riders going to meet three men who might be packing saddleguns, as well as beltguns. Unless those three men were genuine heroes, they'd cut and run. That's what Burke was hoping they would do.

As they pointed northward, there was very little conversation. Burke was especially quiet. His range boss knew that look, and rode back with the other men.

It was still cold, so the riders were bundled inside their coats. The sun was brilliant, but lacked heat, as the small band of armed horsemen approached close enough to the foothills to see JD cattle, which were not in the foothills, but out upon Henry Burke's flat-to-rolling range.

Nothing was said for a while, until that wiry, old rider with the saddle-warped legs threw up a gloved hand to point. Still nothing was said, as the men studied three distant mounted figures with the sun on them.

Joe Holden wagged his head, placed both hands atop the saddle horn, and while leaning slightly forward, cocked his head in the direction of the Demis riders as he said, "Must be real greenhorns to set up there watching their cattle trespass on someone else's range and do nothing about it."

"Sure," Red said dryly. "Sure, Joe. They don't know no better."

Burke cut through the sarcasm as he angled in the direction of the Demis men, and ignored little bands of trespassing cattle which scattered in front of him. "I'm interested to hear what they got to say."

A hundred yards closer Joe Holden said, "There's your answer, Mr. Burke." The three riders had turned, and were riding at a lope in the opposite direction. Burke and his men passed the JD cattle and were riding at a lope when Burke held aloft a gloved hand, then sat with his men, watching the JD horsemen. "Going home," he said, and raised his rein hand. "Now let's go back and push those cattle off our grass."

Late morning heat came and along with it, the annoyance common to any men who had to work cattle—flies. Not just face flies and deerflies, but a sprung-legged, long-bodied kind that didn't just bite, they stung.

Jeff Demis's cattle had a little redback bred into them, but not very much. Some of the old cows had horn-spreads of nearly six feet, long faces, and if they thought the horsemen were crowding them they would come around, heads down, baleful little black eyes hostile, and wring their tails, ready to fight.

Usually a rangeman's reaction to this clear challenge was to accept it instinctively and either go after the critter or shoot into the ground in front of her. But today they did not do this, instead they exercised uncharacteristic patience, while swearing until the air almost turned blue. It was slow work getting all those cattle back into the foothills and heading eastward.

Razorbacked cattle would be driven, but at their own pace. They were unpredictable by temperament, would fight a bear, a wolf, or a mountain lion on sight, and if they had been any different they would never have been able to survive. But while rangemen respected this belligerence, working a herd of cattle that liked to fight was hard on the disposition.

They rode slowly on both wings and in the drag, alternately watching the cattle and scanning elsewhere for those three riders. They did not see any riders at all until late in the afternoon, when they were close enough to the Buckhorn roadway to make out the ruts. Again, it was the red-haired rider who raised a hand and called out. "Yonder through the dust, dead ahead."

Burke was on the north side to keep the cattle from getting too close to the timbered uplands above the foothills. He stood in his stirrups for a long time, then settled back and called to Joe Holden. "Five. That must be the whole crew, plus Demis."

The cattle also saw those five horsemen up ahead, directly in their line of vision. Joe Holden turned back and made a long, looping ride around to get beside Burke. As he hauled back, Joe said, "You want to end this now once an' for all?" He lifted out his six-gun and pointed it over the backs of the half-wild, unpredictable longhorns, his meaning very clear. A couple of thunderous gunshots over the heads of the cattle and they would stampede. Demis and his riders were in a direct line.

There wasn't a horse alive that could out-run a razorbacked cow if the critter was running blind.

Burke squinted at the distant, motionless men. He was certainly tempted. "Naw," he said loudly. "Put it up, Joe."

Joe obeyed, but his expression was rueful as he tipped

down his hat brim and peered up ahead. "You're just puttin'
things off," he grumbled.

Demis and his riders turned back as far as the stage road,
then split up, tow men going north, two other men heading
south. Their obvious intention was to take over the drive as
soon as the cattle crossed the road onto JD range.

One man rode northward, but only to get clear of the
plodding herd. His course was in Henry Burke's direction.
Joe Holden leaned aside to spray tobacco juice, then straightened up and spoke as he watched the approaching horsemen. "He's goin' to give you another chance, Mr. Burke. If I
was in your boots, I'd have run the cattle over them. Stam-
pedes are common. It would have been a damned accident."

Burke did not take his eyes off the oncoming Demis riders
as he said to Joe, "Drop back. Keep an eye on things, but
don't start anything."

Joe obeyed by turning in the direction of the drag. Several
times he glanced over his shoulder with a disgusted
expression.

The dust moved with the cattle because there was no air to
disperse it. It also obscured the horsemen to some extent,
but as the Burke riders began to slack off on their side of the
roadway so that the Demis riders could take over, they pulled
farther to one side, where they were clearly visible.

They were no longer interested in the cattle, they were
watching their two bosses up north, where they came together in the dusty sunlight.

CHAPTER 3

An Omen

JEFF DEMIS was not a tall man. He was lean though, which made him appear taller. He had coarse features, a fixed smile, two gold teeth squarely in the front of his upper jaw, and small, slate-gray eyes nested deeply in folds of flesh. He looked to be Burke's age, about sixty, but could have been younger and badly weathered.

He liked to ride good horses, which was one thing even people who did not care for him agreed upon. Today he was riding a handsome seal-brown gelding with breedy legs, chest, and head. He drew rein opposite Henry Burke and smiled as he said, "Good afternoon, Henry. It's been a while."

Burke returned the greeting because it was required of him, but that was the extent of any neighborly conversation between them. "Good afternoon, Jeff. . . . I don't want to have to drive any more JD cattle out of these foothills."

Demis's smile broadened. "Is that a fact? Well now, Henry, you don't own them foothills." Demis raised a gloved hand to make an expansive gesture. "Open country for a hell of a ways. Free-graze. Only thing kept me out this long was them darned potshootin' redskins, and now they're gone." He leaned on his saddle horn, looking straight at Henry Burke. "You're not goin' to keep me out, any more'n I can keep you out—or anyone else."

Burke's expression was unfriendly. "You got that all off your chest? All right. Now let me tell you something. If I find any more JD cattle on the west side of the stage road, I'm going to have them drove all the way to Messico. If I

18

catch you or any of your men over here, Jeff, I'm goin' to make you wish to Christ you'd never been whelped."

Demis was still smiling, and that was a further goad to Burke, who spat aside. Demis answered, "You don't scare me, Henry. Not one damned bit. I know—I've heard about your hell-roaring days when you'n the territory was young. But that was a while back. Right now, this here is open range. That's what the law says. An' open range means I got just as much right puttin' cattle over here as anyone else. An' I'm going to do it! Now then, if you figure to start trouble, you better go talk to Marshal Sutherland first. He'll explain the law to you." Demis's puffy eyes gleamed. "You commence actin' like this was ten, twelve years back, an' I won't have to fight you. The law'll do it for me."

Henry Burke's reaction to straight-out defiance had always been to match it. He said, "Get down off that horse."

Demis continued to smile as he shook his head. "You're too old, Henry."

That was the last straw. Burke kicked loose his right foot and came down on the left side of his horse. "Get down," he exclaimed.

Demis did not even shift his weight in the saddle as he looked down, smiling. He'd stung Henry Burke, and that delighted him. "Naw. If I get down, I'd have to whip you, you bein' as old as you are, and it's too nice a day for—"

"You son of a bitch, you're not goin' to whip anyone," Burke snarled, yanking loose the tie-down that held his Colt in its holster.

Demis's smile became a little forced, but it did not fade. "I'm not armed," he said.

Burke looked for the belt and weapon. They were not there. He was breathing hard. "All right, get off that horse and whip me, then," he said, and moved up in front of his horse to be close if Demis dismounted.

He didn't. He leaned forward a little though, and wagged his head. "Not today, Henry. I got a lot of work waitin' for me east of the road." He settled back against the cantle and raised his rein hand. "You better go talk to the law," he said, whirled the seal-brown horse, and loped in the direction of the roadway.

By the time Joe Holden and the other riders reached their employer Burke was back astride, staring furiously after the distant man on the handsome, seal-brown horse. Joe hauled down and said, "What happened?"

Burke did not want to talk about it, but he told them the essence of it in a tight voice. "He said he'd drive cattle over here any time he wanted to."

The riders were silent. Joe Holden jettisoned a cud, spat a couple of times, and slouched in the saddle. Jack Waite, a red-haired, bow-legged, turkey-necked older rider, said, "Old man told me one time that when trouble's comin' not to wait for it, to start it first."

Burke's fury was fading, but his anger was not as he looked at Jack. He seemed about to speak, then instead, he exhaled a big breath and turned to lead the group back the way they'd come. An hour later, he said that first thing tomorrow morning they would start a big gather, push all the cattle they could find up into the foothills, and then they'd establish a line camp.

Jack volunteered to be the first man to live up there. Burke did not say whether he would consent to that or not. In fact, he said very little all the way back to the yard, where they arrived as the day was fast fading.

Later, when the men were making their supper at the bunkhouse, and Henry Burke was sitting on the porch over at the main house, sipping spring water and malt whiskey, a falling star raced down the underside of heaven, leaving a sparkling tailrace ten thousand miles long and so bright Henry had to half-close his eyes. He watched it fade, sipped his whiskey, and smiled to himself. Falling stars were not uncommon, but they were rarely as brilliant and awesome as that one had been.

When Henry was a child, his grandmother had been on the porch with him back in Indiana when one of those things had burned itself out in a blazing, high arc. She had told him that was a sign of bad trouble on the way. Later, long after his grandmother and just about every other relative he had was dead, he'd seen a lot of falling stars and had remembered, and sure as gawd made green grass, trouble came.

What made him want to laugh this time was his eventual conviction that two things were inevitable—falling stars and trouble. By the time Henry had reached forty, he was convinced that there was no connection; it was just that life *was* trouble, and stars *fell*.

He finished the watered whiskey and trooped inside to patch together some supper. He ate while thinking of his grandmother. The Lord knew she had seen trouble, nothing but trouble from the day she was born to the day she died. She'd told him stories of Indian raids that had left him with his hair standing straight up. And of British soldiers burning every building on their line of march toward Washington. And of bands of renegades that traveled like small armies.

He smiled to himself. There must be a falling star every darned night. Sometimes maybe even two or three a night. As he arose to head for bed, he was no longer smiling. It was hard not to be superstitious, and the old lady had been dead serious. If she could have been with him this evening and had seen that burning star, she would likely have got right down on her knees because it was about the biggest, longest, and brightest falling star anyone would see in a long time—and sure as hell, trouble was coming.

Henry slept like a log. His wife used to say he could sleep through a house burning down around him. When he awakened, it was still dark. It was also utterly still. He lay with both arms under his head, gazing out the bedroom window at the rash of diamond-chip stars for a long while. He lived a lonely life, but it had not been a dull one for as far back as he could remember.

Horses nickered down by the barn. Henry sighed, climbed out and reached for his britches and boots. He lit the kitchen lamp and stoked up the stove for coffee and steak—and a rat as large as a small cat sprang from behind the stove and dove headfirst into the wood box. Henry took his shell belt and holstered Colt from the peg behind the door and buckled them into place, then picked up a piece of kindling and ransacked the wood box without finding the rat.

The coffee was boiling, and the greased fry pan was smoking. He tossed the scantling back into the wood box and returned to the stove. His wife had kept two cats. After her passing, one cat had just upped and disappeared. Probably caught by coyotes. They were known to prefer domestic cats even to chickens. The other cat died of old age. While they had been alive though, Henry had never seen even a mouse in the house. His wife had been a very practical woman.

He ate standing up, left everything on the table, picked up his hat, and headed for the barn.

It was still as dark out as the inside of a boot, but a rider called Mack, whose real name was Chauncey McElroy, called a greeting to Henry Burke on his way out back with a forkful of timothy hay for the animals in the corral.

Burke took down an old blanket-coat he'd kept in the barn for years and shrugged into it, dislodging a spider and a small frog in the process. Mack returned, hung up the fork and said, "Jack's fryin' breakfast. I'll tell 'em to hurry up, that you're waiting."

Burke nodded, and walked out to the corrals where the horses were eating. They ignored him. That damned scoundrel Demis was forcing Burke to do something he really did not have the time to do. It was early summer—late springtime—about the time to start work over at the marking ground. Most of the cows had calved out in February and March. The time to cut and brand calves was when they were small enough for a man to handle, not in midsummer, when they were too big to be busted to the ground by a knee-drop.

He felt like swearing. Instead, he leaned on the corral, watching the horses, and was still doing that when his riders came trooping from the bunkhouse, bundled against the chill, and carrying Winchesters in saddleboots.

By the time they got to where the cattle were, it would be light enough to see. Burke made the disposition: Two men were to scour to the east. Two more were to ride west. Burke and Joe Holden would start out straight north from the yard. Everyone would make a northerly sweep, pushing everything they found—bulls, steers, cows with spindly calves, toward the foothills. Burke thought they would be up there by ten or eleven o'clock—with a little luck.

Joe was leading his horse outside to be mounted when he said, "You don't suppose Demis went out and turned those cattle and drove them right back, do you?"

Burke had considered that, and although he did not believe the razorbacks could get as far back as they had been through the hills, he told Joe the two of them would make a quick sashay when they were close enough, just to make sure.

Joe was riding beside Burke, just the pair of them a mile out, when the range boss said, "Mr. Burke, I been thinking. Nobody's been to town for a spell. You could send me to town—in front of the men—an' I could take care of that son of a bitch and still make it to town an' back in regular time."

Burke looked at his foreman. "Let's just poke along a day at a time," he said.

Joe said no more, and a little while later, they saw their first cattle. The animals were still bedded down, but they had detected the sound of rein chains and shod hooves, and were peering intently through the gloom. As soon as they saw the horsemen, they sprang up. Some pawed to demonstrate their irritation at being rousted out of their beds, and some wet-cows with little calves got between the horsemen and their babies, and tried to sidle away.

It took a little time to make a gather. They lost a few in the darkness, but by the time they had the cattle lined out, and were picking up more along the route, dawn was on the way.

After sunup, they could hear cattle on both sides in the distance, but were unable to see them for another hour, not until the men making the drive from those directions saw Burke's bunch and began edging their gathers toward it.

The sun was climbing by the time all the cattle were in one gather. Burke had a chew, as he stood in his stirrups to estimate the number they had. It wasn't a thousand head, but it had to be at least the same number Jeff Demis had put up there—six hundred or thereabouts.

He sat back down. That would be enough. Of course he wanted the feed, and in a few days they would drive up another bunch, maybe the same number again, but what he was doing was staking out his right to the foothills.

Jack Waite drifted over to mention the establishment of the line camp. Burke's eyes crinkled a little. Waite was one of those individuals who, like a dog worrying an old blanket, never let up once he got a notion fixed in his mind.

He was a good hand, one of the best Burke had ever had on the ranch. A little too old to still be riding, but to watch him, a person would never think of him as being in his fifties.

"Tomorrow," Burke said. "We'll load a wagon, and that way the camp'll be set up right. Plenty of grub, a decent tent, some tools and all."

Jack nodded about those things. "If you need me, all you got to do is light a little fire and use a wet blanket. I'll see it."

Burke faced forward. It annoyed him that Jack was taking it for granted that he would be the one to live at the new line camp. Burke reluctantly allowed himself to be used like this. He did not really object. Jack would be as good a man in a line camp to watch cattle as anyone else, and a lot better than some. "All right," he said, and looked around for Joe, who was over eastward where there was a little trouble with agitated mammy cows whose tiny babies were having a hard time keeping up. The cows wanted to hang back with them.

THE TAURUS GUN ■ 25

Joe saw Burke coming and drew aside to wait, allowing his companions to worry about the drag. Joe looped his reins, fished for his plug of Star and as Burke turned in beside him, he offered it. Burke took a bite, nodded his thanks, tugged at his gloves, and looked northward. "I haven't seen any cattle or any men, have you?"

Joe hadn't. "No. But the way I got Demis figured, he maybe hasn't pushed any cattle back over here but he sure as hell's got someone spyin' around the countryside. He's that sneakin' kind of a feller."

Burke nodded. "Let's go see," he said, and boosted his mount over into a rocking chair lope.

Heat was coming into the day. Burke had not shed the old blanket-coat, but Joe's jacket was rolled and tied behind his cantle. They rode with about a hundred yards separating them until they got into the gently upended country, then they had to ride closer in order to be able to make a real sweep; not leave too wide a gap between them where they might miss finding Demis's man—if he was up here.

They continued eastward until they had the Buckhorn roadway in sight, without finding anyone. Joe clung to the idea that there was a spy, though. Henry watched the afternoon stagecoach whirl tan dust in its wake, then he finally removed his old coat and tied it aft.

There were no JD cows on the west side of the road, and there were none for as far eastward as he could see. Burke was relieved as they turned back.

He and Joe talked about the line camp. Burke told him he'd agreed to let Jack Waite live up there. Joe was not particularly concerned about who would stay in the camp, so they discussed the things that would have to be brought up tomorrow by wagon, and that led them to a discussion of where to establish the camp. There had to be water close by, and having wood close would be handy too, except that there was very little timber in the foothills, so whoever stayed at the camp would have to use his saddle horse to snake small, dry snags down from the mountains.

By the time they reached the other riders, who were squatting in horse-shade talking and loafing, waiting for the boss and his foreman to come back, the cattle, even the old mammies with wobbly babies, were contentedly spreading out, grazing as they went.

Mack said, "Demis wouldn't want to drive his cattle back an' get 'em all mixed up with ours, would he? Hell, it'd take two weeks to separate a thousand head."

Burke gave the only answer he knew: "With fellers like Jeff Demis, you never know, Mack. . . . Let's head for home."

The sun was still high, they would make it back about dusk. All in all, it had been a fairly routine day. Although every one of them had come armed to the gullet, they had encountered no trouble, and they were all relieved about that.

CHAPTER 4

The Cow Business

BURKE had two line camps. One, far to the west, was occupied when the need for strong feed made it necessary to drive the cattle in that direction. A man was stationed over there to prevent cattle from venturing into the rough areas where the mountains curved around southwesterly. It was months too early for that camp to be manned.

His second line camp was also a seasonal one. But it was about seven miles eastward, its main purpose to prevent cattle from grazing close to Buckhorn.

Establishing a new camp in the northward foothills required a full day, beginning very early—and when the wagon was ready to roll, and the riders had gone after saddle stock, Jack Waite got his right foot stepped on by the shod horse he was leading into the barn. Amid Jack's groans and the rough solicitousness of his companions, Burke had to make the decision of whether to send a one-legged rider up north, or select someone else. He chose Mack, and sent him to the bunkhouse for the personal things he would require.

They left Jack behind, hobbling around and cursing, while his replacement rode up front with Burke and listened to everything the older man had to say about minding a drift toward the mountains, shooting predators on sight, and in his free time riding to one of the low hills up there and keeping an eye to the east.

No mention was made of trouble except once, when Burke gave Mack some advice. "If you got reason to figure I ought to come up here, make a greasewood fire. But don't take on

27

Jeff or his riders by yourself. If they come along driving cattle, just get out of their way and set up the signal fire."

The wagon slowed them down, so Joe and Burke loped ahead to stake out the most likely spot for the camp. While they waited the arrival of the wagon, they left the horses tied in shade and hiked up a gravelly little knob which had three scrub pines atop it. Eastward, there was a faint veil of heat-haze and nothing else. No cattle, no riders, not even any deer. Burke was satisfied, but his range boss wasn't.

"Mr. Burke, he's lyin' back. I'll bet a new hat he's figuring things. He's just plain not the kind that'll let go when he should."

Burke was laconic about these things. "He's not up here, Joe, an' right now that's all I really care much about. Now let's get back, guide the wagon in, and set up Mack's camp."

The rig and its accompaniment of horseback-men were entering the foothills when Burke and Joe rode back to wave it forward. They walked their horses ahead of it to the site they had selected, which was beside a little fast-water creek, and was shaded by a clump of ancient cottonwood trees.

Setting up the old tent did not take long, and actually, at this time of year Mack would spend very little time inside it. While the others were unloading the wagon, Mack began rounding up boulders to make a fire-ring. He was settling in before the camp was fully established. He had enough food to last two weeks, just in case the crew was too busy to bring up more, and he had his weapons, two saddle animals—just about everything that would make his existence comfortable. When the men and the wagon were ready to leave, he was already looking northward for dry snags he could drag to camp for cooking fires.

On the ride back Burke led his riders westerly to look over the cattle they had driven up here previously. What they found was bunches of contented animals already benefiting from the strong feed. They fanned out, hunting for first-calf heifers who might look like they needed help, found none, and came together on the south range heading for home, satisfied that if any heifers got hung up at calving, Mack would be on hand. Pulling hung-up calves was not a pleasant chore, but it had to be done.

Burke had his rooftops in sight when he grinned and raised a gloved hand to point. Jack Waite was leaning on the hitchrack in front of the barn, watching their approach. He had doctored his foot and had it wrapped in what appeared to be a flour sack.

"Disgusted all to hell," Burke reasoned, and he was right. As they rode across the yard to halt in front of the barn Jack said, "Find anything up there?"

Burke was freeing his cinch when he replied. "Peaceful as it could be. Nothing up there but our cattle—and Mack in his camp under some trees beside a little creek." Burke had his back to Jack and winked over the saddle seat at Joe Holden. "Mack's goin' to miss getting black and blue over at the markin' grounds. He'll be livin' like a king up there."

Jack would have stamped toward the bunkhouse, if he'd dared treat his injured foot that way. Burke called after him. "Jack? What does that foot look like? Maybe you ought to go over to Buckhorn and see old Doc Hudson."

Jack turned back. "The toes wiggle, an' I couldn't feel no busted bones. It's as swollen as a gourd, but it'll be all right."

They cared for the horses, then pushed the wagon back under its three-sided shed, and separated. The riders headed for the bunkhouse while Burke hiked to the main house. For a change he was hungry, also for a change he did not mix a glassful of branch water and malt whiskey when he went to work in the kitchen.

He was feeling good. Not optimistic, but satisfied. Joe had not had to tell him that Jeff Demis would not give up so easily. But right now Henry Burke's cattle were up there, along with a line-rider to keep an eye on things, so from here on it would be up to Jeff. Maybe, not very likely, but just maybe Jeff would stay out of the foothills.

Henry ate fried spuds cooked nearly black, some reheated steak left over from breakfast, and as tough as a boot sole. While chewing, which he was obliged to do for extraordinarily long periods of time, he thought of the time early last spring when the Buckhorn physician and the town marshal had passed through his yard returning from an unsuccessful elk hunt, and he had put them up overnight. Marshal Sutherland had sat down at the supper table like someone who was not very particular when he was hungry, while Dr. Percival Hudson had not even sat down. He had leaned on the back of the chair looking at the food as he had quietly said, "Henry, I don't want you to misunderstand me. You're a fine host, and we been friends a long time . . ."

Henry had looked up, eyes ironic. "Yeah, I know, and you're not goin' to eat that fried steak and burnt potatoes and week-old coffee. Perc, a man your size can't draw on his fat for long. It's goin' to be a long night an' an even longer tomorrow before you get back to town—and there is no place in between where you can eat."

A compromise had been reached. Henry supplied Doctor Hudson with fresh meat and unpeeled potatoes, showed him how to dump out the heavy accumulation of ancient coffee grounds and make a fresh pot for himself, then Henry and Abe Sutherland had finished their meal in silence. Later, they had taken two glasses of watered whiskey out front, and sat out there in the late dusk talking quietly while Percival Hudson made his own meal and ate it alone in the kitchen.

What kept Henry amused as he ate supper now was the sequel to that affair. He had met Abe Sutherland in town a month or so later, and Abe had told him Perc Hudson had said he was never again going to go hunting west of the Burke place. Hereafter he would only hunt where the ranch he laid over at on his way back had a woman on the place who did the cooking.

Joe came up through the warm night to rap lightly on the front door. Henry yelled for him to enter. He was making his usual slipshod attempt at tidying up after supper when the range boss appeared in the kitchen doorway to say, "You want to start the gather tomorrow for the marking ground—or wait a week or so until we can bring down the herd from the foothills and do 'em all at the same time?"

Henry had grudgingly made his decision about this long before they had returned from up north. "We'll commence a gather tomorrow, Joe, and work 'em through the marking ground down here. Then we'll go up yonder, establish a working area and work those cattle up there. Yeah, I know, it's goin' to cause a waste of time, but as long as we're established up there I don't like the idea of bringing those cattle down here to work them."

Perhaps Joe had anticipated something like this because he slowly raised his head. "All right." He lingered, eyeing the untidy kitchen. As his gaze drifted to the wall behind the wood box a large rat raised its head, whiskers twitching, and regarded the two men without moving until Joe said, "Mr. Burke, if you'll move aside—you got a rat behind the wood box. I'll shoot his head off."

Henry's head swung swiftly. He and the rat regarded one another, and Henry said, "No. If you shoot—even if you hit him, Joe—you're goin' to blow a hole in the wall."

Joe's steely gray eyes did not blink nor move from the rat. "If that's a female, you're goin' to have to move out before autumn."

"I'll get him," Henry muttered. "I've been watchin' him for a week. I think I got it figured where he hides out. One of these days I'll get him. . . . Can Jack ride, because if he can't we're goin' to be shy two men—him and Mack. That means we got to hire another two, or work ourselves to a frazzle at the marking grounds."

The rat disappeared. Joe blinked and raised his gaze to his employer. "Jack can ride. We'll rig up a blanket-sling for his foot. But he won't be worth a damn on the ground. It's up to you, but if one of us heads for Buckhorn to try to find a couple more men, that's goin' to slow things down even more."

Henry's answer was practical. "We can gather for two days, Joe. They're scattered all over hell this time of year when the feed's strong and every crevice has water runnin' out of it. We couldn't begin to really work them through for two days anyway. Maybe you should go over to Buckhorn tomorrow. Check with Buster at the saloon. He usually's got a line on riders lookin' for work."

Joe continued to gaze at his employer. He'd had something like this in mind a few days back; an excuse for making a discreet sashay through the Demis place. He said, "Mr. Burke . . ."

Henry began to wag slowly his head from side to side. "Leave it be. For the time being, anyway. If they caught you over there, then we'd be shy a range boss as well."

"They're not goin' to catch me. They're not even goin' to see me."

This time when Henry spoke he had an edge to his voice. "Joe, just leave it be."

The range boss did not lower his gray gaze as he slowly nodded his head, then he straightened up off the doorjamb and started turning as he said, "All right. I might as well stay here, let someone else go to town to find a couple more riders. How about Jack? He could see Doctor Hudson about his foot."

Henry liked that suggestion. For a fact, Jack would not be worth much on a big sweep or at the marking ground. "All right. Tell him what he's goin' over there for."

After Joe left, Henry stopped puttering in the kitchen and went to scrape the hearth ash before feeding in some shavings and bone-dry kindling. As he set his evening fire, he thought about the range boss. He and Joe had worked together for a long time. He knew, without anyone telling him, that Joe had settled with trespassers and others over the years, little unpleasant chores Joe had not mentioned to him.

As the blaze licked upward and spread on both sides of the wood, Henry stood up watching it, his mind still occupied with the foreman. It was obvious that Joe considered the Demis threat very real and dangerous. What troubled his employer was the persistence Joe had demonstrated in pushing his solution to the problem. Joe had been almost insistent lately. One other thing was clear to Henry. Whether Joe had ever done anything like murder before, he was certainly willing to do it now.

In the years of their association, nothing like this had ever come up. Always in the past their concern had been for the ranch, the livestock, the riders, the weather; things which impinged upon the outfit and its well-being.

But now, as Henry stood watching his fire, he wondered about Joe's long-ago backtrail. Joe certainly would not be the first killer who had taken to the cowman's existence like a fish to water.

Henry went back to refill his tumbler and take it to the hearth with him, where he stood wide-legged, feeling the heat play up and down his back. He was fond of Joe, even though at times Joe's stubborn opposition irritated the hell out of him. One thing mattered—no, two things: Joe was a top-notch stockman, as well as a very knowledgeable range boss, and he was as loyal to the brand he rode for as the day was long.

Henry sipped his watered whiskey and shrugged into the gloom of the musty old parlor. In half a century of knowing rangemen, he had probably encountered as great a variety of them as anyone else. He had never known any Sunday-school teachers among them. Otherwise, he had known and worked with men whose temperaments ranged from easygoing and cold-blooded, to quick-tempered and good-natured. Joe undoubtedly fit in there someplace. If this damned Demis affair blossomed into something bad, Henry would know enough to keep his range boss on a short rein.

He finished the whiskey, considered the sticky glass, and

blew out a fiery breath. If his wife were still alive, she would have raised Cain about him drinking every blessed day.

The lump in his throat could have been caused by the damned liquor. It could have been caused by something else. He noisily cleared his pipes, took the glass to the kitchen, sank it in the big dishpan half full of cold, greasy water atop the stove, and went off to bed.

One thing a hard day and whiskey did for a man once he got inside a warm house, was make him sleepy. Henry had made that discovery only a year or so after his wife had died. He did not always drink after supper. Sometimes he drank before supper, and occasionally he drank *for* supper, but there were also times when he did not need anything to keep him from lying awake in the night, staring into the darkness.

He was still sleeping when nickering horses down by the barn awakened him in pitch darkness. He did not carry a watch. He'd had one, but it had gotten a little squashed a few years back, and he'd never bought another. Anyway, he could tell by the degree of coldness and by the smell of the air that it was time to roll out. Someone was already down there pitching feed.

He lit the lantern to scrub and shave by in the washhouse out back, and returned to the kitchen for something to eat.

By the time he was ready to leave the house, after pausing long enough to buckle the old shell belt and holstered handgun around his middle, there was a strong aroma in the cold air of food frying at the bunkhouse.

He paused on the porch, studying the sky. It was full of stars, but there was no moon. This was going to be another magnificent early summer day, perhaps with enough heat later on to make horses sweat, but at least they would have a decent day to start the gather with.

A man astride a dapple gray animal started eastward from the yard. Burke could not make out the rider, but he knew the horse. Jack Waite had been bringing that big colt along expertly for three months; he would do almost as much in a hackamore as an old experienced using cowhorse would do in a bit.

Burke watched Jack until darkness dulled out the color of the gray horse, then went down to the barn. He arrived late. All the animals were rigged out and patiently waiting for their riders to finish breakfast and return.

Burke got his own animal, this time a leggy, big, muscled-up seven-year-old chestnut gelding, and without haste, saddled and bridled him. Burke had a few breedy animals—not as many as Jeff Demis and a few other cattlemen, who made a hobby of breeding up and buying only the very best horseflesh, but he had enough of that kind. Burke was a cowman, and while he now had the wealth which would enable him to ride flashy horses, as he had been telling himself since the death of his wife, he was too old to change; he was perfectly satisfied to straddle good using stockhorses and leave it to others, such as Demis, to preen like damned peacocks atop their elegant thoroughbreds and Arabs and whatnot.

CHAPTER 5

The Dawn Visitor

THEY had to put in a long, tiring day. Not just because the only riders were Burke, Joe Holden, and Bob Cheney, but also because the cattle were scattered over thousands of acres.

They were rarely in sight of each other, but each man knew roughly where his companions were by the uneasy lowing of driven cattle. By the time the heat arrived, the horses had had to sashay back and forth over a considerable distance in order for their riders to be sure they were not missing any critters. The horses had covered many times more than the amount of territory they would have covered if there had been a full crew, so about noon, when Burke could see Jack and Bob, and the sea of cattle was moving sluggishly in the correct direction, he stood in his stirrups and wigwagged with his hat.

The three of them met atop a low land swell near some white oaks. They hobbled the animals, removed their outfits and sat in oak shade while the horses cropped grass.

Burke said he thought they had done well. Joe, who was leaning against a tree, nodded his head while skiving a sliver off his plug. Bob Cheney, who was a quiet, rather nondescript rider, about thirty years old and dark, rolled a smoke as he said, "Sure hope Jack finds some help in town. We got a hell of a lot of critters to work for just the three of us."

Joe cheeked his chew as Burke told them he was confident that between Jack Waite and Buster Munzer at the saloon, they would come up with something. Bob smiled about that.

"Yeah. That's what I been worryin' about. . . . Something. Green kids, or worse."

They let this topic die, and sat for a long while watching the horses and beyond them the cattle, fill up. The cattle were beginning to spread out, which was normal. Joe said, "Looks like the makings of a good year."

Burke thought so. "If the good Lord'll give us a little rain when we need it."

Bob Cheney bumped ash off his quirley. "If Jack don't find anyone, maybe Mack could come down an' lend a hand for a few days. Them cattle up there aren't goin' anywhere."

Burke was picking lint off his plug as he replied to that. "If it comes down to it, I expect he could. Jack sure isn't goin' to be much good on the ground. He can do the roping. He's good at that. The rest of us'll work the fires." Burke considered his plucked plug. It still resembled a very dark brown, fuzzy young rat. He shrugged and bit into it.

They saddled up an hour later and resumed the drive, but now they were required to spread out even more because they were approaching country that was marked by a number of brushy arroyos, where a few wily old wet-cows took their calves the moment they saw that a drive was underway.

Henry Burke did not use dogs, as many stockmen did, to go down into those thickets and chouse out the cattle. There were times when his riders cursed about this, because the real savvy old critters would lunge as hard as they could until stopped by dense underbrush, then they would stand in there, watching the riders. A man could sit his horse ten, fifteen feet from them and the cows would not budge. They knew horses were reluctant to plow head-on into thorny thickets, and their riders were even more reluctant. Dogs, on the other hand, were smaller and more agile. A good cowdog would work his way into a thicket and bite an old cow's nose or legs. Mounted men swore a lot and tried many things, from bouncing rocks off cattle to firing guns into the brush behind them. A lass rope was useless; nooses did not settle around heads and necks buried in underbrush.

Of course, the cattle could be run out of those places, but it took time, was very hard on dispositions, and usually resulted in bleeding scratches. Then too, there was always the possibility that the critter was not going to let her baby go anywhere. Some old cows would fight a man on foot quicker than they'd fight a bear, and that possibility was usually uppermost in a rider's mind as he stepped to the ground cursing, to try and work in close enough the kick the cow out.

Today no one got charged, but each of the men encountered those old cut-backs and received scratches getting them out. It required a good deal of time to get the entire herd past those brushy gullies. The same damned old cow who had been kicked out a mile back would whip around and go down into the next thicket, so the process would have to be repeated.

As Bob Cheney said when they were ready to leave the cattle to bed down while they headed for the yard, if those old biddies weren't valuable, a man would be tempted to shoot them and leave them to rot in that damned underbrush.

They spent an hour washing horses' backs out behind the barn, and checking the animals for bad scratches, then they turned them into corrals and fed them. It was close to dusk by the time they walked out front and separated.

Henry was tired as much as he was hungry. He made a decent meal, and afterwards went out to sit in his sprung-bottom old porch chair and relax all over.

Some time tonight Jack would return with whatever scrapings he could find in town. Bob Cheney's skepticism was probably justified. It was a little late in the year for good hired men to be unemployed. The other kind were always around. Henry raised his worn old boots to the porch railing and studied the sky.

If Jack brought back a couple of saddle tramps, one of them could be sent up north to the foothills line camp, and Mack could be brought down to the marking ground. The other one could tend the branding fires and, providing he wasn't completely blind, he could do the wattling. Things that required the least skill.

Henry sighed loudly. He would have liked a glass of water and whiskey, but he was too tired to stir out of the chair to get it. Tonight he would sleep like a dead man.

Which was exactly what he did. In fact, for the second morning in a row everyone else was up and doing chores before he even opened his eyes. He felt perfectly well and active, but he still had a few aches from yesterday.

He went hopefully down to the barn, where a lantern was hanging. Jack would be there with the men he had brought back with him. Burke's surmise was partly right—Jack was there, helping with the feeding as he hopped in the lamplight like a monkey on a rope.

He had a professional bandage on his foot, its outer covering very white. Beneath this was a plaster mold that made the foot look like a stump.

Burke looked around. He even walked out back, where Bob Cheney and Joe Holden were pitching feed. When he returned to the barn, Jack was sitting on an old wooden horseshoe keg, waiting for him. Jack said, "Had a little trouble, Mr. Burke."

"You couldn't find anyone?"

"Oh yeah. I found a couple of young fellers. Maybe a little green, but plumb willin' and needing work."

"Where are they, at the bunkhouse?"

Jack continued to gaze at his employer in the feeble light. "No . . . Buster knew about them. They'd been around town for about a week. There was a note tacked to the front wall of the saloon sayin' they were stayin' at the rooming house and needed work really bad. I went up there and talked to them on the porch out front. While I was explainin' what

you paid and all, Mr. Demis come along with some big feller
I never saw before. He heard me talkin' and commenced to
grin like he does . . . Demis, not the big man. The big man
never opened his mouth, just stood lookin' and listening. . . .
Demis asked how much I'd offered, and when those young
fellers told him, Mr. Demis upped it five dollars a month.
. . . The young fellers walked away with him."

Joe Holden walked up, looking solemn, and halted, with
both thumbs hooked in his shell belt. He looked at Jack, not
Henry Burke, and he did not say anything until Burke spoke.
"Did Buster know of any other fellers, Jack?"

Jack hitched up off the horseshoe keg. "Nope. In fact, he
told me except for those two greenhorns there hadn't been
anyone come in lookin' for work in more'n a month."

Joe, who had heard this story last night when Jack had
returned, put a smoky gaze upon his employer. "He's doing
it, Mr. Burke. The son of a bitch is getting set up to make
trouble for us." Joe sounded almost accusing.

Bob Cheney, who had returned from out back and was
hanging the hay fork from its pegs, finished what he had
been doing and faced out across the graying yard as he said,
"You fellers hear anything?"

They looked first at Bob, then faced around, also peering
across the yard westerly. Someone was loping a horse in their
direction. Bob spoke dryly. "Kind of early for visiting, isn't
it?"

Burke led the way out as far as the tie-rack. By then it was
possible to make out the rider, but still too gloomy to recognize him—until Joe Holden straightened up in surprise.
"Well, hell," he exclaimed. "It's Abe Sutherland. . . . Now
what do you expect got him out of bed a couple of hours ago
to come out here?"

Not another word was spoken until the large man on his
big buckskin horse slackened to a walk as he crossed the yard
toward the men in front of the tie-rack. He looked stonily at

the four of them, nodded, and swung to the ground as he gruffly said, " 'morning."

Burke's curiosity was not so great it inhibited his hospitality. "Coffee's still hot, Marshal."

Abe led his horse inside, piled his outfit in a corner, and stalled the buckskin. As Bob pitched hay to the big horse, Abe Sutherland pulled off his gloves, stuffed them in a coat pocket, and looked from Burke to Joe and back as he said, "I rode out early because I didn't want to have to shag my butt all over the countryside lookin' for you. Glad I caught you before you rode out."

Abe groped inside his coat as he added a little more to what he'd already said, "Henry, I sure don't like to do this." He held out a paper which Burke took, but the light in the barn was not good enough to read by, so they all trooped over to the bunkhouse. There, as Marshal Sutherland shed his coat because the bunkhouse was still hot from the breakfast fire, Burke sat down at the table, spread the paper and pulled in the coal-oil lamp. Reading was not one of Burke's greatest talents. He shoved back his hat, furrowed his brow, and moved his lips as he read.

The other men stood in uncomfortable silence. It was Marshal Sutherland who finally broke the hush. "It's legal, Henry. I didn't want you to do something rash before you knew about this."

Burke finally raised his head, very slowly, and stared at the marshal. For a while he simply stared, then he tapped the paper as he said, "It can't be legal, Abe. I heard at Buster's place a couple of years back a man can't take up more'n a hundred and sixty acres."

Abe looked at the stove, then stepped up to it, and closed the damper. As he faced around, he was scowling. "That's partly right, but there's ways a man can homestead a full section—six hundred an' forty acres, or one square mile." Abe pointed. "Read that bottom part again. It gives metes and bounds."

Joe Holden looked baffled. "Metes and bounds?"

"Surveyor talk," the lawman explained, and he faced the table again. "It gives the legal descriptions, Henry, for the full four square miles Jeff Demis put in for—and it was approved by the Denver land office." Abe stepped over to drop down opposite Burke at the scarred old table. He was watching Burke closely. All the way out here in the cold darkness, he had known what Henry Burke's reaction to this might be, which is why he had made the ride. He wanted to stay as close to Burke as a tick until the shock and fury had passed. He knew Burke. The parts he did not know from firsthand experience, he had heard from older men in Buckhorn who had been around during Burke's younger years.

When Burke exploded in anger, he was not at all the man he normally was. Now, as he ignored the heat and sat hunched over the table in his old coat, his stare at Abe Sutherland was like ice. "When did he do it?" he asked very quietly.

Abe reached over to indicate the date on the paper. "He filed on the land about a month back, which would be about the time he ran his cattle west of the road into the foothills. But that there is the date of the approval—about four, five days ago."

Joe Holden went to the door, opened it, and left the bunkhouse. Possibly the heat had driven him outside. Bob Cheney wiped sweat off his face, but remained where he was.

Burke looked down again at the paper as he said, "Where did you get this, Abe?"

Abe shifted on the wooden bench. He did not like any of this, but this part he liked least of all. "Jeff came by my office yesterday. He had a big feller with him and a couple of young riders he'd just hired. He handed me the paper and said maybe it'd be better if I rode out and explained all this to you. That way, he wouldn't be put in a position where he might have to—get into trouble with you, which he said he don't want to do."

Burke stood up, his color gone, his eyes fixed on Abe Sutherland. Bob Cheney was transfixed. He had seen Burke annoyed, but never angry. Not like this, anyway. Burke looked like he was going to explode.

Abe also shoved up from the table. He groped for something to say, found nothing he thought would do any good, and wisely remained silent until Burke began to swear, his voice neither loud nor gruff. Finally, he said, "No, by gawd. He's not goin' to get away with this. We ran him off, an' his cattle, an' we put our own cattle up there. In fact, we set up a line camp."

The marshal leaned to retrieve his legal paper, folded it slowly, and put it back in his shirt pocket. Then he raised his eyes to Burke's white face. This was something Abe had faced many times, angry defiance of a legal process. He said. "Listen to me, Henry. In the eyes of the law, it's been done an' it's legal."

"I don't give a gawdamn, Marshal. I been grazing up there since the holdouts were taken away. Before that . . . where was your damned legal papers when those In'ians were killin' and eating my beef, shooting my riders, makin' life miserable for me and everyone who rode for me? The damned government said In'ians was their wards. Where was the damned lawyers and government men when their wards were raiding my horse herds and all?"

Abe looked around for his coat and held it in one arm. "Sue the government," he said sourly. "Sue the Bureau of In'ian Affairs, but don't go up there and—"

Burke's mouth drooped, his eyes blazed at Marshal Sutherland. "Sue! What kind of talk is that? Sue the government, sue the In'ian agency people! Abe, I never sued anyone in my life. I'm not goin' to start actin' like some damned fee-lawyer's little whinin' weasel now."

Abe looked steadily across the table. "What are you going to do, Henry?"

Jack Waite spoke from the shadowy farthest corner of the bunkhouse where he had been sitting in silence on his bunk. "He's goin' to finish the gather he started yesterday, Marshal." Jack hobbled over closer to the lamplight, his face totally expressionless. "We got a hell of a lot of work to do. An' in case you'd like to know, I hired those two young bucks who was with Demis yesterday, an' he came along and with me standin' right there, he offered them five dollars more a month. And he was grinnin' like an idiot when they walked away with him. . . . So you see, we're damned shorthanded and we got a lot of work to do. An' standin' around in here isn't gettin' any of it done."

Jack hobbled to the door, jerked his head for Bob to follow him, and went out into the cold to join Joe, who was watching the sunrise come.

Marshal Sutherland began putting on his heavy riding coat as he studied Henry Burke's face. As he fished in a pocket for his gloves, he said, "Henry, listen to me. Whatever you're thinking, don't do it. You got any idea what kind a position you'll put me in if you go after Jeff, or stir up trouble over this?"

Burke stared. "Trouble for you? Do you know what that son of a bitch did to me? After all these years of me actin' as a buffer for him and everyone else, including you folks down in Buckhorn—keepin' those broncos away from everyone— now Demis comes along like a sneak in the night and does this. Abe, before he's very much older, he's goin' to wish he'd never done it."

Abe started to speak, but the door opened and Joe Holden poked his head in to say, "Mr. Burke, it's sunup and we got enough work to last us until long after dark."

Burke gave Marshal Sutherland a bitter, very slight nod and walked out, leaving the lawman alone in the bunkhouse.

CHAPTER 6

The Coming Storm

EVEN Bob Cheney, who rarely got fired up about anything, was furious—but like the others, he said nothing. In fact, by the time they had completed the gather and pulled back to let the cattle get settled near the old marking ground with its scattering of a woodpile, its big rings of boulders with six inches of black ash inside, its logs for balancing hot branding irons, and its pieces of flat rock men had sharpened castration blades on for years, the working day was about finished. Shadows were puddling, which meant dusk was not far off.

They headed for the yard. The cattle would drift a little, but not very much, because it would be dark shortly and they would bed down. Come morning, the men would be back out there to build the fires and await first light. The cattle would not have much chance to drift once the horsemen returned.

Burke had barely spoken all day, not even to his range boss, when Joe Holden came up, sat his horse beside the older man, and said, "Marshal Sutherland did what he figured was best."

Burke did not look around. "I expect George Washington said somethin' like that about Benedict Arnold."

Joe watched his employer push his horse ahead, in the direction of the yard. The range boss signaled with his hat for the other riders to do the same, and rode without haste until Bob and Jack came up. Then Joe said, "I can't figure Demis out. I've yet to hear a single person say anythin' good about him. But he's still alive."

Bob said nothing, he was concentrating on not spilling

tobacco flakes as he built a smoke. Jack Waite, still raw about the way Demis had walked up and hired those two young fellows in town, threw out a bitter remark. "Well, Joe, he just damned well may not be alive a hell of a lot longer."

But Joe Holden's anger and outrage were controlled. Unlike the other two hands, he just simmered that first day. After supper that evening, he strolled over to where Burke was sitting on the porch. He leaned on an upright as he gazed at the dusk-shadowed profile of his employer, and said, "I don't think one bit better of Jeff Demis than you do, but he's got a fair-sized outfit, which he built up himself, an' to me that means he don't do too many things on the spur of the moment."

Surprisingly, Burke agreed. "Yeah, looks that way, don't it? That day we turned his cattle back . . . Joe, sure as hell he'd already filed on the foothills by then. I can see it all now. The way he grinned an' acted, wouldn't get off his horse and fight; just sat up there and told me to go see Abe Sutherland." Burke turned his face toward the range boss. "He'd already filed, an' he wasn't goin' to tell me that, he was goin' to let Abe do his dirty work for him."

Joe nodded slightly. "That's what I'm saying. He's a miserable, conniving, underhanded snake, but he's not a fool." Joe stepped to the railing and sat on it. "Mr. Burke, what sticks in my craw is that now that he's froze you out up there, legal and all, he's settin' at home waiting for whatever you do next."

"I know that."

"Wait a minute. Let me finish. He's figured out the things you'll do. Like ride over there and call him out. Well, his answer to that would be to have his riders lined up in the barn or behind some sheds. He's sure as hell figured you might go chargin' up yonder with your crew and dare him to drive cattle in again. An' he'll have something figured out to do about that, too."

Burke gazed at the range boss, gently scowling.

THE TAURUS GUN ■ 47

Joe smiled faintly. "If I was in your place, I'd figure what he'll figure, then I'd figure a way around it. Like playin' checkers."

Burke continued to stare and scowl. "What you got in mind?"

But Joe had nothing in mind, or if he did have, he did not think this was the time to mention is, so he said, "Set still for a few days. Work the cattle, maybe. It'd be good for all of us if we worked it off at the marking ground. Then, when we're back to normal, set down and out-figure that measly bastard."

It seemed to be good advice, but Burke did not stop scowling, nor did he say anything to indicate he might agree with his range boss. Instead, he yawned, got to his feet, and said, "We got a hell of a day ahead of us, Joe. Good night."

Joe ambled thoughtfully back to the bunkhouse. He paused on the small porch with its warped wooden overhang to listen to a pair of distant wolves call back and forth, then he went inside.

Burke went out back with a lamp, hauled some water, and took an all-over bath. He climbed into clean underwear, and returned to the house with his clothing over one arm. He had not expected to sleep well, but he did; slept like a bear and awakened feeling fairly normal, all things considered.

After shoveling in some food and washing it all the way down with black coffee, he dumped on his hat and went to the barn for his old riding coat.

Bob and Jack were pitching feed. Burke watched the way Jack hobbled and went over to take the pitchfork but Jack would not relinquish it. "Foot's a lot better. Don't hurt at all unless I bump it." Jack looked down. The white bandaging was dirty, something he ignored as he said, "Doctor Hudson knows his trade."

Burke also gazed at the foot. It looked like a club, but as Jack hitched around to continue forking feed, Burke shrugged. He was not quite convinced the foot did not hurt but if he knew anything at all, it was the make-up of range riders. Jack would have sold his soul before he'd have missed pulling his weight today. Marking was just about the most important job on a ranch, and it was only done twice a year.

Burke turned as Joe walked up behind him and said, "Good morning. There's a million stars up there. It's going to be a good day."

Nothing was said about their conversation on the porch last night. Burke went to the small storeroom on the south side of the barn, just inside the big, doorless front opening, to rummage for branding irons. Ordinarily, he would have taken a wagon, but they would not be so far from the yard that they could not lope back to eat. Otherwise, the things they'd need today could be taken on their saddles.

He was still in the little room when the riders walked past, on their way to breakfast at the bunkhouse. He had accumulated just about everything he wanted, and was putting it near the doorway, when a man shouted out in the yard.

It was not the shout of an angry man, it was high and shrill. Burke felt that shout go down his spine like a set of steel fingernails. He dropped everything and bolted from the barn.

The men were midway to the bunkhouse, standing motionless, looking northward.

There was no mistaking a greasewood fire. If the wood was green, it would burn with intense heat only providing it was fed into a fire which was already burning, but when it was dry, it burned so fiercely that it could melt the bottom out of a stove. This fire was blazing with a pure white intensity. It was so bright that despite the pre-dawn darkness, it showed brilliantly for ten miles.

Burke stopped breathing for several seconds, then turned. "That's McElroy. I told him if he ran into anything bad, to set off a fire we could see down here. Get your guns and saddle up."

The riders rushed to the bunkhouse. There would be no

time for breakfast. Burke was leading in a horse when the men came around the side of the barn, heading for the corral. There was noise, but none of it was made by conversation.

It took a few additional minutes to buckle Winchester scabbards under saddle fenders. When the men were leading their animals outside, Burke had to trot to the main house for his saddlegun. That added a little more time, but the riders stood with their mounts, looking northward. When Burke rose up and came across leather, his crew did the same.

They walked their horses a mile, staring at the fire, then broke over into a lope and held to it for three miles before dropping back down to a walk again. By then they were close enough so that, although the firelight seemed to be diminishing somewhat, they could make out faint breaks in the land up there where firelight bounced off obstructions.

Not a word was said. When a horse snorted, it sounded unusually loud. To the east there was a ghostly smear of dove-gray all along the horizon. It went unnoticed as Burke led off at a lope, then reined down to a fast walk as they came within gun range of the foothills. Here, finally, they could smell smoke.

Here, too, they encountered cattle. They were not bedded, but were milling in groups and individually, the way troubled cattle do when they are in a strange place without daylight. Some were walking eastward, others were obeying instinct by cropping grass, but they did not keep their heads down for long. They raised them while chewing, and swung them in all directions as though seeking some reassuring object.

Joe Holden said, "JD cattle."

It was true. The cattle who did not bolt at the sight of the riders, but swung to face them, had wide spans of horns. Burke spat and eyed the nearest animals. He did not have to see the brand to know whose cattle these were.

He eyed them, but had his course set for the vicinity of the fire, which was dying down now. Another characteristic of greasewood fires was that although they burned fiercely, unless they were constantly fed, they died down fast. This one was dying as Burke led his riders toward it.

A streak of red appeared above the horizon. Below it, the grayness was beginning to have the look of burnished copper. Daylight was close. Burke's crew had covered ten miles in close to record time, during which the cold had increased, and the promise of daylight had become steadily more pronounced.

Bob Cheney raised an arm but said nothing. The line camp tent was flat down and wrinkled. The entire camp looked as though a cyclone had struck it. There were cooking pans, tinned food, tools, and blankets strewn over a large area.

Burke halted, pulled off a glove, groped inside the old coat for his plug, bit off a corner, and was putting his glove back on when Joe Holden spoke quietly beside him. "They ran their cattle right over his camp." Joe straightened to look around. The fire was about fifty yards back, in the direction of the forested mountains. Burke swung down, handed his reins to Jack Waite, and started walking. When he reached the fire, there was still enough heat to prevent a close approach, so he made a rough circle, halted behind the fire, spat, and swore with relief. One thing was clear. Before Mack could light the stack of greasewood he had evidently racked up for just such an emergency, he'd had to run north from the camp Demis had stampeded his cattle over, which meant that Mack had survived the stampede.

He went back, squinted at the red half-disc balancing just behind the eastern rim of the world, and said, "Let Jack mind the horses. Be careful where you walk. Somewhere out here, Mack left tracks."

They had no luck until the sun was fully up, the world was flooded with brilliance, and the new day was advancing. Joe found the sign and called to Burke. Evidently Mack had had just about enough time to leap up and run. The tracks had been made by a man in his stocking feet. They were completely obliterated until the searchers got closer to the greasewood fire than the stampeding cattle had gone. From there, they went arrow-straight northward toward the forested highlands. With good visibility and fresh dew on the grass, it was an easy trail to follow.

Once, the stocking-footed tracks were crossed by shod-horse prints. The rider had been going west. Mack had been running north. No one paid particular attention to the horse tracks. If they had been left by one of Demis's riders, he had probably passed by long after Mack had gone, the rider's purpose was perhaps to prevent the longhorns from turning northward into the forest.

They halted once and shouted McElroy's name. When there was no reply, they started along Mack's trail again. Twice more before they reached the first tier of timber they halted and shouted. There was no reply either time.

Burke and his range boss exchanged a look. No one in his stocking feet could run so far in mountainous country, uphill every inch of the way, that he would be unable to hear men shouting his name.

It became more difficult to discern the stocking-footed impressions once they passed from dewy grass to spongy layers of pine and fir needles, so they were slowed down, but not stopped.

Behind them, out in open country, Jack had dismounted, tied the horses, and was now poking among the ruin of the camp. The sun was well on its way toward its meridian, but the day was still cool, and Jack was still wearing his coat.

Northward in the forest, with huge old trees so close together that their stiff, spiny tops blocked out all sunlight, it was still cold. Burke gestured for Bob and Joe to fan out among the trees. The trail had not deviated, which signified to Burke that his range rider was up ahead, and tracks or no tracks, if they widened their search, they would find him.

They did.

Bob stopped dead in his tracks where some scaly old prehistoric rocks jutted from the ground to form a small half-circle, no higher than a man's waist. Bob swallowed twice, then called. Burke and Joe turned in the direction of the call. When they found the rocks, Bob was down on one knee, white-faced with shock. He raised his eyes to them and said, "How'n hell did he get this far? Look—shot through the body from in back."

Burke sank to the ground, and eased the inert body over onto its back just in time to catch a flicker of both eyes, then the lids dropped to a half-closed position.

There was nothing to be done or said. They stood looking at the dead man for a full minute. Bob got back to his feet and finally spoke. "There wasn't no blood on the trail."

Burke ignored that statement. There had to have been blood, but they had groped northward toward the timber before daylight. After the sun rose, they had been in the forest where no light reached.

Joe Holden removed both gloves, folded them under his shell belt, brought out his plug, bit off a cud, and returned the plug to his pocket. He spat once, then went over to where Bob had been kneeling and knelt. He spoke in a sepulchral voice. "I don't see how he did it—got this far. That bullet sure as hell busted up his insides pretty bad." Joe raised the dead man's head, cuffed up some fir needles for a pillow, then eased the head down again. He and Mack had team-roped at the marking ground. They had ridden together a lot. They had picked on one another, argued, drank at the saloon in Buckhorn, and hazed the other men together.

Joe lifted the soggy shirt, examined the wounds, one in back, and a more ragged one in front, then eased the torn cloth down and turned aside to expectorate before getting to his feet.

"Whoever did that, Mack," he said, without raising his

voice, "is goin' to burn in hell for a thousand years. I promise you."

Bob went back for one of the saddle animals. Burke sat on the ground and Joe Holden leaned on a big tree. Burke eventually said, "He didn't wait, Joe."

"Wait for what? Who are you talkin' about?"

"Jeff. He didn't wait to see what we'd do. He jumped in first."

Joe jettisoned his cud before speaking again. "If you'd done like I said this wouldn't have happened, Mr. Burke."

Burke kept his back to the range boss and said nothing. If he'd allowed Joe to bushwhack Demis, *this* probably would not have happened, but something else just as bad surely would have.

Bob came back with the horse. They loaded Mack, after wrapping him in a blanket Jack Waite had insisted that Bob take back with him. They tied the body so that it would not slide off, and started back down out of the mountains. By the time they reached open country, Jack was coming up with the other animals, and when he stopped, he pointed at the ground.

There was blood. Now, with the sun high and heat coming, it was turning black in the grass.

Bob Cheney rode double behind Joe Holden. Burke led the way back down, past the ruined camp, past the little knobs and land swells, out to open country. He turned off on a southeasterly course, in the direction of Buckhorn. No one said a word.

The cattle at the marking ground would be drifting. By the time they got back from town, they'd have to make the whole damned gather all over again.

CHAPTER 7

Burke's Backlash

MARSHAL Sutherland had been out of town most of the day looking for a horse thief who, as it turned out, did not exist. The horses an excited stockman had reported stolen, had been spooked out of their fenced pasture by a cougar. They were five miles east by the time Abe tracked them down, and irritably turned them back. He drove them fast all the way so he would be able to tell the stockman what he thought of people who cried wolf before scouting around first, and still get back to town before nightfall.

He was not in a good mood when he put his horse up at the livery barn and walked up the back alley, booted Winchester under his arm, to the rear door of his jailhouse.

Old Henry Burke was sitting inside, slouched and rumpled in the fading light. Abe had a bad feeling in the pit of his stomach as he walked in, nodded, leaned his Winchester against the wall, and went to light the lamp that was suspended by a bent nail from the ceiling.

"Thought you were working cattle," he said. He shook out the match, lowered the mantle, adjusted the wick, and watched critically as the flame flared briefly, then settled down.

Burke too watched the flame. "That's the way things started out," he said dryly, still watching the lamp flame, and shoved up out of the chair. "Take a little walk with me, Abe."

Abe eyed the older man for a moment. He was tired and he was hungry.

Burke held the door and waited. After they were out in

the late dusk, Burke turned northward and did not say a word until they had passed through Doctor Hudson's little white gate. They did not approach the front of the house, but went down the south side of it, past a bed of red geraniums, to the small converted buggy shed out back.

There was a light burning as Burke opened the door. Doctor Hudson looked up irritably, then recognized the intruders and stepped away from his white-painted combination operating and embalming table. He reached for a towel as he said, "Henry, Joe said to tell you he and the other riders would be at the saloon."

Marshal Sutherland looked at the dead man on the table, who was bare from the waist up, and whose stocking feet extended about six or eight inches beyond the lower end of the table.

Doctor Hudson continued to dry his hands. He too looked at the dead man as he said, "I washed him up. He looked like a stuck hog when they brought him in." Without putting the little towel aside, Hudson stepped back beside the table and jutted his chin. "From in back, Abe. I'd guess he was maybe running away when the bullet hit him."

Abe looked from Hudson to Henry Burke. "That's McElroy," Abe said. Neither of the older men spoke. Abe went up closer and leaned in to look. Doctor Hudson rolled Mack up onto his side and pointed. "Neat hole in back. Unless it's a buffalo gun, they usually don't make much of a hole going in, but where they come out, if the bullets encounter any bones and are split or deformed, they make a much worse hole coming out. Like the hole in front." Hudson eased the body back down and nodded at Burke. "Tell him," he said. As Burke began speaking, Doctor Hudson finally put down the little towel.

His shed always smelled of carbolic acid, but he had embalmed so many people back here over the years that the smell of formaldehyde was also noticeable. This time he had used no embalming fluid. It would not be required.

Burke was halfway through his recitation when Marshal Sutherland looked around for a chair and sat down, heavily, listening to Burke and looking at Mack.

When Burke finished, Abe Sutherland asked a question. "Was he dead when you found him?"

"Not quite," Burke replied. "But he died within moments after we got up there."

"Then he didn't tell you what happened at the line camp, or who shot him?"

Burke gazed bleakly at the lawman. "He didn't have to tell us, Abe. Not about what happened up there. Demis's cattle are all over the place, all mixed up with my cattle. They didn't get over there by themselves. About who that was who crossed Mack's trail on horseback, I got no idea, but as sure as I'm standin' here, that's the man who shot him in the back."

Marshal Sutherland folded his big hands in his lap. It crossed his mind what the stage company manager, George Dunhill had said to him last month at the Antler Saloon about bad trouble coming. He blew out a ragged breath and stood up, no longer hungry, but still tired. Even more so now. "I'll go up there and poke around," he said, sounding dispirited.

Burke had a question. "What good will that do? All you're going to find is razorbacked cattle mixed with my herd. They'll have trampled out everything useful to you."

Marshal Sutherland was a stubborn man. "I'll go anyway," he said.

Burke was looking at his dead rangeman when he replied. "You do that. Me, I got something else in mind."

Abe's broad features hardened, but he hung fire until he had the words in orderly sequence. "You go home, Henry, an' you stay there. Go work your cattle. Do whatever you got to do, but do it on your own land, and stay out of the foothills." At the slow way Burke turned to face him, Abe reddened. "I mean it."

Burke's gaze did not waver from the angry lawman's face. "Sure you mean it. An' I mean what I just said." He gestured with one hand toward the embalming table. "Remember what you said about suing people? I told you that wasn't my kind of law. All I want, Abe, is the son of a bitch who shot Mack in the back as he was tryin' to get away in his stocking feet."

Doctor Hudson went to the door and held it open. He had heard all he intended to listen to. "Good night, gents," he snapped. "I have work to do."

Abe exited first. As Burke came out, the marshal said, "Henry, for chrissake, leave this to me. I'm paid to do it. But more'n that, the law is behind me. I'll get him, whoever he is, and most likely he'll hang. It's murder when you shoot an unarmed man. It's worse when it's done from in back."

Burke listened without comment, nodded, and headed out around the geranium bed for the dark roadway. There were lights at the saloon, just about the only lights still burning among Buckhorn's business establishments.

But he did not go there. He stood at the edge of the plankwalk, listening to the saloon's noise and considering its bright lights, thinking of the things he might have done to prevent McElroy's killing. Uppermost among those things were Joe's repeated offers to take care of Demis. For two reasons, Burke had demurred. For one thing, Demis had a wife and two children. For another thing, until today the idea of killing Demis, regardless of how much Burke loathed the man, had not set well with him.

A surprised, friendly voice spoke up from behind as Larry Spearman, who minded Buster Munzer's bar part of the time, stepped up and said, "A man could die of thirst standin' over here lookin' at the saloon." When Burke turned his face, the barman knew instantly he had made a mistake. He cleared his throat and stepped down into the manured dust to cross over as he said, "Just a joke."

Burke said, "Larry, my foreman and riders are over there.

I'd take it kindly if you'd tell them I'll be waitin' down at the livery barn."

Spearman had an opportunity to redeem himself, and seized it. "I'll tell them. I'll keep tellin' them until they leave. Good night."

Burke nodded and turned southward. He was passing the jailhouse when the lanky man named Dunhill emerged, his thick-lensed glasses reflecting the weak light. At sight of Burke, he stopped dead still and nodded his head. Everyone in town who had not seen Burke's riders come down Main Street with a dead man over a horse, had heard about it later. By this late in the day, they had heard the whole story. George Dunhill, who was rarely at a loss for words, was this time. He made a sickly smile and allowed Henry Burke to walk past without making a sound.

The nightman was snoring in a tipped-back chair in the small, cramped, smelly saddle and harness room when Burke reached the barn, listened to the guttural snoring, and went looking for his horse.

He had the animal saddled when his crew came in. They had eaten at the café and had downed a few jolts at the saloon, but they seemed to Burke to be completely sober as they nodded in passing, fanning out to find their saddle mounts.

The nightman was one of those individuals who could sleep through a war. He did not stir, and only once did his cadenced snoring briefly break off. He coughed. Then the cadence was resumed.

Burke entered the little room and put some crumpled old greenbacks on the table. He returned to the runway, followed his men to the back alley where they all mounted, and rode northward until they came to an intersecting roadway heading west out of town. They headed in that direction, for home.

Whiskey made men say things they ordinarily would not say. Jack Waite spoke angrily of riding over to the Demis place and settling up for Mack. Before anyone could growl approval of the idea, Burke made a contemptuous retort. "We're not skulking bushwhackers, damn it. When our turn comes, we'll go right up to his face in broad daylight."

Joe Holden glanced at his employer, then looped his reins and felt around for his cut plug.

By the time they reached the yard, it was not only dark, it was also cold. They had been gone a long time. Some corralled horses out back let them know about it. They were very hungry.

Burke headed for the main house, mixed a glass of water and whiskey, and took it into the bedroom with him. As he perched on the edge of the bed yanking at his boots, he thought derisively of Abe Sutherland. It would be a total damned waste of time for him to ride up yonder. Even if he found those old rocks, all he'd find was black blood and some tracks.

Henry did not finish the whiskey. He rolled in, turned his back on it, and considered the two ways he knew of to settle with Demis. One was to go back to the foothills, cut out as many of his cattle as they could, and push them east in a dead run so's they would shrink ten pounds by the time they crossed the stage road.

That really would not solve anything. It would give Henry and his riders some satisfaction, but it really would not solve anything. Moreover, there was an excellent chance they would run into Marshal Sutherland up there, and that would cause more trouble.

Henry flopped onto his back, staring at the dark ceiling. The other thing he could do was hunt Demis down. That would solve things. One way or another. He probably should have done it a week ago.

He thought of Demis's wife and her two children, and groaned aloud. He tossed a little, then slept.

In the morning, he did not feel particularly rested as he

chewed tough-cooked steak, and spuds fried the color of cinders. He got rid of some of the bad taste with hot coffee.

When he reached the barn, the only man there was the range boss. It seemed to Burke almost as though this had been planned. He looked around. The stalled horses had been fed, so presumably the horses out back had also eaten.

Joe hadn't done that alone. Burke eyed the lanky man leaning on the saddle pole. "Y'know, Joe, now that our cattle are mixed up with Demis's, if we didn't have another thing to do for a month or more other than cutting ours out—and making the damned gather all over again, and working the cattle through, we'd still have enough to keep us humping 'til winter."

Joe nodded, while fidgeting with his gloves, tugging first at one, then at the other one. "Yeah. Trouble is, this other mess came along, and I don't see us puttin' it off." He stopped pulling his gloves and looked steadily at Henry Burke.

The older man neither bobbed his head nor spoke. He walked down to the stall where his big horse was scarfing up the leaves that had been shaken off the stalks of his hay. From down there, Burke said, "It'd just be a waste of time to go up yonder, chouse his razorbacks away, and maybe put a little fear into whoever he might have up there."

Joe nodded, still leaning on the saddle pole.

Burke turned. "We're not goin' to put it off, Joe."

Joe smiled flintily. "Good—because Mack was a special friend of mine." He was waiting for what else Burke had to say. It was a very short wait.

"I hate to do this, Joe, because of his woman and their kids, but it's not me brought this on. It was Jeff right from the start. . . . I think maybe we'd better find out where Jeff is, and leave whatever happens after that up to him."

Joe straightened up, smiling broadly. "Maybe you'd like to know that last night we talked this over at the bunkhouse, an' what you just said pretty well matches what the rest of us figure has got to be done." Joe started out of the barn. "Right after breakfast," he stated, and shook his head ruefully, because yesterday they'd left the yard with empty guts.

Burke got his old coat from its peg, then went back to the house for his Winchester. He was determined, finally, but having made the decision did not leave him feeling pleased. It wasn't the fight he worried about, it was the possibility of leaving two kids orphaned and their mother a widow.

The men gathered at the barn, bundled in their coats and wearing gloves. All they knew was what Joe had told them, and that simply meant that Mr. Burke had made up his mind he was not going to wait for any more Demis-caused disasters. But what exactly Burke meant to do they could only speculate about, until he led his saddled horse outside.

Out there, in the pre-dawn chill, he told them, "I know it's a hell of a waste of time because we got plenty of work waitin' to be done, but what they did to Mack was the last straw. Thing is, I got no idea where Demis will be. I know he likes to hang around town. I also know this time of year, he's got plenty to keep him on his own range. So Joe, you'n Bob take advantage of the dark and get over where you can see his yard. Just keep watching. Don't let him see you, an' whatever you do, don't start a fight. Jack and I'll head for town, in case he heads over there."

Bob Cheney said, "One thing wrong with that idea, Mr. Burke. If anything happens out on the range or in town, it'll be two against whatever he's got with him, which might be his whole crew. After what he done up yonder, he's not goin' to be easy to walk up to."

Burke was patient. "All we're goin' to do is find him. Find out where he's spending most of his time these days."

Jack Waite said, "How about the foothills? He sure will want to know whoever he left up there isn't going to get the same dose of medicine he gave Mack."

"Abe Sutherland said he was going up there. I'd just as

soon not run into him right now, an' the cattle will be fine until we get around to bringin' them home."

They mounted and left the yard in pairs. It was still about half-dark when Burke could smell the smoke from breakfast fires over where Buckhorn stood, even though he could not see the place yet.

Jack had said little on the ride. When they could finally hear dogs barking, he spoke. "Abe Sutherland won't find anything in the foothills."

Burke nodded. "That's what I told him, but I like the idea of him being up there in case we run into Demis. I like Abe. But he's got a job to do, an' I'd just as soon not have to buck him head to head."

They entered town from the lower end, put their horses up at the livery barn, and went for some hot coffee at the little cubbyhole café with steamed-up windows. Daylight was arriving; Buckhorn was coming to life.

The café owner was a fat man whose cooking was not great and whose coffee was strong enough to float a horseshoe, but because he got a lot of traveling peddlers through his café, he always had fresh jokes to pass along to his male customers.

He was in the midst of telling Burke and Jack his latest joke as they toyed with their coffee when George Dunhill walked in, looking cold. The café man had to break off in mid-joke to draw off coffee for Dunhill and take his order for breakfast.

Dunhill eyed Burke askance. He was uncomfortable in Burke's presence. He knew about Burke's murdered rider. He also knew old Henry Burke was not someone a man would want for an enemy. When Burke smiled and nodded, Dunhill did the same. Then, perhaps to make conversation, he said, "They tell me this is a busy time of the year for you stockmen. Well, lately it's been no bed of roses for me. Today, for example, as soon as I finish here I have to unload some crates of freight for Jeff Demis."

Burke gazed steadily at the tall man with the thick eye-glasses. "Is that a fact. What kind of freight?"

"A couple of crated wagons sent from the Studebaker works back east. There are nine crates. I'm short-handed at the corral yard, and those blessed crates are heavy."

Burke continued to sit slouched, gazing at Dunhill. "Why don't you send word to Jeff to come get his crates. He'd most likely be willing."

"I did that day before yesterday. His wife was in yesterday with their buggy to buy some bolt goods. She told me her husband got my message and would come in today."

CHAPTER 8

The Quandary

BURKE sat hunched in thought as George Dunhill ate his breakfast. Now that he knew where Jeff Demis would be, he speculated about Jack Waite's ability to find Joe and Bob over on the Demis range east of the stage road.

There was no reason now for them to sit over there, and Burke suspected that his range boss would be very disappointed if he was not on hand when the face-down came.

But Jack was lame, even though he tried valiantly not to let it show. But perhaps more to the point, Demis's range was large. Nearly as large as the Burke range. Finding two men out there who had been instructed to make themselves as near to invisible as possible would create serious problems, not the least of which was that Jack might have to ride all over hell to find Joe and Bob, during which time Demis would arrive in town.

Burke finally dumped some silver coins beside their cups and led the way outside. He would keep Jack with him here in town. As they stood in the cold sunlight Perc Hudson saw them and started across the road, calling as he walked. When he reached them, he looked twice at Jack's bandaged foot. The cloth was filthy. He raised his gaze and said, "What have you been doing, using your foot instead of a shovel to dung out the barn?" Before Jack could reply, the doctor jerked his head at them. "Come on up and we'll examine the foot and change the dressing."

Jack glanced at his employer. Burke shrugged and struck out after the medical practitioner. When Hudson would have taken them both into his examination room, Burke smiled from a chair in the parlor and said he would wait out there.

He had a few things to unravel. It had not been his intention when they split up in the yard to force a fight. At that time, he had simply wanted to know whether or not it would be possible later on to catch Jeff Demis alone somewhere.

Now, as he sat cross-legged gazing out the front window, hat perched upon his knee, he decided that if Demis was coming, whether Joe Holden was there or not, if the opportunity presented itself, Burke was going to call Demis.

In the back of his mind was a very irritating thought. Unless he got this damned thing finished once and for all, right now when the opportunity came along, he was going to be maybe a month behind at the ranch. Demis was not worth what that would cost Burke.

Buster Munzer, the Antler Saloon's proprietor, came in and exchanged a look and a nod with Burke. Buster found a chair and sank down in it as he held aloft a thickly bandaged hand. "I've always heard whiskey was bad for folks, but since I don't hardly ever drink it myself, this here hand got to be about the worst kind of retribution the good Lord can cause me."

"How'd you do it?"

"Pickin' up the pieces of a broken bottle."

That exhausted the subject. Burke was not really interested in it, anyway. He went back to brooding, until Buster interrupted with a question. "You sick?"

"No. Jack Waite's gettin' the bandage changed on his right foot. A horse stepped on him."

Buster nodded. He had already heard about Jack's injured foot. "Sometimes," he opined, "things seems to come in bunches."

Burke nodded politely. "Seems like it."

"Couple days back, one of George Dunhill's hostlers at the corral yard got a foot run over by a stagecoach. Right there in the yard. Couple of days before that Jeff Demis's tophand, feller by the name of Richard Ward, had a horse fall with him. Busted his ankle, and that's pretty close to the foot." Buster paused as though considering what he had just said, then shrugged it off as he resumed speaking. "Have you seen the new feller Jeff hired to take Ward's place?"

Burke shook his head.

Buster settled back in the chair, lowering his bandaged hand to one knee very gently. "His name's Tom Grant. He isn't more'n average height but so help me, Henry, he's as broad as a brick wall and built like one. . . . Never smiles, never has much to say."

Burke vaguely remembered someone saying something about a man with that build. "Does he go around with Jeff?"

Buster grinned. "Like peas in a pod. They're gathering now, one of the other hands told me, but if Jeff comes to town, there's Tom Grant ridin' beside him. Larry Spearman an' I got a joke about it. We was wondering when Jeff an' his wife go to bed, if Tom Grant don't slip in on the far side."

Henry sat in silence, gazing at the saloon man. Doggone Joe Holden anyway, he had been right. Demis had indeed figured what reaction might follow in the wake of what he had done up in the foothills. That grinning, underhanded whelp had figured out that Burke would come after him.

He had hired a gunman.

He asked Buster if Demis's new hired hand visited the saloon. Munzer smiled. "Together, Henry. If Jeff comes in, so does Tom Grant. But they drink different. You know Jeff, he'd drink swill if it had a jolt in it. Tom Grant don't drink anything but my best malt whiskey. . . . It goes with the rest of him, I think. He don't wear heavy cowhide boots like everyone else does, no, he's got five or six rows of different colored stitching on his uppers, and real nice little toe caps, different color from the feet. His belt an' holster is hand-carved. Beautiful work, Henry. His gun's got silver-inlay, all engraved, down the backstrap. Grant sure spends money on himself. Larry an' I got that impression the first time he came in. But he's not a real friendly cuss, so we don't josh him."

Burke pulled in a big, deep-down breath. It was too late, he told himself. He'd done the wrong thing; he should have brought Joe and Bob Cheney to town, too. It was too late to change that. He'd made up his mind down at the café to call Demis as soon as the man got to town. If he did that, he was going to have to go up against a damned gunfighter!

He arose and stepped to a roadway window and stood there with his hands clasped in back, gazing out. He had been as good as the next man with weapons thirty, forty years back. Now his hands were gnarled from labor, his reflexes were slower; he'd noticed that a couple of years earlier when he'd teamed up at the marking ground with one of his riders. He was still as accurate with a lariat, but shades slower getting the rope ready for the cast.

He watched the box-like wagon of an itinerant peddler and fix-it man go past in the road, complete with fry pans, scissors, odds and ends nailed to the wagon's side, advertising the peddler's trade and wares.

He and Jack could go to the livery barn, saddle up and leave town. And if he did that, as soon as Jack got back, he'd tell Joe and Bob what Dunhill had said at the café about Demis coming to town. Holden was not going to approve of Burke tucking tail, even though Burke had made a particular point of telling them in the yard that this was a scouting trip. He had emphasized to Joe and Bob that no one was to provoke trouble, just scout the Demis place so they would have an idea of Demis's routine and habits for a later showdown.

Burke turned. The saloon man rose restlessly and paced the room as he spoke. "You got any idea who shot your rider? There's a lot of speculation in town about that."

Burke said, "Is that a fact?"

"Yeah. Over at my bar I've heard just about every notion—

from Mack havin' been waylaid by a couple of In'ians who still live back in the mountains, to Mack havin' surprised a renegade killer on the run from the law."

Burke watched Munzer pace.

The pacing halted as Jack and Doctor Hudson emerged from the examination room. Jack's foot had a fresh, clean bandage, without the plaster cast he'd been wearing. When Burke's gaze went to the injured foot, Doctor Hudson said, "There never was serious damage, but there was some bad bruising. I didn't put the cast on him because it was a serious injury, I put it on because I've been patching rangemen for many years; I know how they behave. I immobilized the foot so the bruised tendons and ligaments would get a good chance to heal." Doctor Hudson crossed the room and beckoned for Jack Waite to walk. He favored the foot from habit, then stopped favoring it and moved out in a normal stride. He smiled at Burke and Perc Hudson. "Good as new."

Hudson got a pained and exasperated look on his face. "It's not as good as new. I told you that in the examination room. It feels that good, but you must still be careful with it. It can be easily re-injured. . . . Henry, that'll be one dollar."

Jack winked at Buster Munzer, as though to imply that doctors always said things like that and they didn't mean a damned thing.

Burke handed over the cartwheel and led Jack back to the roadway. "Better head for the emporium an' get you a slipper," he said, rather absently.

As they were approaching the broad doorway of the general store, he rallied a little from his former mood and said, "You reckon they'll sell us just one slipper?"

They wouldn't, and Burke did not ask them to. Jack shoved the useless slipper into his rear pocket, made several short excursions around the big old gloomy room, and was satisfied.

Outside, a range rider from the southeastern range who had repped for Burke's outfit and knew Jack well, came along. He looked at the slippered foot, then at Jack and said, "Pigeon kick you?"

Jack grinned. "Nope. It was an eight hunnert-pound wood tick. Fell out of a bush right on my danged foot."

The cowboy accepted that. "You got to watch 'em. I've seen 'em that large many times."

As the rider winked at Jack and resumed his stroll northward, Burke made his decision. He would not leave town. Beyond that, he did not speculate.

A top-buggy whose tassles had been cut off unevenly, entered town from the south. It was a sturdy rig, old with cracked, faded black paint and very little of the yellow left on the wheels or the underside of the running gear, but it was well-made. Henry recognized the buggy as soon as he saw it. He also knew who had manufactured it: the Studebaker buggy-works back East.

He had not seen the woman who drove the rig in several years, but he remembered her. After their initial meeting seven or eight years ago, he had wondered how a woman that handsome, and with what he had assumed at the time was good intelligence, could have married as thorough a no-good son of a bitch as Jeff Demis.

He was still watching as the rig swung left around a big, laden freighter drawn by eight Mexican mules. As the buggy passed Burke and Jack on the plankwalk the woman turned, met Burke's gaze, and neither nodded nor spoke as she faced forward, her features expressionless.

He watched her drive north, thinking that she did not look one bit different today than she had looked years back. She had wings of silver over each ear, otherwise her hair was a reddish chestnut color. She sat erect on the buggy seat, her shoulders squared. Burke remembered thinking years ago that despite having had two children, as well as having lived the hard life of a range cattleman's woman, Mary Ellen Demis's figure was better than the figures of nine-tenths of the much younger women he had known.

Jack interrupted his thoughts. "You hungry?"

Burke brought his attention back with an effort. "I guess so," he said, and led the way to the café.

Buckhorn was bustling. It usually was before noon. The café counter had men eating all along it, except for some empty places toward the upper end, which was near the fat man's cooking area. It was also directly in front of the roadway window.

The fat man was too busy to lean down and tell one of his jokes. He took their orders and hustled back behind a cotton curtain with huge cabbage roses printed on it, which blocked off his kitchen.

Burke waited until their java arrived, then cupped it in both hands as he said, "Jack, you recollect that big man who was with Jeff the day he hired those two riders away from you?"

Jack nodded. "Sure do."

"Did he wear a carved belt an' holster, and fancy boots?"

Jack did not remember the boots, but he remembered the belt and holster. He also remembered the gun. "Yeah. An' he had one of those silver-inlaid an' engraved six-shooters you see every now an' then when some fancy gunsel shows up."

Burke reared back so the platter of food could be placed in front of him. After the café man departed, Burke pushed the coffee cup away and spoke again. "You've run across gunfighters, haven't you?"

Jack nodded while leaning in to inspect his meal. "A few. At least folks told me that's who they were." Jack's head swung sharply, his habitually narrowed eyes widening. "You reckon? Where'd you get such a notion?"

"By putting two and two together. But that don't mean I'm right."

Jack leaned back, forgetting his meal for the time being. He stared at his employer, then faced forward. In a quiet voice he said, "By gawd, Mr. Burke, I think you're right.

That day when he came along with Mr. Demis I was too mad at what Mr. Demis did to pay much attention to his friend. But thinkin' back . . . that big feller just stood there, thumbs hooked in his fancy belt, lookin' and listenin' and not saying a word or even acting very interested." Jack paused, then said, "Jeff Demis got himself a hired gunfighter?"

Burke went to work on his meal while Jack sat gazing at him for a full ten seconds before going to work on his own plate. But as he ate he thought, and when he had reached some conclusions, he leaned in slightly and spoke in a low-ered voice.

"Suppose he's with Mr. Demis when he comes to town?"

Burke went on eating as he replied. "That's what I've been thinking. I expect he will be. Unless I miss my guess, Jeff's hired himself a gunfighter because he knew tryin' to drive his cattle in them foothills was going to raise hell and prop it up."

Jack took another mouthful of food, swallowed it, and leaned in again. It never occurred to him to suggest they leave town. He said, "Well now, sure as I'm settin' here Mr. Demis is goin' to see you in town, and knowin' how he's acted in the past, and suspicioning that he's got himself a gen-u-wine gunfighter, he'll go out of his way to humiliate you in front of the townsfolk, then leave it up to you and his gunfighter."

Burke continued to eat.

Jack spoke again, even more softly this time. "I got the answer, Mr. Burke. We know Demis's comin', and we suspect he'll have his bodyguard with him. Now then, neither you nor me is up to facin' some professional man-killer, so when I'm finished eatin', I'll just stroll down to the livery barn, an' when no one is lookin' I'll snake out my Winchester from the saddle boot, go out into the back alley, find a real good place where I can see in every direction up an' down Main Street, an' when Mr. Demis and his bloodyhand come along and see you—commence makin' loud talk and insults, why

I'll just give 'em a chance to drop everything, an' if they don't I'll take care of the gunman first, then Mr. Demis."

Burke continued eating. Jack watched him for a while, then straightened up to re-attack his own meal. It probably was in the old rangeman's favor that although he had just discovered he might get killed, he could still eat heartily.

Some diners left and more filed in to take their places, until the café was full. The café man whipped past, sweating like a stud horse.

They paid up and returned to the roadway. Burke gazed southward, saw only that laden freight rig with the Mexican mules about a mile below town, and turned to gaze northward. He saw Mary Ellen Demis's buggy standing in front of Doctor Hudson's place. He might have speculated about this, but Jack was speaking. "Mr. Burke . . . we took too long eating." Jack was jutting his chin at two men strolling up the plankwalk from the direction of the livery barn. One of them was Jeff Demis. He was on the road side. The other man was no taller than Demis, perhaps five feet ten inches, but he was almost twice as wide, and massively thick, and he moved with surprising lightness for an individual of his heft.

Burke was briefly transfixed by the sight of the man with the silver-inlaid six-gun. Jack broke in again to say, "There's a dogtrot behind us. We could duck down there, cross over southward and come in behind them."

While Jack had been saying this, Jeff Demis's head turned slightly. He saw Burke and Jack Waite. He grinned, while speaking softly from the side of his mouth. The big man on Demis's left side turned his head, scanning in the direction of Henry Burke and his wiry, faded tophand.

CHAPTER 9

When the Time Comes

DEMIS and Grant walked slowly to the front window of the harness-works, then halted and faced inward, seemingly admiring a carved saddle on display and a fine set of black driving harnesses with nickel buckles.

Jack Waite snorted, but said nothing. Neither did Burke. His enemies across the road were discussing strategy, sure as hell. They weren't interested in a fancy saddle or driving harness.

People passed, oblivious to Burke and one of his riders standing in front of the café, staring intently at two men over in the shade on the opposite side of the roadway.

George Dunhill strolled past the pole gates of his corral yard, mopping sweat with a blue bandanna, halted, and looked up and down Main Street. He saw Demis and recognized him despite the shadows and the distance. He tucked away the bandanna as he walked purposefully in the direction of the harness-works window.

Burke did not see him approaching until Jack mentioned it. By then it was too late to advise Dunhill to stay away. Also, Demis and his hired gunman had turned around, evidently having perfected their strategy. Burke had a moment to watch their faces before George Dunhill hailed them and walked on up, creating a diversion that no one really wanted.

Jack Waite muttered under his breath. He had yanked loose the thong that held a rider's holstered Colt in place. He did not appear to be the least bit intimidated by the size or the reputation of Jeff Demis's gunfighter.

Burke heard a heavy tread behind him on the duckboards, without heeding it. At any moment he expected the discussion over yonder to end and the fight to begin. He too had his gun riding free in its holster. He'd also had time to consider the situation. He knew where that dogtrot was Jack had mentioned, and he also knew that a wise man probably would have ducked down it to emerge in the far alleyway. So far, it appeared that none of the pedestrians on the plank-walks or the drivers and riders in the roadway had any idea what was about to happen.

There were four men who knew: Jack Waite, Jeff Demis, Henry Burke, and Tom Grant. One would have been too many.

Burke spoke from the corner of his mouth. "Concentrate on the big man. Both of us will concentrate on him. If we're still upright when the smoke clears, we can look after Jeff."

Jack grunted without speaking.

Dunhill fished out his blue bandanna and mopped the back of his neck. Demis was bobbing his head and grinning. Whatever they had discussed over there appeared to have been satisfactorily concluded, except that with someone like Jeff Demis, a man was never sure, because he bobbed his head and grinned at just about anything that was said.

Burke took down a big, slow breath, and exhaled it. Dunhill was turning back in the direction of his corral yard. Demis and his gunfighter were speaking softly, ready to face the men on the opposite plankwalk. Behind Burke, the man whose heavy tread had been ignored moments earlier spoke gruffly. "What in hell do you think you're doing! If Abe was in town, he'd collar all four of you and lock you up. Henry, don't be foolish."

Burke did not turn, neither did the wiry, bandy-legged man at his side, but both of them recognized Doctor Hudson's voice, and Burke answered curtly without taking his eyes off Demis and Grant. "Don't stand back there behind us, Perc."

Hudson's indignation made his next remark ring with authoritarian clarity. "You pair of idiots, haven't you heard who that big man is, over there?"

They had indeed heard. Jack Waite replied. "Yeah, we've heard, Doctor. . . . Like Mr. Burke said, you better not stand behind us."

Hudson, who was also a large, heavy-boned, burly man, was not noted for great patience, and right now he was getting red in the face as he stared at the men across the roadway. Demis was grinning. Grant was expressionless, standing loose and watchful. Doctor Hudson called over to them, "Jeff, you and your friend go on about your business."

Demis's grin was locked in place, a death's-head smile. "Perc, it's you better move away. Go deliver a baby or something."

Hudson took one step forward and halted on Henry Burke's left side, angry and defiant. The calling back and forth had caught the attention of a number of people on both sides of the roadway. They halted to turn and watch. Here and there on both sides of the roadway, people moved swifly and discreetly into the closest doorways.

Behind Demis, the harness-maker appeared in his doorway, wiping both hands on a brown apron. Up the roadway on the east side, one shop south of the Antler Saloon, another merchant appeared in his doorway. He was Gus McPherson, the local gunsmith, a short, bull-necked, grizzled man. He did not have to stand there long before he understood what was happening. He stepped back inside his shop, took down a Henry rifle, checked the slide for loads and returned to the doorway where he stood, holding the rifle in both hands.

Jeff Demis's smile looked strained. His narrowed eyes were fixed dead ahead, on Henry and Jack Waite across the road. Evidently Doctor Hudson constituted nothing more than an annoyance, because Demis placed his right palm upon the handle of his sidearm.

The barrel-built man said something in a husky whisper that made Demis's gaze shift fleetingly northward in the direction of the gun-works. His grin became a grimace.

Again the gunfighter whispered from the corner of his mouth. Doctor Hudson's angry voice interrupted, loud enough to be heard for a considerable distance. Now too, the mounted and wheeled traffic had halted to the north and south of the area where the armed and angry men faced one another across the width of the roadway.

Hudson said, "Jeff, George's got some crates for you up at the corral yard. He's waiting for you."

The gunfighter turned to speak to his companion. The pair of them walked away northward toward the corral yard. They did not look back, not even as they were entering the palisaded yard of the stage company.

Perc Hudson faced Henry Burke. For a moment he simply glared, then he threw up his hands, rolled his eyes in monumental disgust, and walked away without saying a word.

The gunsmith retreated from his doorway, replaced the Henry rifle and paused at his workbench long enough to sift through an assortment of brown paper cigarette stubs until he found one long enough, relit it, and went back to work.

Burke and his hired rider exchanged a look and walked toward the saloon. At the doorway, Jack Waite made a dry comment. "I ain't too sure we could have done it, Mr. Burke."

Burke had no comment about that until they had both downed one jolt and were solemnly watching Larry Spearman refill the little glasses. As Larry moved off, Burke leaned in, looked at his rangeman, and wagged his head. He did not say a word.

It was too early for the regular saloon customers to be arriving, but several men drifted in, ranged along the bar, covertly eyed Burke and Jack, and ordered something wet. Burke watched their faces in the backbar mirror; if either he or Jack opened their mouths, they were going to be swamped with questions and offers of free whiskey.

When Burke and Joe departed, the loafers along the bar raised their voices in a babble of talk. Spearman did not become involved. Like most people in Buckhorn at the time of the confrontation, he had not known anything had been happening until it was over.

Burke stood on the walk in front of the saloon considering the wide, sagging pole gates of the corral yard, which were opposite them and maybe a hundred feet northward. There was no one in sight up there. Jack grumbled, "Next time we'll have the crew."

Directly opposite the corral yard gates, the gunsmith was standing in his doorway. He called, beckoned with an upraised arm, then disappeared inside as Burke and Jack turned northward.

The gunsmith had hot coffee and three tin cups set up on his counter. He ran a thick hand through some gray hair and shook his head at Henry Burke when he said, "I'd have dropped one of 'em, and maybe both before they'd knowed where I was firing from." He jerked a thumb in the direction of the Henry rifle.

Neither Burke nor Jack Waite had known the gunsmith had been standing in his doorway. He explained that, and justified it curtly. "Jeff Demis is no good an' never was, not since I've knowed him, and that goes back a long way. . . . That hefty gent with the fancy gun—I've seen at least a dozen like him. Cold-blooded, deadly bad, Henry. They got no feelings one way or another. Many years back, I earned the right to hate men like that. I'd have dropped him like a stone the minute he moved his right hand."

Burke was no more surprised that there had been an unknown ally backing them from a recessed doorway than Jack Waite was. They were grateful, finished their coffee and returned to the roadway. There was no point in remaining in town, and by the time they reached the yard the day would be close to its end.

As they ambled in the direction of the livery barn, Jack

pinched up his badly weathered and deeply lined face as he said, "I got an idea, Mr. Burke. We don't have to split up, like we done today. What you'n me learnt is that Jeff don't go anywhere without his gunfighter, an' somethin' else we learnt was that if Jeff's called to town to pick somethin' up, he'll come. . . . Now then, suppose Dunhill or the feller at the general store was to send word that Jeff's got a package to be picked up?" Jack spread his hands wide and looked very pleased with himself. "Like baitin' wolves. We'll send him word, he'll come to town with his gunfighter, and our whole crew will be waitin'. . . . Like shootin' fish in a rain barrel."

Burke walked along in silence. Not within anyone's recollection had he given immediate approval to any suggestion. He gave none now, but he winked at Jack Waite as they stepped down to cross to the same side of the road as the livery barn.

The morning traffic had dwindled, in the roadway as well as the plankwalks. Early shoppers had completed their sojourn at the general store in time to arrive back home before the heat arrived. The same thing applied to horseback-men and light rigs and buggy traffic. It did not apply to the big freight outfits; they operated fifteen-hour days, always at a snail's pace, summer or winter.

The area where Burke left the east plankwalk to cut diagonally across the west plankwalk, was free of both pedestrian and wheeled traffic. When he and Jack were approaching the middle of the sun-bright roadway, a furtive silhouette appeared, then disappeared in a blend of shadows behind the buildings on the west side of Main Street. It had been visible only briefly in a wide space between two buildings. No one had seen it.

Jack cocked a squinty eye at the position of the sun before reaching the far plankwalk. He engaged in some elemental arithmetic and determined that Joe Holden and Bob Cheney would most likely have supper ready at the bunkhouse before he and Burke reached the yard, something Burke had also considered likely.

They encountered the liveryman on his way out as they were going in. The liveryman grinned, made an unnecessary little wave, and said, "They're rested, grained, an' ready to ride, Mr. Burke. You can pay the dayman."

Burke turned to watch the liveryman hastening away. In all the years he had known the liveryman, this was the first time he had ever known him to hasten away rather than stand and talk. It was also the first time he had ever been told to give his money to someone else.

Jack was already entering the runway with its enveloping, even distribution of hay-fragrant gloom. The only two openings in the barn faced northward, toward Main Street, and southward out back, where there was a wide space between the barn and a network of old, gnawed corrals on the far side of the alley.

Burke followed his rider into the cool gloom. They hesitated in front of the harness room, where their outfits were straddling a pole, but since there was no sign of the dayman, they decided to find their own horses. They spread out, Burke looking into the stalls on the left side of the runway, Jack doing the same on the right side.

They were roughly opposite one another and about seventy-five feet from the doorless rear opening when Burke recognized the big head of his mount watching from the open upper half of the stall door. He turned to see if Jack had found his animal yet.

A sharply incisive voice spoke from inside the rear barn opening, where sunshine made a harsh background for anyone inside the barn who had to look out there.

"*Burke!* You got guts for an old man!"

Burke saw Jack Waite freeze across the runway from him. He also saw the bear-like silhouette of a thickly built man standing slightly to one side, barely inside the runway, so that anyone looking at him had the full force of the brilliant sunlight in his face.

The thick man straightened up a little, with his head very slightly canted. "No one goin' to interfere this time," he said. "No one's goin' to do a lot of talking either. . . . You better fight, Mr. Burke, you'n that scrawny cowboy of yours, because whether you do or don't is all the same to me."

The shock to Burke's system was identical to the shock of suddenly being immersed in cold water. He was completely motionless for several seconds as Tom Grant was speaking.

Jack Waite moved first; he had a half-open stall door on his right side. He went for his gun as he was springing to enter the stall. The door was not open wide enough. The gunfighter's head was still very slightly to one side and Burke did not see him draw, but the explosion was deafening. Jack had only half-drawn his weapon when the bullet hit him, slamming him violently against the edge of the half-open door.

Burke swung sideways as he drew. He might have thought he had a couple of seconds before Tom Grant changed position after shooting Jack. He didn't have.

Grant's muzzleblast appeared as an arrow-like flash of flame in the gloom. The man's speed was uncanny. So was his aim, except that this time his target was flattening sideways. Grant had only a fraction of a moment to steady up the swinging barrel as his finger tightened inside the trigger guard. He made the correction, but the bullet cut across Burke's body, tearing cloth instead of plowing into flesh and bone. But it was enough; the wrenching impact of the tearing cloth made Burke stagger drunkenly. He tried desperately to raise his gun as he cocked it, but Grant was unequalled at his trade. The second time, Grant corrected his aim while simultaneously squeezing the trigger. He had Burke squarely in view.

That slug caused a blinding flood of redness to explode

behind Henry Burke's eyes with a sensation not unlike that of water boiling.

Burke's desperate reflex made his trigger finger jerk convulsively. His gun exploded, the bullet plowed into the runway's hardpan earthen floor as Burke twisted sideways under the violent impact, sinking down to the woodwork on his left side.

CHAPTER 10

Abe Sutherland's Memorable Day

PERC HUDSON was white-faced. He refused to look at Abe Sutherland, who was standing slightly to one side and behind so that the light of two hanging lamps would shine directly onto the white-painted wooden table in Hudson's old converted buggy shed.

Outside it was as dark as the inside of a boot, and while the noise of raised voices from inside the Antler Saloon came as far as the roadway, in the buggy shed there was not a sound, until a rattle of rowels and rein chains in the alley signified the arrival of several mounted men. Hudson did not raise his head as he said, "Tell them to wait outside. And Abe—if that's who I think it is: Joe Holden, you better keep an eye on him."

With the departure of Marshal Sutherland, Doctor Hudson straightened up, grimaced because he had been working in a bent-over position too long, and looked fiercely into the gray, slack face of Henry Burke as he said softly, "You darned idiot. I warned you. Fat lot of good it did."

There was no response. In fact, Hudson had to grope for his listening device to be sure Burke's heart was still beating. The sound he heard was not reassuring. He put the listening device aside and rinsed both hands in a little basin two-thirds full of pink water, then returned to his work, lips sucked flat, pale blue eyes bleakly intent on what he was doing.

Beyond the table—where no direct light reached, only

shadows, Jack Waite lay wrapped from head to toe in an old army blanket. The bullet that had ended his life had struck him squarely in the middle of the chest, over the breastbone it had shattered to splinters.

There were several raised voices outside. Perc Hudson ignored them. He had been bending over the wooden table for three hours, and the closer he came to the end of his efforts to control the damage done to his old friend, the more depleted and inadequate he felt.

The long bullet gash across Burke's middle had done little more than scratch the skin. Hudson had no way of knowing Burke had been sideways when that slug had caught him.

The second bullet had done extensive damage. Perc Hudson had been working desperately just to stop the hemorrhaging. After that, he used tweezers to pick out bits of shirt lint. He worked with sure hands and a steadily sinking heart. The last time he straightened up to gingerly ease his strained back into its proper position, the men outside had either departed or were no longer talking. Either way, the silence was deeply enduring.

He had to remove his eyeglasses and wipe them before discerning which bottle on the shelf was embalming fluid and which was corn whiskey. He swallowed several times and shoved the bottle away, dipped his hands and wiped them again, pulled up a tall stool, and hunched atop it beside the old man on his table.

He did the bandaging in this position. It required a good half hour, after which Doctor Hudson leaned back, rested both elbows on the edge of the table, and put his head in his hands. He was as exhausted as he could ever remember being.

There was a deferential scratching at the door. Hudson raised his head. "Who is it?"

"Bob Cheney. I ride for—"

"Come in. I know who you are."

Cheney stepped inside, closed the door soundlessly, and

for some reason removed his hat. He looked once at the doctor, then stood like stone gazing at his employer.

Hudson returned to the corn whiskey jug, tapped it again, and was putting it down as Cheney whispered a question: "Is he dead?"

Hudson looked at Burke. "He wasn't ten minutes ago. . . . Where is Holden?"

"Down at the jailhouse with Marshal Sutherland."

Doctor Hudson expelled a rattling breath. "I'm tired. Someone's got to stay here with him, but I've got to lie down for a while."

Bob Cheney nodded his head, went to the high stool, and sat beside the table.

Doctor Hudson nodded and headed for the door. Cheney stopped him with another whispered question. "Can he make it?"

Hudson checked an irritable reply. "I don't know. I've done everything I know to do. I don't know whether it's enough or not. If he so much as groans, come wake me."

Cheney whispered again. "He sure don't look good, does he?"

Hudson had a hand on the door latch when he replied. "No. Mostly, they don't when they been shot like he was. Remember—any change at all, just a wiggling finger or a moan, you come to the house for me."

Outside, the stars were standing in vertical array, there was a thin moon, and the night smelled of woodsmoke, as it always did from suppertime onward in Buckhorn.

Two lights shone out onto Main Street. One was in Doctor Hudson's parlor; the other one was down at the jailhouse, where its reflection showed in the roadway as a series of light and dark stripes. The window through which the light spilled had bars in front of the glass.

The jailhouse was warm. It took no more than two cords of wood to see Marshal Sutherland through an average winter. The jailhouse walls were inordinately thick, which accounted for the structure's ability to retain heat during cold nights, and for its ability to remain fifteen degrees cooler inside than it was outside, almost any midsummer day.

Abe Sutherland's office almost always smelled of coffee, whether he was there or not, and whether someone had recently boiled up a brew or not.

It smelled that way now, but with justification because Abe had made a fresh potful about the time he opened the door to permit Joe Holden to walk in.

Joe had declined to have his coffee laced, so Abe Sutherland had splashed whiskey into his own cup and put the bottle away. He and Joe had been discussing the shooting at the livery barn. Abe could tell him nothing he had not gotten secondhand around town, because he had not returned to town until dusk.

Joe had listened well, then had fixed the lawman with a flat look and said, "It don't sound right, does it? Mr. Burke an' Jack was braced by Demis and that gunfighter of his the width of the road. That time it came to nothing. Less'n an hour later someone shot Jack and Mr. Burke in the livery barn, back near the alley—and Demis and his gunfighter had already left town with a wagonload they got from George Dunhill, full of crates from the corral yard."

Abe leaned on his desk. "That's about it. That's the story I heard when I got back this evening."

Joe eyed the big man skeptically. "No one saw the gunman? Abe, where was the liveryman?"

"At the café, havin' dinner."

"Where was his day man?"

"He'd gone over to the blacksmith's shop to get a couple of horses that'd been shod."

Joe's brows knitted. "Was it dinnertime? And couldn't those horses have been brought back earlier in the day, or later?"

Abe sighed. "Joe," he said patiently, "sure, I expect they

could have brought the horses back later in the afternoon, but they didn't. All that means is that they didn't get around to doin' it earlier or later. . . . You're lookin' for something I don't think you're going to find. I asked up one side of the road an' down the other side. A lot of people saw Jeff and his gunfighter leave town with that damned loaded wagon—and no one saw a gunman in the alley, or anywhere else down by the livery barn."

Joe reset his hat. "Who else could it have been? Abe, he was a dead shot, and fast. Both of 'em had their guns out."

Abe nodded. "Yeah. But Joe . . . listen to me for a minute; I'm not saying Jeff's man didn't shoot them. What I'm trying to get across to you is that I can't just ride out there and haul Jeff and this other feller back and lock them up for murder—unless by gawd I got something I can sink my teeth into as evidence, and so far I haven't found it. But—it only happened today. Tomorrow I'll turn the town inside out. If there was anyone who saw anything I'll find—"

"You talked to George at the corral yard?"

Abe leaned back and rolled his eyes. "He was one of the first people I talked to. He said Jeff and that big feller were together all the time the wagon was being loaded. He said they left together, both of them sittin' up there on the seat like crows on a fence." Abe eyed Burke's range boss thoughtfully, then rocked forward to lean on the desk again. "I'll find him. If it wasn't some darned renegade passin' through and they maybe stumbled onto him fixing to rob the liveryman's safe, and by now he's fifty miles away and still riding, I'll find him."

Joe Holden turned a thinly disguised look of scorn on the larger man, and pushed up out of his chair. They gazed at one another for a moment before the range boss said, "Yeah, you'll find him, an' by the time you do, Abe, that son of a bitch is goin' to be face down and stone-cold."

Abe heaved up to his feet wearing a bleak expression. "It's goin' to be done legal, Joe."

Joe nodded agreement. "Sure it is. Legal the same way he killed Jack and maybe killed Mr. Burke." The range boss's gray gaze was veiled. "He's goin' to see it coming the same way Jack and Mr. Burke did. It won't be from an ambush, it'll be straight up and head to head. Plumb legal."

Abe's brows dropped. "Let me tell you something, Joe. Tom Grant isn't a cowboy. He dresses like one, maybe, except for his fancy gun and boots and all, but you go up against him and you're going to be number three."

"You know him?"

"No. Just his name, what he looks like, and how he acts. That's enough. But Jeff knows him sure as hell or he wouldn't have hired Grant to keep himself from getting shot by you or Henry, or someone else like you and Henry. He's a gunfighter, an' he's a very good one. How do I know? Because in my trade I've run into gunfighters before, and if they're past eighteen or maybe twenty, and are still above ground, they are deadly fast and accurate. There's not a range rider alive who can go up against someone like that and live to tell about it—including you."

Joe Holden's expression had been changing from angry to bleakly sardonic as he listened. But he said nothing after Sutherland had finished. He simply stepped to the door, then looked back to smile before departing.

Marshal Sutherland remained standing behind his desk, gazing at the door after it closed. He felt a slight chill, rather like a premonition, attributed it to his weariness, ignored it, and went around to blow out the lamps before heading for his quarters up at the rooming house.

Henry Burke had been correct. Abe had wasted a day riding into the foothills. Even though he had found those scabrous black rocks where someone, presumably Mack, had lost a lot of blood, that was all he found because, as Burke had prophesied, the cattle had trampled everything, including what had remained of the line camp Burke and his men had established.

He had seen a solitary rider up there. The man sat his horse, watching everything Marshal Sutherland did, and when Abe had finally ridden down to talk, the rider was unable to tell him much. He had not, he said, been with the crew that had returned the Demis razorbacks to the foothills. He had been sent up afterwards to keep an eye on them.

Maybe it was a lie, but one thing was a fact; there had been nothing up there to help the marshal in his search, so he headed back for Buckhorn, having ridden all over hell for nothing.

He was on the boardinghouse porch, one hand reaching for the door latch when a familiar voice spoke from farther back. "A word, Abe."

Abe turned to face Doctor Hudson. He said nothing, not even "good evening." Hudson stepped up onto the porch. "I think we're going to lose Henry."

Abe Sutherland nodded woodenly. He was not surprised, and right now he was too tired to feel as miserable over the loss of an old friend as he would feel after ten hours of sleep.

"It's not going to require a hell of a lot of intelligence to figure out who shot them, and I've been in this country long enough to understand that once the feeling becomes unanimous, there is going to be serious trouble."

Abe leaned on the doorjamb. He did not intend to stand out here arguing with Perc Hudson over what had happened and the inadvisibility of people banding together like vigilantes to do something about it, so he simply said, "It's been a hell of a long day, Perc. I'll stop by in the morning. Good night."

Doctor Hudson reached out. "One more minute, Abe. Jeff Demis's wife came to see me this morning."

Abe faced around, his eyes showing some interest.

"What she told me is supposed to be a confidence. In my trade that's one of the cardinal rules. But—I don't know how other people handle these things, I only know that I'm not going to stand by doing nothing and feeling sanctimonious because I kept the faith, when what she told me is sure as the devil going to get someone killed."

Marshal Sutherland settled against the doorjamb again, his interest increasing.

Doctor Hudson paused, then said, "She argued with Jeff about hiring that gunfighter. The result of that discussion was her main reason for visiting me this morning. He hit her in the stomach with his fist; she couldn't keep her breakfast down. He told her if she stuck her nose into his business one more time he'd overhaul her until she wouldn't be able to stand upright without help."

Abe glanced right and left. They were alone, the town was dark, the roadway was empty. He pointed to a pair of old chairs and sat down in one as Doctor Hudson went to the other one. Abe said, "How bad was she hurt?"

"Well, I gave her some stomach powders. Mostly, I think time will take care of it, but he hit her a hell of a whack. She's puffed up and black and blue."

Marshal Sutherland settled deeper into the old chair, stretched his legs and blew out a big breath, then quietly said, "Someday, Perc, someday . . ."

"Yes. And I hope I'm there when it happens. Anyway, she told me she overheard Jeff and Grant talking about slipping over to the Burke place and firing the buildings."

Abe looked up. "When?"

"If they set a date, she didn't hear it. But what kept me from sleepin' tonight is what will happen. Henry may be out of it, but he's got some pretty rough'n tough men working for him. I don't know much about that young one, Cheney I think his name is, but I know a little about Joe Holden."

The lawman nodded his head without speaking. He was thinking of the enigmatic smile Joe had showed as he had been leaving the jailhouse a while back.

Hudson leaned forward, looking directly at the larger man. "Joe Holden killed three men in Idaho in fair fights."

Abe Sutherland's tiredness vanished. "Where did you hear that?"

"Do you remember last year when one of George's coaches lost a wheel north of town, up where those boulders come down to the road, and four people who were inside got hurt?"

The marshal nodded. He remembered that incident very well. The driver had crawled halfway to town with a broken wrist and a shattered kneecap before a rancher had come along and brought him the rest of the way, flat out in the back of his wagon. He also remembered Doctor Hudson going up there to care for the other injured people. "You patched them up."

Hudson said, "You probably don't remember that one of those folks was a big, bearded freighter named Murray Slavin."

Abe said, "Broken collarbone?"

"You do remember. He sat on my porch after I'd done what I could, waiting for the next southbound stage. He saw Henry ride in one afternoon with his crew. He recognized Holden. He was in the town where Joe killed those men. Abe, he was positive it was the same man, and asked what his name was. I told him who Holden was and Slavin said, 'That's him. That's the same name, and that's the same man, as sure as I'm sitting here.' "

Abe sat in silence for a long while, then shoved up to his feet as he said, "Thanks, Perc." He did not mention the smile on Joe's face down at the jailhouse, or the little premonition he'd had.

Hudson also arose. He watched the lawman step to the door and said, "Abe, what bothered me most tonight is that you can't do this by yourself. It's snowballed into something that could cause a damned war."

Abe smiled from the doorway. "I'll see you in the morning, Perc. I'm obliged to you. Good night."

This time he meant it. Hudson watched him enter the

building and close the door very quietly after himself, then he too headed home.

Before returning to his bedroom, he went to the carriage shed. Cheney was sound asleep on the floor, and Henry did not seem to have moved even a finger. Hudson did not linger. If Henry were dead he did not need a doctor, and if he were still hanging on weakly, there was nothing more Perc Hudson could do for him.

Whatever happened now was up to Henry Burke, the tough, whiskey-drinking, hardworking, lonely old cowman who had not changed one whit in temperament or appearance since Percy Hudson had first met him years earlier.

CHAPTER 11

No Promises

MARSHAL Sutherland had a large breakfast at the café, and crossed to his office to fire up the stove and make a pot of coffee before it was too hot to have a fire. Then he stood gazing at his wall rack of weapons.

He was standing like that, with his back to the roadway door, when it opened and Joe Holden walked in looking fresh, shaved, and fed. Abe studied the range boss. Joe had been around the country quite a spell. He had never caused trouble—not that Abe knew of, anyway.

He waved Joe to a chair as he said, "Coffee'll be a while."

Joe did not sit down. He said, "Mr. Burke wants to see you."

Abe blinked. His expression brought a smile to the other man's face.

"Figured he was dead, eh? Lots of folks did."

Abe picked up his hat, turned down the stove damper and followed the range boss outside. The sun had just topped out, there was sparkling clear daylight all the way to the top of the most distant crags. But it was still cold. As they walked, Joe said, "I sent Bob Cheney back to the ranch to do the chores, an' bedded down here in town last night. To be honest, Abe, I expected to have to hire a rig and haul Mr. Burke home to be buried this morning. I may have to do it yet. He looks like hell. He's weaker'n a kitten. Perc Hudson spooned a little whiskey down him while I held his head up. First thing he said was that he wanted to see you."

Joe stopped speaking and stared at a heavy top-buggy parked in front of the Hudson place. Abe was sure Joe would recognize the outfit, so he spoke quickly. "It won't be Jeff. His wife's got a stomach complaint. Perc is treating her for it."

Joe did not say another word as they passed through the little white gate. He would have walked straight up the steps to the front porch, but Abe grabbed his arm and hauled him down the south side of the house, in the direction of the carriage shed.

Doctor Hudson was beside the table, holding a big watch in one hand and Burke's limp wrist in the other hand. He looked up to nod at the newcomers, pocketed his watch and said, "Henry, don't move and don't talk more than one minute." Hudson turned, looking sternly at Joe and Abe. "One minute—exactly—then clear out of here. I'll be back as soon as I can."

He closed the door after himself as Marshal Sutherland approached the table. Burke's color had been artificially heightened by the whiskey. His eyes were deeply sunken, drowsy-looking but clear. He seemed to be able to think clearly, because he did not waste a moment of the time Doc had allowed him. "He was down the runway near the alley, where Jack an' I had sun in our eyes. Jack reached for his gun. He shot him. I tried to turn sideways to make a narrower target. He shot and dang near missed, but the bullet tore my clothes and made me lose my balance. The next time he shot—I don't rightly even remember the noise."

Abe leaned down slightly. "Who?"

"Grant. Tom Grant."

"You're sure—the sun in your face and—?"

"Abe, I come real close to bein' dead sure."

Abe reached instinctively to place a large hand over one of Burke's smaller, more scarred and wrinkled hands, then turned and jerked his head for Joe to follow him outside. Joe hesitated as he and Burke exchanged a glance, but Abe stepped between them and jerked his head at Joe.

Doctor Hudson was approaching rapidly from the direction of the house. He stopped and raised his eyebrows. Abe smiled. "He's tough."

Hudson did not dispute that, but he said, "Tough may not be enough. Tough won't stop gangrene if it starts. What did he tell you?" They told him. Hudson looked away without speaking.

Joe watched as Doctor Hudson entered the shed and closed the door after himself. He and Abe exchanged a glance, Joe's expression was sardonic. "I told you," he said.

Abe shoved big hands deep into his trouser pockets. "I didn't doubt it. But like I said last night, the law demands proof."

"All right, you got it. So have I."

Abe jerked his head and led off in the direction of his office. Down there, the coffee was finally hot, so he drew off two cups, took one behind the desk with him and handed the other cup to the range boss. As he sat down he said, "Joe, I wish you hadn't sent Bob out to the ranch."

The range boss gazed dispassionately at the big man behind the desk. "Why?"

Abe sidestepped a direct answer. "Ride out and bring him back to town."

"Why?"

Abe drank some coffee, put the cup aside and leaned on the desk. "Because I want you and Bob in town today. . . . I'm going out to the Demis place."

Joe's eyes widened slightly. "Alone?"

"No. I figure to make up a posse from here in town."

"Abe, what's Bob Cheney got to do with this?"

". . . I got reason to believe Demis is goin' to take his gunfighter over to your place and fire the buildings."

Joe's knuckles turned white around the tin cup he was holding. "When?"

"I don't know, which is why I don't want anyone out there."

Joe leaned to place his cup on the edge of the desk, then

he stood up. "He's crazy, Abe. He's already up to his gullet in trouble with us."

Abe also arose. "Go get Bob and fetch him back to town with you."

"It'd be better if Bob an' me stayed out there. If they come, we can take care of it. Abe, there are a dozen places a couple of men could sneak around and set a fire. Somebody should be there to fill some buckets and—"

"And rush out with buckets to put out a fire and get shot? Joe, you and Bob get back here to town."

"What about the buildings, for chrissake?"

"I'm goin' to string out some possemen between Demis's yard and the Burke place. Put them in hiding. I'm not goin' to let anyone from east of the road get anywhere near the Burke yard. But just in case someone slips past, I don't want anyone in those buildings. I'm goin' to do my absolute damnedest to prevent any more killing."

Joe Holden looked around, then sat down again. Now he looked more baffled than angry. "What in hell's got into that darned fool?"

Marshal Sutherland had asked himself the same question before breakfast. The answer he had come up with, the only one that seemed to fit, had nothing to do with logic. Nor did he care to discuss it right now. "Whatever's got into him," he told the range boss, "isn't as important to me as preventing him from burning Henry out. You go get Bob away from there, and come back to town with him. Joe, I got about all I can handle right now. I don't need you going over there on your own to challenge that gunfighter." Abe straightened up to his full height. "I need your word on it."

Joe reddened faintly. He stood, returning the lawman's stare for a long time before speaking. "I'm not goin' to promise anything," he said, "but all right, about half what you say makes sense. The other half is—Mr. Burke's been awful good to me. But if I see that gunfighter or Jeff Demis on my way back here with Bob, it's goin' to be no holds barred."

Joe left the office and Abe did not spend any time worrying. He had gotten more in the way of concessions from the range boss than he had expected to get. Nor was he entirely out of sympathy with Joe. After hearing Henry's version of the shooting in the livery barn, he was not convinced he wanted Tom Grant in his jailhouse, unless it was under a blanket on the floor of the back room.

He closed the door after himself, shot a look northward, and saw that heavy top-buggy still parked in front of the Hudson place. He went first to the gun shop, where he recruited a posseman without much difficulty, then he went southward to the blacksmith's shop. There, he got a fishy stare from the smith, who was a cantankerous individual at best. At worst, he was thoroughly disagreeable. His name was English, he wore pocked glasses and chewed unlighted cigars. But Abe was not after the smith, he wanted to recruit his son, who was also the older man's apprentice.

The blacksmith flatly refused to give his son the time off. The son, who was larger, more massive and better-dispositioned than his father, unbuckled his shoeing apron, tossed it across an anvil, and asked where the posse would meet, and when. Abe's reply was curt. "In front of the livery barn in fifteen minutes. Bring your beltgun and Winchester." As Abe was turning away, he caught the older man's angry glare and shrugged. "I wouldn't be doin' it if it wasn't absolutely necessary."

Abe rounded up six men, including George Dunhill from the corral yard. What surprised the marshal was Dunhill's willingness, until George said he had never ridden with a posse before and thought it would be "sporting."

Abe had no answer to that.

One of his posse-riders was Buster Munzer, owner of the saloon. When they met down at the livery barn and went inside after horses, Abe collared Buster and ran his hands over him. Buster had two bottles of whiskey. Abe set them up on a high shelf usually reserved for rice brushes and curry combs, and almost smiled at Munzer's expression. But there was no argument. Neither of them said a word. Buster went after his horse, looking glum.

Marshal Sutherland had been bothered by something since returning to town last night. He now went down through the barn looking for the liveryman, whom he found across the alley at his trading corrals. Abe asked him why no one had been in the barn yesterday when the fight occurred.

The liveryman, a thin, rawboned man, made a nervous gesture with his hands. "A man's got to eat. I went over to the café."

"How about your dayman? Was he hungry too, at the same time?"

"No, but you know how they are, never around when you want them, and loafin' all the time unless a man watches them like a hawk."

An indignant, high-pitched voice seemed to come out of the air. Actually, the dayman was in the haymow. He poked his head out, glaring. He had heard every word his employer had said, and had not liked any of it. "Tell him the truth, why don't you?" the dayman said sharply. "Tell 'em about that big feller handin' you ten silver cartwheels to go over to the café."

Abe Sutherland scowled down at the liveryman. "Is that true?"

"Well. But I was goin' over there anyway. Like I already told you, I was hungry."

Abe tipped his head back in order to see the red-faced dayman. "How much did he pay you to go for a walk?"

"I didn't go for a damned walk," the dayman replied, looking venomously at his employer. "I was loafing. Hostlers always loaf. Ask him if you doubt me."

Abe could hear horses being led out of the runway. He said, "Once more—where were you when the shooting started? An' you give me another cute answer and I'll come up there and sit on you. . . . Where were you?"

"All day I'd been meanin' to go fetch back some horses the smith was shoeing all around. Four head. Every time I thought I'd have the time to do it, old spindle-shanks there beside you would come up with something else for me to do. Marshal, that's the gospel truth."

Abe brought his gaze down to the liveryman. He stared until someone called his name from up front, then he turned without a word and walked swiftly up to where his possemen were waiting. The liveryman watched him all the way. He even scuttled up front and watched Marshal Sutherland lead his riders northward through town. Then he hurried back as far as the loft ladder, which was a peeled lodgepole pine with slats nailed across it, and scooted up it.

His daytime hostler had anticipated him. He was standing beside the crawl hole, leaning on a three-tined hayfork. He was older than the liveryman, and thicker, but even so, there was no surplus weight on his frame.

He let the liveryman get head-and-shoulders through the crawl-hole, then straightened up, swung the hayfork with an almost casual manner, and stopped it about three inches from the liveryman's head.

He glared downward. "You wasn't really an' truly fixin' to fire me now, was you Mr. Reilly? Because if you was, it'd make me think my Uncle Jasper was right when he said there's nothin' less decent and trustworthy than an Irishman. . . . Was you, Mr. Reilly?"

The liveryman eyed his dayman's face, then the poised three-tined fork, and rocked back and forth on the lodge-pole ladder. "Dan, you wouldn't stick me with that fork."

"You're wrong. I'd stick you quicker'n I'd stick a hog. I put in long days an' never loaf nor hide out, yet there you stood when you figured I wasn't nowhere around, tellin' one lie about me after the other."

"No, Dan. Now you listen to me. I didn't specially say your

name, did I? Of course I didn't. But I've had an awful lot of hostlers work for me since I first set up in business, and mostly they was stupid, clumsy, and loafed every chance they got." The liveryman looked up. His hostler's expression was flintily unrelenting. The liveryman changed tactics.

"You'll be about the best worker I've ever had, and that is a blessed fact. I've been toyin' with the notion of givin' you fifty cents more a week."

The hostler said, "Thank you. Fifty cents more a week. All right. Now tell me something: Why did you take those ten silver cartwheels from that stranger with the fancy boots and all? Because you knew there was goin' to be a gunfight and you didn't want to be around when it happened."

"No," the liveryman exclaimed ringingly. "It wasn't any such thing."

"Well then, why did you take that money from him?"

"I got to be truthful with you, Dan. You only been workin' here a couple of weeks, ain't it?"

"Yeah. Close onto two weeks. What's that got to do with—?"

"Just let me finish, boy. Just give me one more minute. . . . The reason I accepted those cartwheels and went over to the café was because over the years I've taken money—never that much though—from a lot of young bucks who wanted me to go up to the saloon for something like an hour or so, while they an' some lady friend used the hayloft."

The hostler tossed the hayfork away. It landed tines-down in the hay and remained upright as the liveryman climbed down, followed by his hostler. As soon as they were both on the floor, the liveryman pulled out a huge white handkerchief and blew his nose, making a sound like a Canadian goose. Then he peered over the edge of his hands at the hostler and said. "You downright sure fifty cents more a week won't turn you into a drunk, or a profligate gambler, or a poolhall loafer?"

Dan was sure. "You wasn't fixin' to go back on your word

to me, was you now, Mr. Reilly? Because if you was, there's something else I can tell the marshal."

"What else?"

"That about half the time you buy stolen horses off saddle tramps, you know they're stolen, and I can prove it."

The liveryman pocketed his handkerchief. "Dan, boy, you don't realize what you're saying."

"Yes I do. . . . But an extra benefit of you payin' me fifty cents more a week . . . I got bad eyesight and a real weak memory."

CHAPTER 12

A Very Long Day

ABE SUTHERLAND rode slowly out of Buckhorn on the north roadway, his companions recalling earlier episodes as possemen. The only man who had never been a posseman before was the stage company's local superintendent, George Dunhill. He started out in an adventuresome spirit, but the farther he rode and the more he listened to his companions, all of whom had done this before, the less enthusiasm Dunhill showed.

Abe had a long ride ahead. He knew all of this might turn out to be a wild goose chase. He had nothing except a hunch, and personal knowledge of Jeff Demis, to keep him going.

But whether Demis attempted to burn out the Burke place today or next week, what Marshal Sutherland particularly wanted to accomplish today was the apprehension of Tom Grant.

Abe had no illusions. He was good with weapons, had practiced with them for years, and although he had gone up against his share of yeasty rangemen, he had never faced a professional gunfighter.

His estimate of how this day might end for him and his possemen was either in a furious and bloody fight, or without one. He did not believe there would be much of the faunching, backing, and filling, which ordinarily happened when angry and hostile cowmen met. This time, he was going up against a man who was noted both for his reticence and for his deadliness. But there was not much point in dwelling on what might happen; he'd do better to wait and see what did happen, and be prepared.

When they were several miles above town, the riders brought up the subject of Burke's condition. Buster, who could usually be counted on to have the latest bar gossip, opined that old Henry would never walk again. When that statement was challenged, Buster gave as his source a liquor drummer he'd ordered stock from, who had it directly from a battered old book on gunshot wounds and their residual effects, that he had found once on a stagecoach while traveling between Fort Laramie and Cheyenne.

The young blacksmith eyed Buster skeptically. "What did Doc Hudson say? I'd believe him before I'd believe some darned book."

Buster had to admit that Perc Hudson had not been in his saloon since the shooting, and on that note the possemen sank back into thoughtful silence.

The young blacksmith had made a point. The most reliable authority on Burke's condition was Perc Hudson, and although he had been unable to avoid being questioned every time he had to leave his house, he had avoided specific or speculative answers with a medical practitioner's canniness.

Except to one person.

Mary Ellen Demis had been at Hudson's place when noisily excited townsmen had brought in dead Jack Waite and badly shot-up Henry Burke. No one had told her what had happened. No one would know the details until Burke regained consciousness and told Abe Sutherland, but Mary Ellen possessed unusual prescience. When Doctor Hudson had returned to the house after working on Henry, she had hot coffee waiting. As he sank down at the kitchen table, blood on his shirt and cuffs, she had sat opposite him, looking ill. Hudson's stomach powders, or her tough constitution, had alleviated the stomach pains, but as she had sat opposite Hudson, silent as he drank the coffee, she felt her pain returning and clenched both hands atop the table, a symptom which did not go unnoticed by the man opposite her. He put down the cup and said. "I'll get you some laudanum. I gave Henry a little. It will help, Mary."

She shook her head, gold-flecked brown eyes fixed on him. "I don't want to sleep. And if I did—it would only be waiting when I awakened, wouldn't it?"

He regarded her kindly. He knew better than anyone what she had been living with for years. Right now, he knew what she was thinking so he said, "We don't know what happened."

She did not yield. "Yes we do, Doctor. When I drove into town this morning I saw Mr. Burke and one of his riders out in front of the café. . . . As I told you earlier, my husband was coming into town today to pick up some freight at the corral yard."

"Well, but that doesn't—"

"Doctor, since I was a youngster, people have been saying I was a little strange."

Hudson inclined his head, not over her strangeness, but over what he had heard about Mary Ellen's reputed ability to predict things, and her rumored capacity to read human beings the way other people read books. He had never paid any attention to those stories; he had heard them before, but Perc Hudson was most of all a man of science, grounded in basic learning, the kind of man who neither believed in nor was sympathetic to what was called "second sight."

In this case, the strongest proof that Mary Ellen Demis had no such powers was the fact that she had married a man two-thirds of the people in the territory had known for years was a no good son of a bitch.

But Perc Hudson liked Mary Ellen. He liked her candor, her honesty, and most of all he admired her dauntless spirit, so he smiled as he said, "You wouldn't have to be strange, Mary, to put two and two together: Jeff does not like Henry Burke, and Henry feels the same way toward Jeff. However, the fact that they were both in town this morning—"

"Doctor, I know my husband. I watched him change from

a sly man to a hating, jealous, scheming individual over the years. I don't think he could have shot those men, but since he hired Tom Grant, my husband does not go anywhere without him, and Grant is not just a killer, he's as unprincipled as Jeff is. . . . I would bet my life Tom Grant waylaid Mr. Burke and that range rider and shot them. I *know* that's what happened."

The next morning, when Doctor Hudson returned to the shed, Joe Holden and Abe Sutherland had arrived to speak with Burke. Hudson had not remained out there with them because he was worried about Mary Ellen, but after giving her more powders and having her lie down for a while, he had returned to the shed.

Now he knew she had been right. So as Marshal Sutherland and his possemen rode past on their way out of town, Perc had allowed Mary Ellen to return to the kitchen, but he would not allow her any coffee, just some heated milk—and he told her what he now knew as she sipped the milk and gazed at him across the kitchen table.

Aside from Sutherland, Joe Holden, and Perc Hudson— and excluding Burke, the man who had tried to kill Burke, and the man who had sent the killer to do that, Mary Ellen was the only person who now had the full story. She dutifully drained the milk glass and would have arisen, but Perc Hudson scowled. "Just sit there," he said. She smiled wanly over his solicitousness. "No, I have to get back home."

Hudson came to the opposite side of the table and looked steadily at her. "Mary, I think it would be wise if you stayed in town today."

She arose. "I can't. The children are out there."

"Mary, listen to me. Jeff knows you were here. Even if you didn't tell him, he saw your buggy out front."

She gazed at his face as she said, "I don't think he will hit me again. And the children—"

"You don't think he'll hit you again. That was a very bad blow. Guessing he may not do it again isn't something you ought to bet on. Mary, a man who will hit a woman with his fist once will do it again. Next time, you may not be able to get to town."

"But what about the children?"

He had no answer. He knew both the Demis youngsters, a pretty, dark little girl of about ten, and her brother, who was fair and tall, and about thirteen. He had treated them both for a number of childhood ailments. He avoided answering her question by refilling the glass with hot milk from the stove. As he faced around, she was holding her underlip with her teeth and fighting to prevent the swimming wetness in her eyes from spilling over.

He put the glass on the table as he said, "Has the milk helped the stomach pains?"

She nodded, unwilling to release her lower lip long enough to speak.

He went around, took her hand in his, and said, "Mary, I need some help right now. It won't take long."

He took her out back to the shed, halted at the door and looked critically at her. She was no longer holding her underlip, and her eyes were clearer. He squeezed her hand. "I can't do what I am asking you to do. The relationship between a doctor and his patient does not have the same— whatever it is—that the relationship between a handsome woman and a wounded man has."

Her eyes widened. ". . . Mr. Burke?"

"Yes. He's very ill. He may not live, and I dosed him so that he'll be asleep when we go inside. What I need from you is to be sitting there when he awakens."

"Doctor . . . " she murmured in mild protest.

He squeezed her hand a little harder. "Hold his hand, Mary. He probably won't talk, but hold his hand and smile at him . . . like he was one of your children when they were very small. Will you do it, please?"

She freed her fingers, smoothed her skirt, raised one hand to her hair, and looked steadily at the closed shed door. "It's probably the least I can do. But I'm Jeff's wife. Seeing me at his bedside may make him worse."

Perc Hudson smiled gently at her. "Not if I know Henry Burke." He opened the door. It was hot inside the shed. Henry was indeed sleeping; he was also perspiring, and his face was red. Hudson did not comment on that, but his heart sank. It looked like the high flush of fever. Gangrene caused people to have that high, greasy-looking color.

He had been worrying about infection since he had cleaned Henry up before operating on him. He always worried about infection; it was almost an obsession with him, and with good cause: a large percentage of the patients he had lost had died of blood poisoning with him helplessly watching.

He lingered long enough to see Mary Ellen's eyes darken as she gazed at Burke. She clasped both hands across her stomach. She lost color, and when she turned slightly to face Hudson she was holding her underlip with her teeth again. He raised a big, gentle hand to her face, eased away a single tear, leaned over without even thinking, and kissed her cheek, then said, "He needs you very, very much. I'll be back as soon as I've taken care of a few things at the house."

Outside, he paused to take several very deep breaths, to scan the sky, which was flawless, and to listen to the sounds of the town, which seemed normal. Then he went back to the house and arrived in the parlor just in time to greet a large, buxom woman pushing a very recalcitrant youngster ahead of her. He was about the same age as Mary Ellen's son. But he was shorter, thicker, and darker.

He had broken his arm. For the second time his exasperated mother told Doctor Hudson the break was the result of the child's natural clumsiness—inherited from his father, the town blacksmith, whose entire family was clumsy, and the lad's own direct disobedience, since he had been told repeatedly not to climb that big apple tree in the backyard.

Doctor Hudson took the boy into his examination room to

see if the cast and splints he had put on the arm several days earlier were still performing their function. They were, although the boy complained bitterly about being unable to scratch under the cast, and it was obvious that despite the doctor's admonition about not using that arm or doing anything strenuous for a few days, the lad had ignored him. The cast showed definite signs of having been in the mud.

Hudson washed the hand and cast with alcohol and returned the boy to his mother, who was standing near the front window when they emerged from the examination room. She looked inquiringly at the doctor, who assured her the arm was healing properly. He did not repeat his earlier admonition to the lad. It would not have done any good.

Reassured, the buxom woman led her son to the door and looked back, wearing a resigned expression. "It is a tribulation being a mother, Doctor. This one with a broken arm, and his older brother riding with Marshal Sutherland's posse—Lord knows where they're going or what they'll run up against."

Doctor Hudson was sympathetic and encouraging. "Marshal Sutherland is a prudent man. As for this one—climbing apple trees and breaking arms are natural parts of growing up. He'll be fine too, given a little more time."

The woman nodded toward a small table. "Your payment is over there. Good day, Doctor."

He retrieved the silver cartwheel, pocketed it, and went to the window to look toward the roadway. The lad and his mother were crossing the road toward home. Hudson gave a sharp exclamation. Mary Ellen's buggy was still tied out front. The horse patiently drooping. It was certainly hungry by now, and probably thirsty as well.

He went out to untie it and lead it around back and across the alley to his shed and horse corral. It did not take much time to drop the shafts, pitch the driving-harness into the buggy, and lead the horse to where he could eat from a manger and drink from a stone trough.

As Hudson was returning across the alley toward his back door, he passed the doctoring shed and heard voices. He stepped close and leaned to listen, without touching the door. An old man who lived in a tarpaper shack at the north end of town came shuffling down the alley on his daily search of the trash barrels, saw Doctor Hudson eavesdropping, and made a loud clucking sound as he wagged his head in disapproval.

Hudson straightened up as the old man shuffled southward, holding the long stick he used to prod all the way to the bottom of the refuse barrels. Some of his most successful scavenging had been at the bottom of the barrels. That was where the heavier items seemed to settle.

Doctor Hudson went back to the house, reheated the coffee on his cookstove, tipped a dram of brandy into the cup, then sat down to wait for the coffee to heat. He got tired of waiting and drained the cup without any coffee in it, just the brandy, which felt like it was peeling the lining from his gullet on its way down.

CHAPTER 13

A Matter Of Tempers

HENRY BURKE awakened thirsty, sweaty, and lethargic. There was more ache than pain unless he moved, then the pain came fiercely, so he was very careful to move only his head. He gazed straight into the gold-flecked, tawny-tan eyes of Mary Ellen Demis, and despite the residual lethargy from his laudanum, he was startled.

She smiled weakly and gently tightened her grip on his hand. "You had a long rest," she told him. "Are you thirsty?"

He answered a little thickly. "Yes'm. Thirsty."

She brought him water and supported his head as he drank. As she eased his head down, Henry licked his lips, considered the ceiling until the effect of partial dehydration had been alleviated, which actually did not take very long, then brought his eyes down in a search of her face.

He regarded her for a long moment before speaking. "I'm obliged to you for bein' here. But it sure surprised me. . . . This confounded table is harder'n cast iron."

She believed him, but made no move to do anything to correct that condition. She did not have to be told not to move him or to allow him to move himself. She said, "Doctor Hudson'll be along directly. I'll tell him. Maybe he can ease a quilt under you."

Henry was sweating anew after his intake of water. His eyes appeared to be focusing better, and for a fact when he spoke, the slow drag was less noticeable. He gazed at her for a long time. "Miz' Demis, I likely won't make it, and knowin' that makes it easier for me to say things I guess I otherwise wouldn't never say. Years back, the first time I saw you, I thought you was the handsomest woman I ever saw. Since then, I've seen you maybe a dozen times, and I thought so those times too. Now I still think it."

She raised a hand to her face while looking toward the door as she said, "It's hot in here, Mr. Burke." She was blushing.

He agreed about the heat. "Sun must hit this roof real early and keep on hittin' it until late. . . . Miz' Demis, I used to figure out what I'd say to you if we ever met, maybe in town or out on the range."

Now, she returned his gaze. "You're a sick man, Mr. Burke. You shouldn't talk, just rest. You'll need a lot of rest."

His gaze turned sardonic. "I just darned well may get so much rest I'll still be restin' when that angel blows his trumpet."

She responded sharply. "No such a thing. You're going to be fine. It may take a while, a long while, but you're going to mend as good as new."

His sunken eyes laughed at her. "Well, you're encouragin' for a fact, but not as good as new. I'm not plumb sure I'd want to be that good again." He changed the subject. "Anythin' goin' on in town?"

She looked at her hand holding his. "A posse rode out a while ago."

He looked closely at her. "Which direction?"

"North."

He continued to look at her, and this time it was Henry who gently squeezed fingers. Mary Ellen did not appear to have noticed. She still did not look at him.

"How are your boy and girl?" he asked, wanting desperately to keep her with him.

Her face brightened a little. "They are fine. Betsy can read as well as I can, and do sums. Jason's breaking his first colt. I watch him from the kitchen window. It's dangerous, Mr. Burke. Mothers worry."

He was sure they did that. "The riders'll keep an eye on him."

Without intending to, he had taken their conversation to the one place he would have preferred avoiding, the Demis ranch.

Mary Ellen's response to his last statement was said softly. "The riders are busy at the marking ground."

Henry remembered his own situation on the range. They had been falling behind before he had been shot. Now it would be worse. He pushed those thoughts to the back of his mind as he studied Mary Ellen Demis's profile. She did not look her age, except perhaps for the silver streak running from her temple back past her ear. Her throat had a strong, flawless sweep, her face had fewer lines than the faces of many younger women. But what held Henry's attention was something he could not put into words. Mary Ellen, despite years of uncertainty, disillusionment, and pain, showed the world an expression of uncommon serenity. She was a beautiful woman, mainly because what showed in her eyes and face was a total lack of bitterness, something very close to a reflection that behind her silence and gentleness there remained a stubborn faith.

Henry had no idea why she had been in town, which was just as well. He was at a point where the last thing he needed was to get upset, fiercely condemnatory about a man striking a woman, or worse yet, a man striking his wife.

He broke the silence between them. "It's a busy time of year. Did you folks have a good calf crop?"

She nodded soberly. "Yes. Jeff said it was about eighty percent, or maybe a tad higher."

Henry would have nodded his head if he'd dared. That high a percentage of cows dropping calves was indeed good for range ranchers.

She suddenly released his hand, straightened up on the stool, and looked him squarely in the eye as she spoke. "It's very hard to just sit here and not talk about things that are uppermost in both our minds, Mr. Burke."

He wanted to hold her hand again, but she had both hands clasped in her lap. "It will pass," he said. "It's been my experience that things pass, Miz' Demis."

Her reply was tinged with bitterness. "Of course you're right. That's been my experience too. But by the time they pass—sometimes people are drastically changed."

He did not like the way their easy conversation of moments earlier had turned to what was clearly going to end up as a discussion of ugly things, so he said, "I'm older'n you are, and it's taken me a long while to figure out that whatever you can't change is a lot easier to live with if you make an effort to accept it, but sure as the devil it won't last forever, no matter what it is. What folks can't do much about, someone else takes care of."

Her eyes went to his face and remained there. "Mr. Burke—"

"Just plain 'Henry' would suit me fine. I'd take it kindly too."

"Henry . . . that man who shot you and killed your rider is named Tom Grant."

"Yes'm. I know that."

"He is a professional gunman."

"I know that too."

"And my husband hired him because he was sure you would not sit back and allow him to take his cattle west of the road into the foothills."

"Yes'm, I figured it was something like that. But Jeff don't need a gunfighter. We got a difference, but hiring gunfighters isn't goin' to settle it."

"I heard Jeff say that he knew you, and that you would fight him."

"All right, Miz' Burke, that was my idea. But if he hired a gunfighter, why then I'd have to hire one too, an' where do things like that end? I'll tell you, because I've seen it happen before. Graveyards commence fillin' up."

"Henry, did you know my husband filed to homestead the best part of those foothills?"

"Yes'm, I heard that, an' it bothers me because I've run cattle west of the road for a long time, and as soon as the holdouts were corralled, I expected to put cattle up there because I figured I had the best right to that country. It never crossed my mind Jeff would make a legal claim to that land."

"But he did, Henry," Mary Ellen said, looking troubled as she sat erect, clasping both hands in her lap.

He did not like seeing her so upset so he did something her husband, Tom Grant, or wild horses could never have forced him to do. He said, "All right Miz' Demis. He did it legal, which I wasn't smart enough to do, so I expect he's got a right up there. If I ever leave this shed I'll take some men up there, cut out my cattle and drive them south to my deeded land." He smiled weakly at her. "Does that make it easier?"

He expected her to relax, possibly to smile her relief. Instead, she looked him straight in the eye and said, "That's exactly it, Henry—he didn't do it legal." Henry's stare turned stone-steady after that, so she explained. "Minors can't file to homestead. Jeff made the applications in our children's names, showing them to be of legal age, which they aren't. Betsy's only eleven, and Jason is thirteen. He filed in his own name, which was legal, and he filed for a section of that land in my name, which was legal, except that he made out the application in my name, and he signed my name to it. I didn't sign it. I didn't know how he had managed to get four sections. I didn't even know he had filed on them until he told me one night before supper, when he'd been drinking. He was so pleased with himself, he had to boast to someone, and I was the only person handy."

Henry said nothing. His gazed drifted from her face to

the closed door. His reaction to the disclosure of Jeff Demis's deceit was exactly as it had been the last time they had met in the foothills and Henry had invited Jeff to get down off his horse, except that this time Henry could not move, and knew instinctively what would happen if he did move. He did not even clench his fists.

Mary Ellen got him more water. He allowed her to lift his head slightly so that he could drink. Afterwards he lay back, looking upwards. She leaned over to catch his attention and said, "I know we shouldn't have talked about this. I know you're not healthy enough to hear things like this. But it's been bothering me for a long time, Henry. It bothered me nearly as much as overhearing Jeff and Tom Grant talking about burning you out."

Henry's eyes dropped to her face at the same moment Doctor Hudson walked in. The look on Henry's face brought a fast scowl to the other man's face. He shot Mary Ellen a look and jerked his head for her to leave. She obeyed, but went only a few feet beyond the door until she heard Hudson's angry voice, then she walked disconsolately over to the house and went inside. She had not intended for any of this to happen.

Henry looked Perc Hudson squarely in the eye and said, "Did you know that son of a bitch an' his hired gun figure to burn my buildings?"

Hudson's immediate concern was his patient. He did not reply to the question. Instead, he moved to the side of the table and looked downward annoyedly. "I'm going to give you more laudanum. You can't get yourself into an uproar. I've told you that, Henry. You've got one foot in the grave and the other one on a banana peel. Now, be quiet. I want to look beneath the dressings."

"You've looked under there so many times you could draw a picture of me with your eyes closed."

"You're right," retorted the angry medical man. "And I'll

go right on looking under there every chance I get. . . . Have you ever heard of gangrene?"

Henry's smoky gaze became fixed on Hudson's bent figure. "I got it, have I?"

Hudson did not attempt to reply until he had finished his examination and had a fresh dressing in place beneath the bulky body bandage. Even then he did not answer until he had rinsed his hands and was drying them, and what he had to say ignored the topic of blood poisoning altogether.

"You damned fool, Henry. You haven't even had time to heal yet, and here you are mad as a hornet and ready to jump up and go find your horse. She had no right bringing up things she knew would upset you. I'm really surprised at her."

Henry's gaze remained on Doctor Hudson as though the medical practitioner had not spoken. "How bad's the gangrene?"

Hudson tossed aside the little towel and replied as though he had not heard the question. "The only reason you're alive right now is because I stopped the bleeding before you lost too much blood. That—and your damned disagreeable, tough disposition. Most other men would have given up and died quietly. Not you—you've got to argue and get mad and . . ." Doctor Hudson's eyes rolled up, he made a despairing gesture with his hands. "Henry, you've given me more gray hairs since yesterday than any other patient I've ever had."

"For the last time," Henry snarled. "How bad is that damned gangrene?"

"What gangrene? Did I say you had gangrene?"

Their eyes locked. Hudson turned away first. He went to the door and stood there gazing back. "I want to put something soft under you. Otherwise you're goin' to get sores. But I'm afraid to move you. Can you stand another day or two like you are?"

Henry's grim expression lessened slightly, and like Doctor

Hudson, when he spoke now, his voice was no longer angry. "I can stand it for another couple of days, if you'll promise me I'll be alive in a couple of days."

Hudson considered the old cowman and shook his head as he opened the door. "Anyone who eats burnt potatoes and meat fried so hard you could resole boots with it, and drinks whiskey three times a day, is not going to die, if he's held on this long—unless gangrene sets in. That's why I keep worrying and looking under your damned bandage. How the hell would I know if you'll be alive for two more days? I didn't even know you'd be alive this morning. Henry, I'm a medical doctor, not a miracle-worker. Now I'm going to have a talk with Mary Ellen."

"Wait," Henry exclaimed. "You say one mean thing to her and so help me when I'm out of this damned shed I'll make life so miserable for you, Perc, you'll wish you'd never heard of either one of us. I mean it. She just plain couldn't hold it back any longer. Don't you say a damned mean word to her. She did me a favor and I'm beholden to her."

Hudson lingered in the doorway briefly, looking back. "I already wish to hell I'd never heard of either one of you," he exclaimed. He closed the door and started toward the back of the house, halted midway to glare ahead, and back in the direction of the shed, let go a rattling breath of resignation, and went the rest of the way.

Mary Ellen was gone.

He went through the house with rising alarm, ended up in the parlor where his hat, coat, and little black satchel were, and called her name several times. He did not get a response, had not expected to, and with a sizzling curse, grabbed his hat.

He would have noticed if she had been across the alley where he had put her horse and had parked her buggy. Nevertheless, to be certain, he went out back and looked. The buggy was still where he had put it, and her harness horse was standing hipshot, half in shade, stamping occasionally at flies.

He yanked the hat lower and went trotting southward down the alley, in the direction of the livery barn.

CHAPTER 14

The Taurean

SHE was down there and the day hostler was saddling a big, stud-necked, seal-brown mare for her when Doctor Hudson panted his way inside, out of direct sunlight. Mary Ellen and the hostler saw him at the same moment. The dayman looked baffled; since he had been in Buckhorn he had never once seen the local physician move out of a walk, or look anything but calm. Mary Ellen's reaction was different. She moved swiftly to grab the mare's reins and turn to toe into the stirrup. The saddle was in place but had not been cinched. As she made a swift move to mount, the saddle turned under her weight. She nearly fell. The big mare turned a quizzical gaze upon the woman and patiently stood for the upset hostler to free the latigo and boost the saddle back up where it belonged.

Except for this, Mary Ellen would have been able to escape. Perc Hudson had trotted about two-thirds the length of town. The last time he'd done anything that strenuous he had been much younger.

He walked up to where Mary Ellen was standing and, remembering Henry's threat—which did not frighten him one bit, but which had impressed him for its sincerity, addressed Mary Ellen in a calm, almost soothing tone of voice.

"I'll walk you back. It'll take both of us to get a blanket under Henry, otherwise he's going to develop bed sores from that table."

The hostler looked from one of them to the other, then began peeling the rigging off the big, seal-brown mare.

Mary Ellen allowed herself to be accompanied up the back alley, but she did not look at the large man escorting her, not even when he said, "It's all right. I didn't want him upset, but I can tell you he's not like other people. He thrives on being upset—some of the time anyway."

She said, "I want to be with my children."

He did not comment until he had held the back door of his house for her to enter first. Then, as he too entered the kitchen, he said, "All right. I'll go with you."

She looked quickly at him. "And leave Henry unattended?"

Hudson spread his hands. "How else can I go with you? He'll just have to hold on, if he can, until I return. . . . Mary, I don't believe anything will happen to your children. Marshal Sutherland will see to that."

"That posse he led northward was going to our ranch."

He did not dispute this. "Maybe. But if so, they'll have just about got out there by now, so anything that happens will be over and done with by the time you could get out there, even if you had wings."

She stood beside the kitchen table looking at him, and he read her feelings without difficulty: She was a mother first and foremost. What he had said, which she clearly knew to be the truth, about whatever would happen at the Demis ranch happening before she could arrive there, might be logical, but mother-animals anxious about the safety of their offspring had never been influenced by logic, only by emotion.

Doctor Hudson offered a compromise, which she accepted because she had no alternative. He said that if she would help him with Henry, he would find someone around town who would look after the sick man, and he would ride north with her.

As they were crossing the yard toward the little shed, carrying several blankets and a bottle of fresh water, she explained that her reason for telling Henry about Tom Grant and her husband, and their plan to burn the buildings, was that she felt he should know, and also because she felt sorry for Henry, lying half-dead in town, a victim of her husband's duplicity.

Hudson said nothing as they approached the shed. He held the door for her to enter first—and got a shock. Joe Holden and Bob Cheney were inside. They had been talking with their employer when the door opened. Now, they stood impassively mute as they gazed at Jeff Demis's wife in front of Doctor Hudson.

Henry broke the awkward silence. "They just got to town from the ranch. They made a sashay northeastward looking for Jeff or his gunfighter, or anyone else they could catch on our side of the stage road. There wasn't a sign of anyone."

Perc Hudson accepted this with a nod of his head, then looked toward the table. "As long as you gents are here, you can help us lift your boss and spread these blankets beneath him. . . . He must not bend. We can lock hands under him and lift. Mary can spread the blankets."

Not another word was said as the men approached the table, groped gently beneath Burke, and after exchanging a look, began to lift. Fortunately, Burke was not much of a weight for three strong men to raise. Mary Ellen worked swiftly and stepped back. As the men eased Burke down, Doctor Hudson, who was watching the cowman's face closely for signs of pain, was the last to straighten up. As he did so he smiled at Henry Burke. The older man did not smile back until Mary Ellen came close and reached for his hand. Then he smiled, and demonstrated how his mind had improved since the last of the laudanum had worn off. He gripped her fingers and said, "I'm feeling measly. If you'd stay with me . . ."

She looked troubled. Doctor Hudson had something to say, and as he did so, he jerked a thumb in the direction of

Holden and Cheney. "She'll stay with you, Henry, but Joe and your other man and I will ride north."

Burke gazed at the doctor as though he did not understand. Hudson explained. "Mary's worried about her son and daughter. While she stays here and watches out for you, I'll head for the Demis place with these two gents, and see if we can't bring the children back with us."

Burke approved of the suggestion as he watched the shadow of anxiety cover Mary Ellen's face. He tugged gently at her hand. "They'll fetch them back. I know each of them. They set out to do something, and they do it."

It was not what she wanted, but as she turned to speak Doctor Hudson spoke first. "Look after him, Mary. I think he needs it more than your children do. We'll bring the kids back." He jerked his head for Joe and Bob to leave. After they had gone outside, Hudson winked at Henry, hesitated as though to speak, and then turned on his heel.

The moment the door closed, Mary Ellen turned slowly toward Henry. He was watching her, and although his normally ruddy complexion still showed color, it was faded. His cheeks looked sunken, as did his eyes, but they were bright. In Mary Ellen's view, Henry needed food. She told him she would go over to the house and make some porridge. He stopped her. "Maybe later. Right now I got no appetite."

"But you're wasting."

He changed the subject. "I been puzzling over something for some time now. Where did Jeff find that gunfighter?"

Mary Ellen eyed the tall stool, but made no move toward it. "I'm not sure. He rode into the yard one day, and Jeff greeted him like they were old friends. But I doubt that they were. I honestly don't know how they met or where." She paused, eyed Henry solemnly, and spoke again. "But I can tell you something about him, if you'd be interested."

Watching her, he would have been interested in anything she said, even if she said the moon was made of blue cheese. "I'd be willing to listen, Mary Ellen."

She either missed his use of her first name, or ignored it as she went closer to the table. She took a stub of a pencil from her pocket, held Henry's hand palm up, and drew what looked like a figure-8 except that the top of the number had not been completed, ᙠ. She raised his palm so he could see what she had drawn. Henry looked, raised his eyes to her face and said, "If that's a brand, it'd be maybe a circle an' a half, or a chain link and a half."

She eased his arm down. "It's the Taurean symbol."

He stared at her. "Is that a fact? Well now, what exactly is a Taurean symbol?"

"It is the symbol for someone born between late April and late May. The Taurean sign is Taurus the bull." She almost smiled down at him because his expression looked bewildered, and mildly alarmed. "Henry, I'm all right."

He muttered "Uh huh."

"Really. Let me tell you. My husband's gunfighter was born in early May."

"How do you know that?"

"I asked him."

"Just like that; you walked up an' asked him when he was born?"

She nodded. "Not when he was born, what month he was born. He is a Taurean, his symbol is that half-an-eight, and his sign is Taurus the bull."

Henry stared at the handsome strange woman. As he lay there looking at her and listening, he had a sensation almost like disappointment. Then she spoke again and scattered his troubled thoughts.

"I watched him, Henry, watched for the signs to show— and they did. Do you know much about the zodiac?"

"No ma'am, I just know cattle and horses."

"The zodiac classifies people. It's not always accurate, but it is accurate enough times. That's why I wanted to know what month the gunfighter was born in."

Henry's brows drew close. "You figured out Jeff's gunfighter from that?"

"Yes. Would you like me to tell you the kind of man Tom Grant is?"

He offered a delayed answer, because he already knew the kind of man Grant was. "Yes'm. I'd like to know."

Mary Ellen got onto the stool and sat beside the table looking down at Henry. "The worst Taurean characteristics are greed, stubbornness, self-indulgence, self-centeredness, and unshakable opinions. They are resentful, and capable of very strong negative emotions. They like money, fancy clothes, good food, hotel rooms instead of bedrolls on the ground. A Taurean would be perfectly coordinated, and blindly loyal to anyone he worked for. He would take his employer's troubles as his own, and if he was a gunfighter, he would never see any side of an issue but his employer's side."

Henry let his gaze wander from her face to the door, then back again. "I'd admire a drink of water," he murmured.

She helped him drink. After she was back on the stool, Henry studied her handsome, even, golden tanned face and sighed. "Mary Ellen, did you read a book?"

She shook her head. "Not one book, dozens of them. I love books. When you're isolated on a big ranch as I've been for many years, books become your way out. Does that make sense to you, Henry?"

"Yes'm. But I didn't mean all books, I meant books on these signs and all."

"I've been interested in those things since childhood," she told him, and put her head slightly to one side. "You don't believe any of it, do you?"

"Well . . ."

"Henry, it's all right with me if you don't believe. I've known dozens of people who didn't. And I've known people who thought I was crazy, or at the very least a few bricks shy of a load. It doesn't bother me."

He eyed her skeptically. "Mary Ellen, did you ever see any of this stuff come true?"

"Yes, many times. That's why I told you about Jeff's gun-fighter being a Taurean."

"Is that a fact? Well now, just exactly what do you mean—that's why you told me?"

"So you would know that if anyone crosses Tom Grant today, Grant will probably kill him. Taureans are angered by someone contradicting them, or someone who might cross them. They are capable of deadly fits of temper."

Henry continued to look at the handsome woman through a long period of silence. She looked at him, too, until she slid down off the big stool and went to the door to look up and down the alleyway, before closing the door and returning to Henry's side.

She squeezed his hand and smiled at him. "You think I'm crazy don't you?"

"No ma'am. I think you're downright pretty as a wild-flower. But different, Mary Ellen. Different."

"And you would prefer I weren't different. You'd like to see me as a typical ranch woman; boil clothes on Monday, iron them on Tuesday, and between other things cook three meals a day, churn butter, make cheese, and—oh yes, have children so I won't be bored."

"No ma'am, I wasn't thinkin' of any of those things. I was thinkin' that you didn't have to tell me Tom Grant will kill. I already knew that. As for his temper and all the other things you said—I could have told you about them, too. I've known an awful lot of men in my time, good ones and bad ones, and a few very damned bad ones. But I never did know what month they were born in." He stopped because he was sure she was going to either be angry with him for being a disbeliever, or feel hurt. Instead, she laughed. It was a pleasantly musical sound. He had never heard her laugh before.

"If I could have gone out there with the possemen," she

told him, "I could have told them the kind of a man they were going to meet. And they wouldn't have paid any more attention to me than most people do when I talk about these things. Henry, it helps to know about people."

He would not have disputed that. It was just that after listening to her, he had arrived at a pragmatic conclusion: No one had to know Jeff Demis's gunfighter was born in May, or had that odd little topless figure eight for his symbol and a bull for his sign. All they had to know was that he was a deadly man, and they already knew that.

She cut into his reflections to say, "I'm going to the house to make you some broth."

He was agreeable; he was not hungry, but he could drink some broth. "While you're over there, see if Perc has a bottle around. Then you could lace my broth."

She looked back from the doorway, smiling and with a twinkle in her eyes. It did not occur to Henry until after she was gone that she might not have in mind feeding him. She might have said that in order to keep him agreeable until she reached the alleyway, where she'd go due south to the livery barn for a saddle animal. Or she might even hitch her Demis horse to the buggy. If she did this, he would probably be able to hear her across the alley, but there would not be a thing he could do about it.

He sighed, stared at the ceiling, alternately thought about the Taurus Gun, and the handsome woman who had told him her husband's hired troublemaker was the Taurus Gun.

CHAPTER 15

A Tense Meeting

MARY Ellen's husband and his companion had watched their backtrail all the way to the Demis yard, without seeing any pursuit. Tom Grant had been satisfied that there would be no pursuit. As Jeff Demis warped the wagon around so that its tailgate would open into the smithy, where they would unload the crates, Tom Grant said, "I told you there was nothin' to worry about. When I run south to meet you below town they was both lyin' there, dead as stones."

Jeff squinted his eyes, concentrating until he had the tailgate exactly where he wanted it, then he eased up, looped the lines, set the binder and sprang down on the near side. Grant got down from the off side. Jeff straightened up, looking back the way they had come. Grant grunted, wagged his head, and went around to lower the tailgate as he said, "You worry too much. Lend a hand back here. . . . where did you send the riders today?"

Jeff replied as he walked toward the tailgate. "Southeast, to make certain the cattle they worked through are all right."

Grant was a physically powerful man. He lifted down the largest crate without assistance, then straightened up to lean on it as he said, "What'd your wife go into town for this morning?"

Jeff offered an indifferent reply as he positioned another crate for Grant to lift down over the tailgate. "I don't know. Some female trouble I expect. They're always gettin' somethin' wrong with them."

"Mighty handsome woman," Grant said, then grunted down another crate. "Is this here a wagon or a buggy?"

"A little of both. I like heavy buggies. Those filmsy things you see around aren't worth a damn in mud."

"Your kids are watching."

Jeff was balancing the third crate. He turned to look toward the main house. His dark daughter and fair son were as motionless as statues over on the porch. He called over there. "Betsy! See what you can rustle up for us to eat. We'll be through here directly."

The girl called back. "Where is Momma?"

"In town, I guess, or on her way back. I don't want to wait, we're hungry."

"Is her stomach all right?" Betsy called back.

Jeff faced fully around, his expression blank. "It's all right," he replied. "She'll be along. Now see what you can put on the table."

Tom Grant muscled the last of the boxes to the ground and yanked out a blue bandanna to mop off sweat with. He spoke quietly, while concentrating on wiping the inside sweatband of his hat. "Now'd be a good time, Jeff. With old Burke dead along with one of his riders, there won't be anybody over there. We can saddle up an' make the round-trip in maybe under two hours."

Jeff made his mechanical smile. "After dark," he said.

The gunfighter did not think much of that. "After dark the riders'll be in the yard an' your wife'll be home. They're goin' to wonder about you'n me ridin' off in the dark. Tomorrow when they smell the smoke, or someone comes by an' tells 'em what happened at the Burke place, they're going to put two and two together."

Jeff's smile remained fixed in place as he too mopped the inside of his hat. "Let's go eat," he said, and got a look from Tom Grant. "Right now," stated the gunfighter. "No one but your kids will even know we was here and rode out. Burke's place'll be empty."

Jeff's smile did not diminish as he gazed at the larger man on the far side of the tailgate. "I sort of like to set back and watch for reactions. There'll be hell to pay in town."

Grant was unrelenting. "All right. All the better for us to follow that up with the torching."

"I think we'd do better to hang and rattle. See what comes of the killings in town. Are you plumb sure no one saw you in the alley?"

"As sure as a man can be. I looked around an' there wasn't anyone in sight. Of course it was broad daylight." Grant dropped the hat on the back of his head, twisted around as he stuffed his shirttail deeper into his britches, then reslung the silver-inlaid Colt in its carved leather holster, pushing it slightly so that it leaned outward from his body. He watched Jeff taking the team off the wagon pole. Grant trailed them inside the barn and helped remove the harness. When they had finished and Grant was about to bring up the subject of the Burke place again, either Betsy or her brother rang the triangle over on the east side of the house. Jeff smiled and jerked his head.

Another man would have given up. Jeff had clearly shown that he did not want to ride to the Burke place today. Grant walked beside the slighter man looking at the ground. When they were just short of the porch steps, he said, "It'll settle things, Jeff. It'll be the end of the Burke outfit, and that's what you want. Nobody's goin' to go out there with the old man dead and his buildings burnt flat to the ground. Like you said, you can ease cattle down from them foothills and take over his range. There's only one thing holdin' us back."

They were on the porch when Jeff turned to respond, and something caught his attention. He turned away from the gunfighter, looking intently southward. "Horsemen coming, Tom. Down yonder."

Grant twisted and reset his hat with the brim low in front. For a while neither of them spoke. "Wouldn't be some neighbor, would it, Jeff?"

"Not from the south. If it was a neighbor, he sure as hell wouldn't bring along his entire riding crew. How many do you make it?"

The gunfighter eased up beside a porch post and leaned. When he spoke he did not answer Jeff's question. He said, "There's sunlight bouncin' off a badge down there, Jeff."

Jeff's body stiffened. He too stepped to the porch railing to see better. He saw no reflection off a badge, but he did see more riders than any of the outfits had east of the road, or, for that matter, on the west side either. He spoke very softly. "Posse, sure as hell. Someone must have seen you leaving the alley."

The gunfighter shaded his eyes, did some rough calculating. "We couldn't get rigged out and on our way. They'd see us leavin' the barn and make a horse race out of it . . . Jeff?"

"What."

"Send your kids. They know the range. Tell 'em where you had the riders goin' today. But you sure better hurry, those gents aren't losing any ground."

Jeff disappeared inside the house. Grant strolled to the bunkhouse, dropped a half box of handgun ammunition in a pocket, yanked a Winchester from its boot beside his bunk, and paused in the bunkhouse doorway to estimate the distance of the oncoming riders. He cleared his pipes and spat, heard voices in the barn, but instead of going down there he returned to the porch, where he had an excellent view in three directions. He suspected that the possemen would see the children streaking it from the rear of the yard. What he speculated about was whether or not they would follow the kids. If the posse split up, some horsemen to pursuing Betsy and Jason while the others entered the yard, it would whittle down the odds.

Jeff joined Grant on the porch. He was not smiling. "It was a fair fight," he told the gunfighter. "In fact it was better'n fair, them two challenging you."

Tom Grant nodded his head without much enthusiasm.

He had been told more than once by some two-bit town constable holding a big-barreled scattergun cocked and aimed, that there was no such thing as a fair fight between a professional gunfighter and cowmen, or townsmen, or anyone else except another gunfighter. From the side of his mouth, he asked if Jeff recognized any of those riders.

"Too far," Jeff said, and swung quickly at the sound of running horses. He and the gunfighter alternately watched the children riding like Indians, and faced the direction of the oncoming possemen. One rider turned away from the others, and although he was definitely riding in pursuit of the children, he did not boost his horse out of a steady lope.

Tom Grant grunted a curse. The difference between excited children pushing their animals to the limit right from the start, and the slower, steadier, and equally persistent gait of the posseman who was pursuing them was clearly the difference between an experienced horseman and two youngsters to whom this kind of a horse race was new.

The remaining riders bunched up a little after the departure of their companion. They appeared to be conferring, but the distance was too great to be certain of that. Moments later, when they all broke over into a lope in the direction of the yard, it seemed that their leader, Marshal Sutherland, had decided not to risk having any more riders make a break for it from behind the barn.

Tom Grant had been considering some such flight since his return to the porch of the main house. But although the idea had appeal, Grant too was an experienced man. The possemen would probably be able to catch him before he went more than a mile or two, but most critical in his view was bluffing. There were two dead men in Buckhorn. Even if he had been seen loping away from town to rendezvous with Demis's wagon after it had cleared the lower end of town, it would be just about impossible to prove the gunfight in the livery barn had not been as he would swear it had been. The odds, as he had assured himself, were heavily balanced in his favor.

Jeff interrupted the flow of Grant's thoughts. "That big one up front—that's Abe Sutherland, the town marshal. I think the one directly behind him is a feller named Dunhill. He runs the stage company. That stocky feller on Dunhill's left is Munzer, the saloon man. The others . . . I don't know, except that the big one on the flea-bit gray looks like the blacksmith's son."

Grant smiled. "Barkeeper, corral yard boss, blacksmith . . . that sounds about right for a town posse. I've yet to see one of those posses that could hit the inside of a barn if they were standing in the runway."

Demis went to the east end of the porch and craned around, looking for his children. He did not see them, but he could make out the easy-riding horseman who was chasing them.

He returned to the front of the house. There was nothing to do now but wait. Abe Sutherland had seen them on the porch. He stopped, and for five minutes the Buckhorn horsemen talked. When Marshal Sutherland started ahead, four of his riders turned off in the direction of the stage road.

Tom Grant rubbed his chin. "They're either goin' after that feller you put over yonder with your razorbacks, or they're figuring to maybe spread out an' prevent anyone from east of the road to get over to the west side of it." As he said this, he dropped the hand he had been rubbing his chin with to his side. He also said, "Like I told you, Jeff. We should have rode out right after unloadin' the wagon. By now, we'd be close to Burke's place and these men would be over here, a hell of a ways from us. We could have fired the buildings and been on our way."

"Sure," stated Jeff. "And we'd have rode right into them."

Grant was a very stubborn and unyielding man. "Naw. We'd have seen them." He sighed. "Too late now. Jeff, remember, you didn't see me until I run out there, flaggin' you down with my hat."

Jeff nodded. They had already discussed Grant's alibi. "And you told me they was in the livery barn when you passed along out back, and they swore at you, then pushed you into a fight with them."

Grant smiled coldly. "That's it. Simple and straightforward."

The last remark Jeff Demis made before Abe Sutherland and three riders pulled down to a walk at the beginning of the yard, was, "Damn! I hope those kids find the crew and get it back here fast."

Grant looked at his companion, then leaned on a porch upright. "Quit worrying."

Marshal Sutherland, with George Dunhill and Buster Munzer behind him, walked his horse directly toward the pair waiting on the porch. The tie-down thong was hanging loose on his holster. He removed his gloves as his horse plodded on up to the rack in front of the porch, and stopped.

Jeff smiled. "Didn't figure you'd be so far from town, Abe. Somethin' I can do for you?"

Abe braced both hands on the saddle swells, stiffened forward slightly, then rocked back. He hardly more than glanced at Jeff. He addressed the gunfighter. "You are Tom Grant?"

"Yep. The same."

"There was a shooting back in town," Abe said without taking his eyes off the gunfighter. "The way I understand it, you were in it."

Grant solemnly inclined his head. "Sure was. While Jeff was signing papers and whatnot up at the corral yard, I walked down the alley. When I got about even with the doorway of the livery barn down there, two men called me. I had a little trouble, me bein' in sunshine and them about midway up the runway, but I walked into the barn and one of 'em, a sort of red-headed feller, called me a couple of fightin' names and went for his gun. The other feller was across the runway beside a stall door. I couldn't see him real well when I drew on the red-headed one. . . ."

Abe said, "And?"

"And the red-headed feller was way too slow. I nailed him center. From the corner of my eye, I saw the other one going for his gun. All I had to do was move my wrist. That one acted like he was too old to be challenging people. He got off one shot. I think it went into the ground. I shot him twice. The first time I darn near missed, he was turning, but the second one dropped him down like a dead rock. . . . That's how it happened, Marshal. If you got witnesses they'll back me up, because that's exactly what happened."

"Did you know either of those men?" Abe asked.

"Nope. Not that I know of, anyway. It was hard seeing very well after I came in out of the sunshine in the alley. No, I don't think I ever saw either of them before." As he finished speaking, Tom Grant smiled directly at Abe Sutherland, and waited.

The marshal loosened in the saddle, gazed at Jeff Demis and asked what he knew of the fight. "Just what Tom told me," he replied. "I wasn't down there. I came along afterwards with the wagon."

Abe said. "Afterwards? It seems to me you had already left town and Mr. Grant had to run to catch up."

Jeff reddened. "That's right, Abe. I—just had a bad spell of memory. You're dead right." Jeff made a little deprecating hand gesture. "Just wasn't thinkin' right. I was already south of town."

"Did you hear the gunfire?"

Jeff nodded. "I heard it, but until Tom come lopin' up and climbed aboard I didn't know what it was. Just maybe a drunk cowboy. I didn't think about it until Tom told me what'd happened at the livery barn."

Abe swung to the ground and looped his reins. Behind him, Munzer and Dunhill also dismounted, but they remained behind the marshal, each man standing at the head of his animal.

The gunfighter had been watching Marshal Sutherland, wearing a small, mocking smile, but when Abe swung to the ground, the gunfighter stopped smirking and straightened up off the post he'd been lounging against.

George Dunhill, who was riding with his first posse, darted a pink tongue around his lips. Buster's fat face was sweat-shiny. He never once took his eyes off the gunfighter.

The marshal leaned on the horse rack, looking up. Jeff was wearing his mechanical smile with his face pale behind it. Abe turned his attention back to the gunfighter. "You're a good shot, Mr. Grant."

"There are better, Marshal."

"Maybe. You're pretty fast, too."

"A man don't have to be real fast to face down a couple of damned fool range riders full of whiskey, or whatever made them act like that. It was their idea. I didn't want to kill them, but a man's got a right to defend himself."

Abe nodded slowly. "He sure does. What I came out here for was to get you to ride back to town with me. We got to hold a coroner's inquiry. Jeff here can tell you who the coroner is—Doctor Hudson, the local medicine man. It's a sort of routine procedure."

The gunfighter nodded woodenly. This would not be his first coroner's inquiry for killing men. "One question, Marshal. Where did you send those other possemen that split off out yonder?"

"Over toward the stage road. Just in case you decided to run for it. That's common custom, Mr. Grant." As he finished addressing the gunfighter Abe glanced at Jeff Demis. "Where did you send Betsy and Jason?"

Jeff's fixed smile was a death's-head expression now. "To hunt up my riders and fetch them back to the yard."

"You figured there'd be trouble, Jeff?"

"A man never knows, Abe, when he sees a lawman comin' toward his yard with a posse."

Abe hauled up off the horse rack. "We'll go to the barn while you saddle up, Mr. Grant."

The gunfighter looked amused. "I'm not goin' to run for it. I got no reason to. Those two damned fools got themselves killed by pickin' a fight I sure as hell didn't want."

Abe nodded slowly and waited until Grant was down off the porch, then walked along with him to the barn. Jeff remained on the porch, while Abe's two town possemen did not seem to know exactly what they were supposed to do, so they did nothing.

CHAPTER 16

Playing A Dangerous Game

ON the ride back toward Buckhorn, the lawman sent his two remaining possemen to find the others and accompany them down the road to town. Dunhill seemed agreeable to leaving Abe alone with the gunfighter, but Buster didn't. He said, "George can find them."

Abe looked steadily at the saloon man. "It'd be easier to do if you both looked for them."

As Buster and George were departing, the gunfighter gazed calmly at his riding companion. "I don't know your town very well, Marshal. I recognized that round-faced feller—he owns the saloon, but otherwise . . . what I'm gettin' at is that I came along with you willingly."

Abe's reply was short. "Yes, you did."

"Well . . . you got any rednecks down there?"

Abe smiled without a shred of humor. "I don't think so. Not among the townsmen, Mr. Grant. But those men you shot had friends among the range outfits." Abe's faint smile lingered as he returned the heavier man's gaze. "If you're thinking about a lynching, naw, it won't happen. It's never happened since I've been around Buckhorn. But even if there was a few smoked-up fellers with some such notion, I think between the two of us, we could discourage them."

Grant faced forward and rode relaxed as he studied the land forms. After a while he had a comment to make. "Was those damned fools connected with the Burke outfit?"

"Yes. The older one was Henry Burke."

Grant acted surprised. "You don't say. Well, from what I've heard about him, he was quick-tempered."

Abe's reply to that was dryly spoken. "I guess he was, but since I've been around he's never been troublesome. . . . Mind if I ask where you're from, Mr. Grant?"

The gunfighter looked amused. "Don't mind at all. I've been just about everywhere. Some places more than once, but originally I came from Missouri." He paused, riding easy and thoughtful. "My paw had a mill back there. When I was a youngster, my mother died and my paw married a widow-woman. She didn't like me right from the start, so when I was old enough I saddled up in the night and never so much as looked back." Tom Grant sighed, said no more and when it was possible to see movement ahead, he jutted his jaw. "Your posse riders?"

Abe had been watching the oncoming riders during the gunfighter's reminiscence. They were not his possemen. In the first place, they were approaching northward and Abe had told Munzer and Dunhill to join up with the others and turn southward toward town. In the second place, there were only three riders.

While Abe had been watching the oncoming trio, the gunfighter had been watching him. When Abe was able to make a pretty good guess as to the identity of the three riders, Tom Grant said, "Rednecks, Marshal? You don't look downright pleased."

They weren't rednecks, but two of them were mortal enemies of the man Abe was riding with, and the third one, Doctor Hudson, would sure as hell call out something about Henry making a decent recovery before Abe could stop him. He said, "Wait here a minute, Mr. Grant. I know them. They're not exactly rednecks but I'm not goin' to take any chances."

The gunfighter drew rein, watching the distant horsemen. "I'll watch, Marshal. If they bow their necks I'll lope down and lend you a hand."

Abe nodded and eased his horse over into a lope. When he approached Bob Cheney, Joe Holden, and Perc Hudson, they halted and waited.

Abe reined down, wagging his head. "He's ridin' back to town with me. I told him there'll be a coroner's inquest, somethin' that's routine before someone is buried. He believes he killed them both in the barn, and I've let him go right on thinking that."

Burke's range boss was looking steadily past Sutherland's shoulder at the distant rider sitting still in the waning daylight. "Abe, if we was to spook him an' he made a run for it—"

"Joe, you and Bob and Perc turn your noses south and ride back the way you came. There's not goin' to be any more killing if I can prevent it."

Joe's face reddened as he regarded Abe. "That man killed Jack Waite and come within an ace of killing Mr. Burke, an' just maybe he's the one who shot McElroy in the back."

Abe rested both hands atop the saddle horn as he looked steadily at the range boss. "That's not news. By now everyone knows what happened. But *he* don't know he didn't kill Henry."

"The only reason he didn't is because it wasn't Mr. Burke's time," the range boss growled.

Abe's patience was getting thin. "Joe, I'll bet you a horse he'll hang for killin' Jack and tryin' to kill Henry. But I'm not goin' to call him, an' neither are you. I'll get him. I'm going to stick with him like a tick until he shoves his right hand in his pocket."

Joe was a stubborn man. He was still staring bleakly past the marshal's shoulder when he said, "Abe, everyone's treatin' him like he's made of glass just because he's good with a gun. Well, he's not the only one. I'd kind of like to take him on."

"You're not goin' to do it, Joe. You're goin' to turn around and head back the way you came."

THE TAURUS GUN ■ 139

Joe's eyes were wide and blank as he faced the lawman. "An' suppose I don't," he said.

"You'd better, Joe."

"You think you can beat me?"

Abe's jaw rippled. "I don't know, and we're not goin' to find out. Not now, anyway. But I'll tell you what I will do. I'll jump this horse into the saddle with you, then I'll put you on the ground and hammer your head on a rock."

Doctor Hudson did not like any of this. He had not come up here looking for the gunfighter, he had come to keep his promise to Mary Ellen Demis, to find her children and return with them. The moment Marshal Sutherland finished speaking, Doctor Hudson spoke.

"We came up here to find Mary Ellen's children and fetch them back to her in town. Abe, we can't go back empty-handed. I promised her."

Abe's smoldering gaze swept from Joe to Doctor Hudson. "They aren't up there, Perc. Jeff sent them southeast to find his riders and bring them back to the ranch. You can probably find them over eastward somewhere. One of the possemen was behind them. . . . All right, head east. By the time you get back to town I'll have the gunfighter locked up."

Hudson looked doubtful about that but offered no comment, because he was sure it would start another argument. He turned his horse and jerked his head for Joe and Bob to follow him. They did, but the range boss refused to meet Abe Sutherland's gaze.

For a minute or so, Marshal Sutherland watched them ride away. Then he cursed under his breath and loped back to where Tom Grant was waiting. When they were riding southward again the gunfighter said, "Looked to me like you was havin' a little trouble, Marshal."

Abe nodded. "There's always someone who knows my job better'n I do."

Grant watched the loping horsemen heading east, and wagged his head. He seemed about to speak when a thin, high shout carried to him from the opposite direction. Buster and George Dunhill were paralleling the roadway with the other possemen, heading toward Buckhorn.

Abe stood in his stirrups and waved, then sank down, saw Grant's hard gaze on him, showing faint amusement, and grinned ruefully. "Mr. Grant, it's come to me a few times since I started wearing badges, that there sure must be an easier way to serve the Lord."

Grant laughed shortly, looped his reins, and fished for the makings of a quirley. By the time he had lighted up, they had the Buckhorn rooftops in sight, and the possemen were already entering town at a long lope.

The sun was well down and redder than it had been earlier, there were black shades among the timbered slopes to the north, a faded old durable stagecoach went bucketing northward, where it would not reach the high pass through the mountains until very late in the night, and as the gunfighter smashed out his cigarette atop the saddle horn before dropping it, he said, "Anyone out at the Burke place?"

Abe gave a considered answer. "Yes, I expect so. Some of his riders."

"How many does he keep?"

"Four, I think."

"Well, with him an' one rider dead, that don't leave very many, does it?"

Abe thought he knew what the gunfighter was thinking about: burning the buildings at the Burke ranch. Also, if Grant had been close enough to hear the argument back yonder, he would have had to have been as thick as oak not to realize that two of those horsemen had been Burke riders, and that meant there was no one at the homeplace.

His answer was deliberately casual. "Just two, but that'll be enough until things get straightened out. Of course, there won't be much work get done, and this is marking and branding time."

"Does he have kin—Burke, I mean?"

"Not that I know of, but I've never tried to find out. Why?"

"If he don't have, Marshal, why then someone's goin' to walk in and take over a hell of a lot of range land, aren't they?"

"Not legally, Mr. Grant. Most of that land is deeded. I think the only open range on the west side of the road is up in the foothills."

"Deeded or not, Marshal, if he don't have heirs it'll pretty much be up for grabs."

Sutherland looked at the gunfighter. "You mean Jeff Demis?"

Grant suddenly spat and straightened back in the saddle. "Anybody, Marshal. Anybody who can claim it an' hold it. Not just Jeff Demis."

Abe allowed the subject to languish as they angled toward the roadway, went over to the roadbed, and covered the last mile or so about the same time lamp-glow was beginning to appear through Buckhorn.

They were entering town when the gunfighter eyed the boardinghouse. "They got roaches?"

Abe had a room there. "Not that I ever saw. The woman who runs the place wouldn't hold still for anything like that." He eyed the gunfighter, who clearly thought he was going to take a room at the boardinghouse, but Abe said nothing.

They rode the full length of town, got some interested stares along the way, and entered the smokily-lighted livery barn runway.

Neither the liveryman nor his day hostler were around, but when Abe and Grant were about finished off-saddling their animals, an old scarecrow came shuffling out of the darkness and grinned, showing wet, pink gums without teeth. He pointed. "In them two stalls, gents."

They put up the horses because the nightman made no attempt to do it for them. In retaliation, they did not flip him the customary five-cent piece. They closed the doors, left their outfits where they had upended them, and strolled out front.

There were two or three lighted business establishments. One was Buster's saloon, another was the dingy little café with its fogged-up window, and the third was the corral yard, where it sounded as though yardmen were taking a hitch off the pole.

Tom Grant eyed the foggy café window. "You hungry, Marshal? I am."

They crossed diagonally and entered the café, where a number of local bachelors were hunched at the counter. A few eyes swung, but for the most part the patrons were just tired and hungry men.

The café man flicked startled eyes at the lawman and his companion, then assumed an expressionless look, and took their orders. Abe was sweating bullets. If someone walked up now and asked him how old Henry Burke was doing, all hell was going to bust loose.

No one approached. Several men nodded on their way out, but no one stopped to talk.

The meal filled a need, which was about the highest compliment anyone could have said about it, or just about any other meal the café man served, but the coffee was fresh.

The gunfighter finished first, rocked back to roll a smoke, and turned his bold gaze around the room at the other diners. None of them looked back. He lit up and heaved upward to his feet. Abe was not finished, but he pushed the plate away regardless and also arose. What he had been waiting for was happening. The gunfighter shoved his right hand into his trouser pocket for silver coins to pay for his meal.

Abe had his body turned slightly as he reached downward and came up with a six-gun in his fist. The gunfighter was counting coins to leave on the countertop and did not see the gun—not until Abe pushed it into his side below the ribs, and used his other hand to lift away the fancy, engraved Colt.

The gunfighter did not move for two seconds, not even his head. Then, when he turned, his eyes were wide and blank looking, but it was too late to make a kill.

Abe stepped back and gestured toward the door. Only two diners saw what was happening, and they did not make a sound. Abe and the big man who had eaten with him were outside on the plank walk before those two men began sputtering loudly. This was going to be all over town in nothing flat.

CHAPTER 17

Getting the Drop

TOM GRANT tipped up onto his toes, settled back down, and ranged a look up and down the darkening roadway, then he let his breath out and turned to face Marshal Sutherland. Without raising his voice he said, "You son of a bitch."

Abe said nothing, he simply wigwagged for the gunfighter to cross the road to the jailhouse. There were faces glued to the damp café window, but all those onlookers saw was two large men walking, almost strolling, across the roadway. Abe was slightly to one side and behind the gunfighter, Grant was moving along with his head down as though he were in deep thought, which he was.

When they halted and Abe gestured for the gunfighter to move away so he could get around him and open the jailhouse door, Grant said, "You went to a lot of conniving trouble to be sure I'd still be in town for the inquest tomorrow. I wasn't goin' to leave."

Abe stepped wide and jerked his head. He still said nothing. When they entered the office, Abe told Grant where the lamp was and tossed him some wooden matches to light it with. The gunfighter took down the lamp, boosted the mantle, touched fire to the wick, waited a moment before lowering the mantle, then rehung the lamp from its ceiling hook. When he faced the marshal, he was smiling sardonically.

Marshal Sutherland pointed with his gun barrel toward a bench along the north wall. Grant went over and sat down, big hands hanging between his legs, as he continued to watch the lawman with bleak amusement.

Abe went to his desk, put the silver-inlaid six-gun atop some papers, sat down, and leaned with his Colt aimed directly at the man on the bench. "You slipped up," he told the other large man.

Grant leaned back and shoved his thick legs out, crossed his feet at the ankles, and regarded the lawman without any visible sign of anxiety. "Naw, Marshal, you slipped up. You didn't have to go to all this trouble to keep me here. I told you, I did what anyone else would have done. It was pure and simple self-defense, and your pill-roller and your coroner's jury aren't goin' to prove otherwise."

Abe relaxed, removed his hat and put his six-gun on the desktop, within easy reach. "You only killed one of them," he said quietly, and watched the gunfighter's eyes widen. "You killed the cowboy, but Henry Burke is still alive. Hurt pretty bad, but alive. He told me what happened. They didn't jump you, Mr. Grant, you was waiting for them near the alley so's the sun would be in their eyes. It was you started the fight. It was a bushwhack, pure and simple."

Grant had not taken his eyes off Abe's face since he had been handed this nasty surprise. He still stared across the room. "I'm not sure what you're up to," he said, "but I got an idea. I've been in towns before where they tried to concoct something to get rid of me. If it had worked, I wouldn't be sittin' here now, would I? Marshal, that old man was dead. I don't make mistakes like that." Perhaps Grant was beginning to believe his own voice, because he suddenly leaned forward. "What time is the inquest tomorrow?"

"I don't know. The time hasn't been set yet. I'll talk to Doctor Hudson after I've locked you up, then I'll let you know."

Grant was still confident. "You do that. And you remember something, Marshal. There wasn't no one in the barn but me and those two. That's all. No witnesses." He made a thin, menacing smile. "Go ahead and have old Burke at the hearing."

Abe said, "He can't be moved."

Grant seized on that and exulted. "Can't be moved, eh? More likely he's too stiff to set in a chair. You said he don't have any kinfolk."

Abe nodded.

"Then he don't have any twin brother for you to haul in. Maybe you know someone who looks like the old devil." Grant arose from the bench. "Do whatever you got planned, an' when they turn me loose for defending myself, Marshal, you better find a hell of a deep hole and hide in it."

Abe picked up the six-gun, stepped around his desk, and without taking his eyes off the gunfighter, opened the cell room door, moved clear and jerked his head for Tom Grant to walk down the dingy little narrow corridor with strap steel cages on both sides.

In life-and-death situations, everyone makes mistakes— some sooner, some later. Abe Sutherland knew that. That was what he had spent the afternoon and early evening waiting for, and Tom Grant had made one.

Now, it was the gunfighter's turn to hone every instinct and wait. But Abe got the cell door open and stepped away to cock his handgun. Grant walked into the cell, wooden-faced.

When the door had been slammed and locked, Abe holstered his gun and gazed at his prisoner. "I'll see you in the morning," he said. "There's two blankets on the bunk. The slop bucket is beneath it." He hesitated, meeting the gunfighter's deadly stare. "I'll fetch you something to eat when I open up tomorrow."

Grant did not move from the center of the little cell, or speak, but as Abe walked back up toward his office, the gunfighter's gaze never left him until the door had been closed and bolted from the office side.

Abe rummaged in a lower desk drawer for his bottle of rye

whiskey, took two swallows, and was closing the drawer on the bottle when the door opened and he saw Joe Holden framed in the opening. They exchanged a look before Joe stepped ahead, kicked the door closed and said, "We found the children."

Abe nodded curtly. "Good. Have a chair."

Joe sat down, shifted his holstered Colt so it would not gouge his leg, and stared at the blackened little coffeepot atop the stove. "You got him locked up?" he asked the coffeepot.

"Yeah. There is his gun."

Joe leaned to pick the weapon up and examine it. "No front sight, filed trigger-pull. Did you heft it? Balanced like someone worked on it who really new his business." Joe put the gun back on the papers. He cleared his throat and regarded the little coffeepot again. "Doc Hudson was right about something."

Abe leaned back, waiting.

"I owe you an apology."

Abe said nothing. He was not going to make this easy for the range boss.

"I got mad at the wrong man, Doc said, and he was right. I'd still like to take him on—that prisoner of yours. Well, I expect that'll never happen now. You got his gun, an' that's like pullin' his fangs." Joe's eyes swiveled to Abe's face. "How did you do it?"

"I told you. I stuck to him like a burr until he shoved his right hand in his pants pocket at the café to pay for supper."

"What did he do?"

"Called me a son of a bitch."

Joe laughed. "Did you tell him Mr. Burke's alive?"

"Yeah. . . . Is he?"

Joe did not laugh again, but he got a soft smile on his face. Instead of a direct answer he went off on a tangent. "Y'know, Abe, the In'ians had a notion that makin' folks well had to do with gettin' bad spirits out of them and puttin' good spirits in to take their place." His smile widened. "Doc and I talked about this a while back, while Miz' Demis was huggin' her kids and spillin' tears on them." He lifted his hat, scratched vigorously, and dropped the hat back down. Then he returned his attention to the little coffeepot as he continued to speak. "There's a lot of things Doc don't know, but what he does know is downright interesting. He made me think of that In'ian hocus-pocus while we drank watered whiskey in his kitchen a while ago. He told me Mary Ellen's the best medicine anyone could ever prescribe for Mr. Burke. He said she's his good spirit."

Joe's gaze returned to the silent town marshal at his desk. "Abe, you wouldn't believe the change in him unless you saw it. That lady's been feedin' him hot broth. She put a little whiskey in his drinkin' water. She even shaved the old billy goat and washed him up."

Joe slapped his leg and finally laughed. "You got to see them two together."

Abe hid a yawn and leaned down on the desk. "I got to see Perc and Henry in the morning. Perc can convene the coroner's hearing for Jack."

Joe suddenly stopped smiling. "You need Jack for that? Hell, I sent Bob Cheney back to the ranch with him to be buried."

Abe relieved the worried range boss. "No, we won't need Jack. But we're goin' to need Henry to tell what really happened in the livery barn."

Joe's response to this solved a problem for Marshal Sutherland without Joe being aware of it. He said, "Then you're goin' to have to hold the inquest in the shed. Mr. Burke can't be moved. And I got a feelin' that if you wanted to move him over to the fire hall where hearings are usually held, Doc Hudson and Miz' Demis would come down on you like a herd of boulders."

Abe regarded his large hands atop the desk. That old converted carriage house was small. Too small for a coroner's jury to crowd into. He pushed back off the desktop. Small or not, that was where the inquest was going to have to be held. He yawned again and stood up. Joe finally understood and also arose. As he turned toward the door, he said, "I didn't mean all that crap I said up yonder. I was orry-eyed; there was that bastard settin' his horse back a ways. Jack was dead and Mr. Burke darned near was . . ."

Abe blew down the lamp mantle, then went to the open doorway and slapped Joe on the shoulder. "Forget it. In your boots, I'd have done the same thing. . . . You stayin' in town or goin' out to the ranch?"

"Stayin' in town. I wouldn't miss this coroner's thing for a year's pay. By the way, where is Jeff Demis?"

"Wasn't he at the ranch?"

"We didn't go to the ranch. We met his riders heading there about the same time we come onto your posseman talking like a Dutch uncle to the kids. I think maybe the riders would have taken the kids with them, except that countin' your posseman and us three, it made a sort of mexican standoff. They rode on, and we come back to town." Joe cocked his head slightly. "Sure as hell Jeff'll show up in town with his riders tomorrow. . . . Good night."

Abe nodded and watched the range boss cross the empty roadway. He did not speculate on where Joe intended to spend the night; all he cared about was getting up to his own bed. This had been a nerve-racking day."

There were lights in Doctor Hudson's house as the marshal passed by. Tired as he was, he could not repress a little sardonic smile. Perc Hudson had never married. All he knew about children could have fit on the head of a pin without causing any crowding. Unless they had the measles, broken arms, or needed sulphur and molasses to thin their blood, he had nothing to do with them. Abe remembered something he'd once heard Perc say about children; that they should not even be born until they were eighteen.

Abe was tempted to go down the side of the house to the

shed, but after what Joe had told him, he was not very worried. Besides, he wanted to sleep.

The boardinghouse was dark and silent when he went down the hall to his room. A dog was barking on the east side of town somewhere. He listened to that until he got into bed. Buckhorn, like every town with miles of open country around it, had regular four-footed invaders after nightfall: raccoons, skunks, coyotes, and assorted varieties of smaller culprits who upset trash barrels and set off the town dogs.

CHAPTER 18

A Brindle Dog

BUSTER Munzer's saloon, along with the café, the general store, and a frequently overlooked but even more lively source for the exchange of gossip, the tonsorial parlor, had been generating lively and often conflicting stories about the livery barn shootings, the condition of that event's sole survivor, the man known to be locked in Marshal Sutherland's jailhouse, and the inquest that was to be held—all of it based on what Sutherland's possemen had to say, and none of it dependable or really very accurate.

By the time Marshal Sutherland had eaten breakfast at the café and taken two pails with him across the road for his prisoner's breakfast, the conflicting and contradictory stories had been retold so many times that even the few known facts had been hopelessly garbled.

The men who could have given reasonably accurate accounts—the town marshal, Doctor Hudson, and Henry Burke, had not done so, with the result that by the time the sun had risen above Buckhorn's rooftops, local curiosity had reached its peak.

Abe Sutherland, who knew his town and its inhabitants, took the pails of meat stew and black coffee down to the gunfighter's cell and shoved them beneath the steel door without a word. When he straightened up, the prisoner gazed at him from the side of the wall bunk, jerked his head in the direction of the very narrow, barred window in the east wall, and said, "Sounds like the Fourth of July out there."

Abe's response was cryptic. "Yeah. What'd you expect?"

151

Tom Grant continued to sit on the edge of the bunk. He ignored the little pails. "If they got lynching in mind, they better hold off until after the inquest."

Abe eyed the large man. "They're not talkin' about lynching, they're just talking. You and Jeff stirred up a hornet's nest.'"

"Is he out there?" the gunfighter asked, arising to approach the little pails. He leaned to inspect their contents then straightened up with scorn. "That's dogfood."

Abe ignored the statement and replied to the question. "I don't think he's out there, but I'd like to see him. As you can see, I got three empty cells."

"What time is the hearing?"

"I don't know. Don't worry, I won't let you miss it."

He returned to the office, locked the roadway door after himself, and went up to Doctor Hudson's place. Mary Ellen opened the door to him, and blushed furiously as he nodded and walked past into the parlor. She and her children had spent the night. In a place the size of Buckhorn, that might have raised a lot of eyebrows if there hadn't been something much more compelling on peoples' minds. She took him through to the kitchen, where her children were having breakfast, and pointed to the door leading out back.

Before he reached the shed, he could hear Perc's deep voice. He was telling Henry what Abe had come up here to find out; when the hearing would be held and who would be dragooned as the coroner's jury.

When he heard the knock on the door, Hudson suspended what he had been saying until he knew who the intruder was, then went on speaking. "It'll be your testimony that counts, Henry. You're the only one who was there."

Abe said, "Have you already talked to folks around town for your jury, Perc?"

Hudson had, "Buster, English the blacksmith, that old man who clerks at the emporium, George Dunhill." Hudson lifted a cup of black coffee he had brought out to the shed with him. "How is your prisoner?"

"Well, he don't give the impression of being worried, but he didn't eat breakfast."

Henry spoke up. "What'd you feed him?"

"Same as I had, meat stew and coffee."

"He won't eat stuff like that," Henry averred, and at the looks he got, he expanded on it. "He won't eat stew made of leftovers. He's a Taurean. They got notions about what they wear, it's got to be the best, and what they eat, no cookhouse slop or leftovers, and—"

"What the hell are you talkin' about?" demanded Marshal Sutherland.

Doctor Hudson dryly replied. "It's Mary Ellen, Marshal. Your prisoner was born under the zodiac sign of Taurus. She's been drilling Henry on that stuff. For example, those fancy boots Grant wears, that expensive gun belt, the clean clothes, that silver-inlaid and engraved six-gun. Taureans got to have things like that. And they're stubborn, opinionated, and a few other things."

"And," put in Henry, "she says they only eat the best grub. He'll starve before he'll eat leftover meat stew. If you doubt me, Abe, go get him a steak and see if he eats it."

Abe looked from one of them to the other, then hunched his shoulders in a shrug. "I don't care if he starves." He continued to look at them. "All right. What is a Taurean?"

"Someone born under the sign of Taurus the bull," said Henry. "Mary Ellen can tell you all about your prisoner, right down to his streak of killin' ability and suchlike."

Abe hauled up to his full height and ignored Henry Burke. "Perc, what time does the inquest begin?"

"Ten o'clock."

"Where?"

"Right here."

Abe nodded his head about that, then dropped another critical look on Henry Burke. He didn't speak, and that bothered the older man, who got a little pink in the face and defensive. "I know what you're thinkin', because I thought the same way yesterday, but she knows about those things. She really does, Abe. I never had any idea she's as savvy as she is."

Abe finally spoke. "And pretty, Henry?"

Burke's color increased. "Yes, and pretty. And decent, and kind, and—"

"Perc, I'd like a word with you outside."

Hudson closed the door after himself and met Abe's quizzical look. "Oh, he's all right, Abe. In fact he's going to make it, which I wouldn't have bet a plugged dollar on yesterday. Don't he look good?"

"Yes he does, good color and all. . . . What's Mary Ellen done to him?"

Doctor Hudson glanced around before replying. "I'd say that whatever she's done, I'd like to hire her to do to my other patients." He brought his gaze back to the marshal. "I guess you didn't notice it, what with havin' other things on your mind. He's in love with her as sure as we're standing here, and that, old friend, has got to be the best medicine there is."

Abe stared through narrowed eyelids. "He's got to be in his sixties."

Hudson nodded. "All right. What's that got to do with it?"

"Well, she's got a husband."

"So she has, but my guess is that Henry's the first man in a long time who's shown her that all sheep aren't black."

Abe Sutherland glanced in the direction of the house, and let his breath out slowly. "I'll be damned. . . . Well, I'll bring the gunfighter up here—what time did you say?"

"Ten o'clock. Abe, you watch that son of a bitch. Does he know Henry survived the gunfight?"

"Yes. I told him."

"Then you better watch him like a hawk. Unless he's an

idiot, he knows now that he isn't going to be able to talk his way out of this one. Put chains on him. Is Jeff in town?"

"I haven't seen him. I don't think he is. If he's smart, he won't come near."

"He's not smart, Abe. I know Jeff pretty well. He thinks he's smarter than anyone alive, and that's proof that he may be sly and tricky and underhanded, but not smart. Suppose he rides in with his crew?"

Abe had thought about that over breakfast. "He's got the legal right, Perc. All the same, I'm goin' to have the gunsmith and one or two others keep an eye peeled. There is not going to be any more killing."

Mary Ellen emerged from the back of the house to tell Doctor Hudson there was a woman in the parlor with a little boy who had a cast on his arm. Hudson said, "Ten o'clock," and walked away.

Abe went down the alley to the jailhouse and passed on through to emerge on Main Street. He had an hour before the inquest. He used it to visit the stores whose proprietors he could rely on to back up the law if armed rangemen appeared in town during the inquest. When he was satisfied, he returned to the jailhouse, took down his copper key ring and went down into the cell room.

The little breakfast pails were where he had left them, and Tom Grant was lying full length atop his bunk. He neither looked around nor spoke as Marshal Sutherland said, "You don't like stew?"

The reply from the bed was harsh. "That's what you feed dogs."

Abe said, "How about a big steak and mashed potatoes?"

Grant swung up off the bunk. "Those are the first sensible words you've said, Marshal. Over at the café?"

Abe stood dangling his key ring and staring at the gunfighter. He wagged his head and muttered. "I'll be damned."

Grant approached the front of the cell. "When do I get it?"

Abe was inserting the large key into the lock when he answered. "You don't. Now get back until I get this door open . . . farther back."

He herded the gunfighter up to the office, kicked the cell room door closed without taking his eyes off his prisoner, and pitched the keys atop his desk. "We're going out of here and up the back alley to a shed behind Doctor Hudson's house. . . . I want to tell you something, and you better listen: One wrong step and I'll kill you. Don't even stumble."

He herded Grant out into the alley and growled for him to walk northward. From a distance of ten feet, Abe watched the other large man like a hawk. He did not draw his six-gun, but he maintained the distance between them so that if the gunfighter did something reckless or desperate, Abe could draw and fire before Grant could either reach him, or duck from sight among the buildings which lined the alleyway.

There was heat in the morning, but what was more notice-able—to those who were able to observe such things—was that the air was utterly still, and there was a diaphanous cloudiness to the sky, like a very thin, cottony veil. It was going to rain. Maybe not soon, but eventually.

Inside the rickety old fence which separated Hudson's rear yard from the alley, there was a loose knot of idling men. For a while, they did not notice the two men coming up the alley, nor did Abe Sutherland more than flick a glance in their direction.

Grant's head was up. He was looking at the small crowd near an old shed, inside a rickety picket fence. Once he turned his head to the left, when a large, tan dog walked out from among some tumbledown sheds, bony tail curved, flat head fixed on the strollers, muscular, lean body tense as he growled. The dog was clearly not the bluffing kind. Grant spoke from the corner of his mouth. "That son of a bitch is goin' to tackle one of us, Marshal."

Abe said, "Keep walkin' and shut up."

The dog took several stiff steps forward and stopped, his growl deep and menacing. Tom Grant missed a step and slowed as the dog seemed to sink back on his haunches. "Marshal, damn it . . ."

The men outside Perc Hudson's shed were watching silently now.

Abe darted a look at the dog and snarled at it. The dog could have been deaf for all that snarl meant to him. His light brown eyes were fixed on the gunfighter, who was closest to him. He did not blink. He crouched lower and continued to growl. Tom Grant stopped moving, staring back at the dog. Abe swore, but that had no effect on the dog either. He seemed to have made up his mind to hurl himself upon Tom Grant if he took another step forward.

Grant's tongue made a swift circuit of his lips, his body tensed. Whatever was going through his mind was between himself and the slab-sided, tawny dog.

Abe halted. He could have shot the dog. Instead, he made a mistake, he leaned down to pick up a stone. The dog understood perfectly what that meant, and with a savage snarl sprang at the gunfighter.

To the spectators, what followed happened very fast, but with an obvious pattern. Grant did not recoil from the attack. He had deliberately taken one more step forward as Marshal Sutherland had leaned to pick up the rock. Perhaps more than what the marshal did, that step forward triggered the dog's attack.

As the dog came in, hurtling off the ground, Tom Grant sprang at him and aimed a kick that caught the dog head-on. Before the dog collapsed in the alleyway, Grant was already past him in a wildly deperate run toward the tumble-down sheds on the west side of the alley.

Within moments, he was lost to sight of the men standing with open mouths in Hudson's yard. But definitely in his favor, he got among those sheds and beyond them before Marshal Sutherland could straighten up to draw and fire.

Abe heard Grant running beyond the sheds and went in angry pursuit, gun in hand but not cocked. In Hudson's yard, there was a delayed bellow as the onlookers got untracked and also rushed across the alley.

There were residences, several fenced yards, some clotheslines with wash drying on them, and other dogs, all of whom became very excited, not at the escaping gunfighter but at the men who were invading their areas, yelling back and forth as they joined the hunt.

Grant got over among the houses, unseen by his pursuers, raced around the side of a residence, and met the startled stare of a graying man preparing to mount his saddle horse at an iron post out front. The gunfighter did not even hesitate. He charged the man, unnerved him with a roar, grabbed the reins, and struck the graying man with sufficient force to knock him backward, his hat flying even farther back.

The terrified horse flung up its head and pulled back, hard, but Tom Grant was not only a physically powerful individual, he was also a desperate one. He wrenched the horse around, not bothering with stirrups, hurled himself into the saddle, and sank in both heels as the panicked animal whirled half around in a leaping lunge, and landed in a wild run, heading north.

Someone from Hudson's yard saw him and yelled. Someone else came blundering through a clothesline, which he left a shambles as he ran toward the man who had shouted, stopped when he saw the distant rider, yanked out a handgun, and fired three times before Marshal Sutherland got out there.

Tom Grant was barely within rifle range. He was well beyond handgun range. Without a word, Abe Sutherland turned back, ran all the way to the livery barn, where he kept two horses, ignored everything and everyone to get astride as rapidly as possible, then he went up the alley and out the north end of town in a dead run.

There was no sign of the gunfighter.

The lawman veered westerly to pick up the gunfighter's tracks. He found them without any difficulty, still fresh and cut deeply into the ground where the animal had dug hard with each jump to propel himself forward.

Once Abe looked over his shoulder. There were riders at the upper end of Buckhorn, but far behind. He settled forward, searching for sign of the fugitive. As time passed, his agitation diminished, and with nothing else to do as he rode, he went back over the events which had ended like this, trying to imagine how it had all happened.

It was that damned brindle dog, of course, but as furious as he was, he made no personal promise to himself to settle with the dog when he returned to town.

He had taken every precaution he could have taken to prevent something like this from happening—except one, and sure as hell Perc Hudson would never let him forget that: He had told Abe to put chains on the prisoner, and Abe had instead relied upon his own judgment, which had been to remain behind Grant and to shoot him if he did anything suspicious.

Someone yelled from a great distance. Several of the pursuing townsmen had caught sight of Abe, and either thought he was the gunfighter, or wanted to let him know they were coming.

Abe had to slack off, his horse was pumping air like a bellows. It aggravated him to have to do this, but there was no alternative. The hoofprints he was following showed that the gunfighter was still pushing his stolen horse as hard as he could, so Abe knew that either the horse would drop in his tracks, or the gunfighter would also slack off. If he did the latter, then the pair of them were going to have a walking-horse contest—but daylight would not last forever. If Grant could reach the northward mountains, his chances of escaping would soar.

It was hard to read signs over miles of spongy pine and fir

needles. It was impossible to read them after sunset. But the marshal, who had not been born under the sign of Taurus, was also a very stubborn individual.

Several times, he looked back. Those town riders appeared to have thinned out. What had looked like a big crowd of them earlier, now seemed to be no more than four or five horsemen.

He grimaced to himself. The world was full of people who liked the idea of excitement, especially when they were part of a crowd, but after the first breathlessness passed and they had time to consider what they were doing—chasing a very dangerous gunman who was also a killer—enthusiasm had a way of dissipating.

But Abe did not expect them to reach him for a long time, nor was he relying on their support. What he wanted was to catch sight of Tom Grant and keep him in sight until the distance between them could be closed. Then, whatever occurred would be up to the gunfighter, but without a weapon he would be a fool to make a fight of it.

Abe felt perfectly confident that was how this horse race was going to end.

And he was wrong again.

CHAPTER 19

The Midday Riders

AMONG the pursuers from town was Joe Holden, Henry Burke's range boss, and his agitation over the escape of the gunfighter did not interfere with his cold logic.

He was in front of the town riders when they caught sight of a distant horseman, and although several of the excited men behind Joe yelled that they had the gunfighter in sight, Joe thought differently.

There was only one rider up there, and since Marshal Sutherland had been behind the gunfighter when the race had begun, Joe knew the rider they were watching was not the gunfighter.

Joe rode a mile before his hatred of the entire Demis outfit inspired him to raise an arm, and when the crowd behind him slacked off and milled, he gestured and raised his voice at the same time.

"You fellers stay together until you reach the road. Go across the road to the east, then fan out ridin' north, slow. You'll be on Demis's land and somewhere up there, you'll likely find him an' his crew heading for town. Turn them back. If you got to use your guns, do it, but don't let them get past you. If they run back for the yard, you boys stay out of gun range and surround the yard. Keep out of sight as much as you can. Box them in and keep them there until I can catch up to Sutherland and come over there with him."

A squatty, older man said. "What the hell are you talkin' about?"

"I'm tellin' you that gunfighter works for Jeff Demis. If his

161

hired gunman was still in town Jeff'd come down there with his riders to bust him out."

"What about the damned gunfighter?" a rider demanded.

"Sutherland will find him. Me too, if I can catch up to them. But you fellers bottle Demis up, otherwise he might damned well see riders chasing his gunfighter, go to his rescue, and start a damned war. Don't give him the chance. Surprise him an' drive him back. Then let him hole up and sweat. Don't fight, just let him fort up in his buildings and sweat."

The gunsmith was tearing a cud off his chewing plug and could not speak until that had been done, then he said, "Joe, suppose that's where the gunfighter is going? To the Demis place."

Joe smiled coldly. "That's exactly what I hope he's trying to do. You gents make them fort up and keep them like that. As soon as I catch up to Abe Sutherland, if the tracks lead us to Demis's yard, we'll come along."

Joe put his horse into a long lope leaving the town riders staring after him more bewildered than enlightened. The gunsmith finally broke the trance with a growl. "Come on. Settin' here isn't goin' to do any good."

The riders turned off toward the roadway. It was this action that made Abe Sutherland believe most of the town riders had lost their enthusiasm and turned back. He could not see them riding toward the stage road. He only saw one of them still coming, but even that rider was too distant for Abe to make out much about him. Nor did he try. The tracks he had been following were no longer digging in. The stolen horse was walking, and not very fast. He had probably been pushed to the limit of his strength.

But that only fleetingly interested Marshal Sutherland because the tracks, which had been going arrow-straight toward the mountains, now veered abruptly eastward. The fugitive was paralleling the mountains, miles southward of them.

Abe squared up in his saddle to squint in the new direction he was riding. He knew where he was—on Demis's land— and he thought he knew where the gunfighter was heading— toward the Demis yard.

Now he had to worry about Jeff and his riders. If they were already on their way to Buckhorn, he might not have to watch very closely. He suspected that they were. It was certainly late enough in the morning for ranchmen to be undertaking whatever they'd had in mind doing after breakfast. He divided his attention between sweeps of the onward country for signs of the fugitive, and in a different direction for signs of the Demis riders and their employer.

He saw neither until the sun had crept closer to its meridian and his horse's shadow was almost directly beneath him. Then he had a glimpse of what appeared to be a mounted man passing in and out among a small stand of trees which he thought were roughly a mile from the Demis yard.

Now he paid less attention to the possible sighting of Jeff and his men, because if the fugitive was up yonder among those scraggly pine trees, and did not emerge, why then he was setting up an ambush for Marshal Sutherland, whose progress had been entirely visible from the time he had left town.

Abe did not slacken his horse's gait, which was a slogging walk on a loose rein. The distant figure had not come out of the trees—at least Abe saw no sign of this having happened, although if the gunfighter rode eastward in the direction of the yard and kept the trees directly behind him, it was probable that Abe would not see him until he, too, reached the trees and could see beyond them. Which could be hazardous.

But the marshal was confident of one thing; he had run down the man-killer. From here on, it was going to be a duel of wits, of who was sly enough, experienced enough, and clever enough to outwit the other man.

He had been unaware of the position of the sun until it

bore directly downward. His horse was sweat-dark but had his second wind. So far back he looked no larger than an ant, a rider was following, and he was no greenhorn. Instead of staying with the tracks, he turned northeastward with Sutherland in sight. He did not go north until the tracks turned, he cut directly away from the sign and was now riding by sight. He would be able to close the distance between himself the lawman much more quickly this way.

Abe was gauging distances as he rode. He knew the gunfighter did not have a six-gun, but he was less sure that he might not have a saddlegun. He had not waited back in town to talk to the man whose horse Tom Grant had taken, and while it was true that townsmen did not carry carbines on their saddles except perhaps in hunting season, being careless about something like this could make a man arrive a few years early in hell.

Abe tipped down his hat and concentrated his full attention upon the trees. He was getting close to Winchester range. When he thought he was close enough, he reined southward to make a big, half-circling sashay around the stand of trees. As he rode, he watched for movement.

There was none. It was a fact that the gunfighter would not move so much as an arm if he were up there in the shadows among the pines, but his horse would not be that prudent.

Still, he saw nothing as he was rounding on his course beyond the trees, but he could just make out the Demis yard and buildings. The distance was too great for him to see movement. The yard looked empty. He decided to bypass the pines, and began a long approach in the direction of the buildings. If Tom Grant was back there among the pines, he would now have an opportunity to break away on the west side and continue toward the mountains.

Abe rode twisted in the saddle, waiting for this to happen. It never did. He was within a mile of the yard, able to make out objects in the yard, when what sounded like a child's popgun sounded southward.

Five horsemen were loping toward the buildings in a strung out, disorderly gathering, and farther back, so much farther back in fact that Marshal Sutherland could barely even see their movement, there was what appeared to be an even more strung out band of horsemen in pursuit of the nearer bunch.

Abe looked for cover. The only thing in sight was that stand of scraggly pine trees. He tugged free the tie-down thong over his holstered Colt and turned back in that direction. Whether the gunfighter was in there or not, for Abe Sutherland it was the lesser of two evils; those horsemen loping toward the yard would be Jeff and his crew. There were too many of them for one lawman to take on, and he felt uneasy about what they might do when they recognized him. Jeff at least would not be friendly, and for all Abe knew, his riders might not be either.

Since he had seen them, of course they had seen him. Whether they had recognized him as the town marshal from Buckhorn, he had no idea. Maybe they had better eyesight than he had; so far he had not been able to recognize any of those men heading toward the yard. Maybe they didn't know who he was, and maybe they would make no attempt to run him down to find out, but he had no intention of sitting out there in plain sight like a crow on a fence until he knew what they were going to do, so he turned directly toward the trees, eyes constantly moving.

He reached the first trees, pushed past them, and rode into an area where the heat had not penetrated to any great extent, and where pinesap was running, making the area pleasantly fragrant as well as cool.

There was no one else among the trees. Abe swung down, trailed his horse behind him on loose reins and looked for shod-horse imprints.

The signs were north of where he searched first. They

came directly in among the trees from the west, where Abe had been tracking. They were overlapping and scuffed in one place, indicating that the rider had halted to turn and watch his backtrail before moving again. From this shadowy place, Abe followed the tracks directly in the direction of the yard. Where the gunfighter had torn out of the trees, he had been riding fast again.

Abe stood back in fragrant shade, gazing in the direction of the yard. He knew where the fugitive was. As he gazed out there, those other horsemen came up into the yard, scuffing dust as they hauled down. Abe's horse jerked up straight and swung his head as far as he could looking back, both ears pointing.

The marshal also looked back. He had not forgotten the rider who had been behind him, but he had not been interested in him either. Now he was, because not only was the fugitive over among Demis's buildings, but sure as hell Jeff and his riders were over there too, and unless Abe was very badly mistaken, he was now facing a seige situation.

He walked back toward the last trees and watched the oncoming man boost his animal over into a rocking chair lope. It was Joe Holden.

Abe leaned on a tree and waited. When Joe was closer he acted wary, so Abe walked out into sunlight and flagged with his hat.

Joe reached the trees, swung off, and nodded without smiling. "Where is the son of a bitch?" he asked, and Abe jerked a thumb over his shoulder. "In Demis's yard. And something spooked Jeff. Him and his riders came foggin' it back from the south. They're over there too."

Joe reset his hat and leaned to peer eastward past the trees, in the direction of the yard. "What spooked him was a mob of riders from town, most likely. I sent them up here to herd him back up here; keep him away from Buckhorn when you and the rest of us aren't down there."

Marshal Sutherland started back the way he had come as

he spoke. "He wouldn't have done anything in town, Joe. Not with his hired killer gone."

Joe did not comment. When they halted among the trees and he had a good view of the distant ranch yard, Abe had a question for him. "How many riders from town are down there?"

Joe Holden was not sure. "About fifteen, unless some turned back. I told them to scatter out beyond gun range, get around the place so's no one can get out. . . . Shoot if they got to, otherwise to wait until you'n me came along."

Joe brought forth a plug and went to work with his clasp-knife while Marshal Sutherland squatted in front of his saddle animal, watching dust in several directions. The men from Buckhorn remained a long way off, but they were evidently attempting to do what Joe had suggested to them, because they were constantly changing positions and directions. If they were affecting a surround, it was a rather general one. Still, there looked to be at least twelve men out there, maybe fifteen as Joe had guessed, and sure as hell Jeff would have made a count too. He might even have figured out by now what all that sashaying back and forth was leading up to. If he had, by now he was sweating, and that was a pleasant thought to Marshal Sutherland.

Joe squatted, spat and said, "If this was my round up, Abe, I'd set here in cool comfort until dark, then I'd slip over there and set some fires."

Abe turned his head slowly. "It's not your round up."

Joe took the rebuke well, but his reply was sarcastic. "Yeah, I know that. You got a dead-shot over there. Maybe more than one. In broad daylight if you ride over there, someone's goin' to blow your head off. Maybe you don't know Jeff as well as I do; he's as sly and underhanded as they come. Him and his gunfighter aren't goin' to just set there and wait. Come dark, in case you hadn't thought of it, they're goin' to sneak out of there and make it to the mountains."

Abe continued to gaze eastward. "The gunfighter maybe, but not Jeff. He didn't kill anyone."

"No. He just hired someone to do it. Or don't that make any difference in the eyes of the law?"

Abe watched a pair of townsmen ride on a very wide angle on their way around the buildings. If they maintained their course, they would pass within a couple of hundred yards of the place where he and Joe were squatting. "Yeah, it makes a difference in the eyes of the law, Joe. It's called bein' an accomplice. But I don't think Jeff's goin' to panic and run for it. He's got far too much to lose. Besides, he thinks he's too clever for me to be able to put him away on nothin' more'n a charge of complicity. . . . If he plays his cards right, I won't be able to." Abe turned toward the range boss. "You got any idea how he can manage that?"

"No. Unless you mean he can hire a fee lawyer from Denver, maybe."

"Shoot his gunfighter in the back. He's the only man who could try to trade his way out of a hangin' by implicating Jeff up to his damned ears."

The range boss turned back to watch the town riders and the distant yard, which was still, empty, and without any more dust stirring. He let the topic drop between them and instead wanted to know what Abe Sutherland had in mind, adding another sarcastic comment to that question.

"They're all set now, Abe. They're waitin' for dark as sure as hell, and then they'll scatter like birds. Unless you got some clever plan up your sleeve."

Abe said nothing for a long time, not until those oncoming riders had passed along without even glancing toward the trees, and were completing their big encircling ride as they got into position behind the buildings.

He arose in front of his horse. "I'm goin' around behind the yard, try an' get down among the sheds, and see if I can talk to Jeff."

Joe also arose, his face wooden, his jaws working slowly. "It's your round up," he said.

Abe faced him, gave Joe a light slap on the shoulder and turned to mount his horse.

CHAPTER 20

A Standoff

MARSHAL Sutherland had plenty to think about as he rode. He'd been a lawman a lot of years. He had often thought that he had been through it all. But he hadn't; he'd never been in a seige before.

He had serious doubts about being able to talk Jeff into yielding. Jeff Demis was one of those people for whom the prospect of any kind of defeat, even in an argument, was almost as bad as death.

Still, Abe had to make the attempt.

Maybe Joe's way would be best, but it would also place a number of men in a position where they would almost certainly be killed. Loyal though Jeff's riders might be to the brand they rode for, they had broken no laws—yet, anyway—and for that reason deserved a chance not to break any, such as firing on a lawman during the performance of his duty.

The heat was increasing. Mounted men were distantly and irregularly visible, but there was not a sound as Abe figured out a course that would keep some of the buildings in the yard between himself and the main house. The forted-up men would be watching closely, and would be able to see him leave the trees and head toward the yard. For about two-thirds of a mile they would be able to see him, and since he was the only thing moving, they would be watching.

Once he got the log barn between himself and the main house, he thought he might be fairly safe. Unless of course all of Jeff's riders were not over at the main house. If one of them was keeping watch from inside the barn, or perhaps from the rear of the bunkhouse, Abe Sutherland might be riding straight down someone's Winchester barrel.

There was no other way to do it. As he walked his horse along, he trusted more to intuition than to eyesight. By now even the distant townsmen, who were holding their ragged surround, were watching him. When he reined toward the barn, he could see only the two riders who had ridden close to the trees on their way northward, and as he got close enough to see horses watching him from a large pole corral, lined up side by side staring at him, he could no longer see those men.

Nothing happened, but Marshal Sutherland was riding like a coiled spring. He was sweating hard by the time he was close enough to the back of the barn to smell timothy hay. He had his six-gun in his fist, lying lightly in his lap right up until he finally reached the barn and could see stud-rings embedded in the logs out back.

He holstered the gun, talked to his horse as he eased up to the back wall, and swung to the ground to loop his reins through one of the iron rings. The horse was perfectly at ease; he was in shade.

Abe went along the rough logs to the doorless, wide rear barn opening and halted to listen. There still was not a sound. He eased up as close as he dared and spoke quietly. "If you're in there, you better think twice. This is Marshal Sutherland."

The silence ran on.

"Unless your name is Demis or Grant, the law's not interested in you. I'm coming in. You got a few seconds to decide whether you want to spend the rest of your life ducking wanted posters, or whether you want to show good sense."

He lifted out the Colt, cocked it this time, waited a few seconds, and then moved swiftly around the door opening and lunged for the nearest darkness.

Nothing happened.

He stood until his eyes were accustomed to the gloom,

made a very close examination of everything in sight, looking for the shape of an armed man, and let his breath out slowly when he was finally satisfied he was the only person inside the barn.

He had to shift the six-gun to his left hand and wipe sweat off his right palm before gripping the weapon again. He made his way toward the front of the barn, up where sunlight bounced off hardpan dust, moving with careful deliberation. He was in a horse barn. It had no hayloft, so he did not have to worry about someone being above him with a gun.

Where he halted, the smells of heat and dust were strong, and being on the north side of the barn's interior, he did not have to risk poking his head out to see the main house at the southern end of the yard. He could stand in front of a horse stall on the north wall and by only leaning slightly, see out into the yard, all along the east side, where there were other buildings, and southward, where the big yard ended at a hitchrack in front of the main house.

There was a veranda along the entire front of the house. It not only sheltered the front of the house from the weather, it also kept it cool, but for Abe Sutherland's purpose, the long porch was a nuisance because it shadowed the only area he was interested in, making it nearly impossible for him to see anything but the door and two small windows, one larger than the other. What was behind those windows, he could not see. Something he saw over there kept him from calling out for a few minutes.

The sunlight from the yard in front of the house would ordinarily have been reflected against the two windows. There was no reflection. Blankets had been nailed across the windows.

That meant Jeff and his men were in there.

Abe raised his hat, mopped off sweat, reset the hat, and called in the direction of the house in a bull-bass voice.

"Jeff! This is Marshal Sutherland! I want to talk to you!"

There was no reply. After the echoes of his shouting had passed, the silence settled again, as deep as ever.

Abe tried again. "Jeff! This isn't doin' anyone any good. The yard is cut off in all directions. If necessary, I can keep you in there until I can get the army up here. We better talk before I got to do somethin' like that."

Again, there was no reply.

Abe squinted at the front of the house. "I'm not goin' to keep this up," he yelled, and this time there was a response.

"Marshal! What the hell do you think you're doing, having a mob from town chase me'n my riders back here, makin' us fort up like it was an In'ian attack?"

Abe was encouraged. "Jeff, Tom Grant broke away when I was gettin' him ready for the coroner's inquest. Send him out and that'll end it as far as I am concerned."

"Tom Grant? What in hell makes you think he's here?"

"Because his tracks led here, Jeff. Just send him out."

Instead of an answer, Abe got a question. "How many men you got out there?"

"Close to twenty. Now send him out."

"He isn't here."

The marshal remained quiet. He knew Jeff was capable of lying. In fact, he had known the man to lie many times in the years of their acquaintanceship. But in the back of his mind, he was not sure Jeff was lying now. There were ways Tom Grant could have escaped. Offhand, Abe could not come up with any he wanted to believe, but he knew it was possible.

It also occurred to him that Jeff had hidden the gunfighter. If he had, short of a minute search of every building in the yard, it would be difficult to find him.

He finally called back. "You know where he is, Jeff. We're goin' to stay here until you or Grant comes out. If it takes a month, we'll out-wait you."

This time the delay in their shouting match was on Jeff Demis's side of the yard. Of one thing Jeff could be certain,

Abe Sutherland did not make threats. If he said he and his men were going to wait Jeff out, then Jeff could depend on that.

He called back to the marshal. "You can come over here an' search the house. But you got to come alone."

Abe swung as a dour voice said, "You go over there an' he'll keep you a hostage until we all leave—and the gunfighter escapes again."

Joe Holden came strolling up from the rear of the barn, carrying a Winchester in the bend of one arm. He looked woodenly at Marshal Sutherland. "I told you what to do, Abe. You want that gunfighter? Tell Jeff we're goin' to fire his house with him an' his riders inside it."

Abe watched the range boss approach. It should not have surprised him that Joe had left the trees and come to the barn. He had seen Abe do it without being shot, which proved that he could also do it. Instead of taking Joe's advice, Abe told him to go out back, open the corral gates and chase all the horses out. He would do the same with the three or four horses stalled in the barn.

Joe stood motionless for a moment, then bobbed his head and turned back the way he had come. Abe cleared his pipes, expectorated, leaned to see the front of the house again, and remained like that until he could hear horses running. He then went down the south side of the barn where some horses were stalled, opened the doors and drove them out through the rear opening, where they could join the other loose animals.

Not a sound came from the main house. Even if the forted-up men down there could not see the loose animals being chased away from the yard, they could hear them. It was a safe bet there was some hair-raising profanity turning the air blue in the house.

Abe Sutherland returned to his place near the front of the barn to shout again. "Jeff! That's the first step. If you thought about playin' for time until dark so's you could

THE TAURUS GUN ■ 175

sneak out, you better think about how far you can get on foot before daylight and we ride you down."

"Damn it, Abe, I told you—he's not here!"

"Where is he?"

"I don't know."

"Jeff, I tracked him right to this yard."

"I don't give a damn. He's not here now. Come look for yourself."

Abe pulled back a big breath before calling out again. "Jeff, I got men all around you, in back of your house, and among the other buildings. I'm goin' to give you ten minutes to walk out into the yard, then I'm goin' to signal for the fires to start. If you come out after that, we're goin' to shoot every damned one of you. . . . Ten minutes!"

Joe Holden returned from out back. He was smiling bleakly as he took a position where he could also see the front of the main house. From the corner of his mouth he said, "I'll go get some of the men and get them ready to start burning."

"You stay right where you are," growled the marshal. He glared at the range boss. "Instead of helpin'," he said, "you're makin this harder."

Joe did not respond. He was watching the front of the house. As the period of time wound down, he shifted his carbine to both hands and held it loosely.

A voice sounded loudly from the house. "I'm comin' out. Abe, did you hear me? I'm coming out."

Abe replied. "Come ahead. Walk toward the barn. Leave your weapons behind."

"You damned sure your men back a ways know I'm comin' out unarmed?"

Abe swore. "Damn you, Jeff. Just walk out of there. Quit stalling and start walking. No one's going to shoot at you."

The silence returned, thick enough now to cut with a knife. Men who were a fair distance from the yard had heard the shouting back and forth. Not one of them moved nor made a sound.

Abe unshipped his six-gun and held it dangling at his side. If there was one thing he knew Jeff Demis was perfectly capable of, it was treachery.

But when the door opened under the veranda overhang, Jeff stepped out. Someone closed and barred the door behind him. Jeff was motionless for a long time, turning his head from side to side, perhaps looking for sunlight reflecting off an aimed Winchester.

"Walk!" Abe yelled.

Jeff finally left the porch and started in the direction of the barn.

He did not walk rapidly, and he continued to look left and right. When Marshal Sutherland thought he was close enough, he called out. "In the front of the barn."

Jeff obeyed. As soon as he stepped from sunlight to barn-gloom, he seemed enormously relieved. He saw Joe Holden holding his carbine in both hands and swung his gaze back to Marshal Sutherland. "You gave your word, Marshal."

Abe holstered his six-gun and gestured for the range boss to ground his saddlegun. He then jerked his head for Jeff to walk deeper inside the barn. As they went past, the range boss said something about continuing to watch the front of the house, and moved into the place Abe Sutherland had vacated.

He could hear every word Jeff Demis and the lawman said. Jeff made a fluttery gesture and repeated what he had said before. "He's not over at the house, an' I don't know where he is. When we got into the yard with those raggedy-pantsed town tramps hootin' an' yellin' behind us, Tom was not there." Jeff made a half-hearted gesture. "Maybe he's holed up in one of the outbuildings. Maybe the wagon shed or the smokehouse. Did you search for him?"

Joe interrupted without taking his eyes off the front of the house. "He's here, Jeff. That horse he stole in town, it was in the bunch I turned loose out back. I know that horse. He's one Mr. Burke sold to some feller in town. I remember when we broke him out at the ranch. . . . Jeff, your gunfighter wouldn't go off on foot, and he didn't have the time to do it any other way after the marshal got up here."

Abe eyed the cowman, who could have answered but who preferred to ignore what Joe had said. "I'll go with you, Abe. We'll search every damned outbuilding, every nook an' cranny. But you'll be wastin' time if he's on horseback headin' for the mountains. Once he gets up there, no one's goin' to find him unless it's an In'ian. You want to search the buildings?"

Abe shook his head. Jeff was too cooperative. "Get your riders out into the yard, Jeff. Tell them to do like you did—walk out bare, no guns. No hideouts stuck in their boots. Yell to them."

Jeff neither complied nor spoke as though he would. He said, "Where's my wife and kids?"

"Safe in town with Perc Hudson."

"Abe, you've gone 'way outside your authority, pickin' on me like this. I'll have the governor down on you."

Abe smiled. "All right. You do that. But right now, you call to those riders of yours and tell them to come out of the house—with no guns. *Do it!*"

Jeff walked partway back toward the opening, and probably would have walked even farther if Joe Holden hadn't slowly brought his Winchester up from the ground, and held it across his body with both hands, a thumb on the hammer, a finger inside the trigger guard.

Abe growled. "Call 'em out, Jeff!"

Jeff obeyed by cupping both hands and shouting. He had to repeat himself three times before the door opened down at the main house and his riders filed out, looking disgusted.

CHAPTER 21

Man to Man

WHILE Jeff Demis was up front watching his riders come down off the porch, Abe jerked his head at Joe, who walked back to where the lawman was standing, looking quizzical. The marshal lowered his voice. "He's in the house, sure as hell. I'll stay with you until we get his riders looked after, then you stay here and watch them while I go over to the house."

Joe said, "Alone?"

Abe had no chance to reply. Jeff was walking back from the front of the barn, followed by four crestfallen-looking rangemen. Joe stepped back, still holding his carbine in both hands, and watched as the marshal lined up the riders, had them raise their britches above their boot tops, and then empty the contents of their pockets into their hats.

He pointed to someone's outfit on the saddle pole. "Toss me that lariat, Joe."

Joe obliged, and moments later there was no question about whose rope Abe was cutting into short lengths. A hawk-faced, lean man glared as he said, "That rope cost me six bits, Marshal."

Abe gazed steadily at the lariat's owner as he pocketed his knife and said, "You first. Face down, with your arms behind you."

One of the remaining cowboys twisted his head toward Joe, who grinned at him. "I told you, Levi. Once at the saloon, and the last time on the range: Hiring on with someone like Jeff Demis was like stickin' your foot in a bear trap."

The cowboy faced forward without making a sound. Jeff had something to say, though, as Abe Sutherland finished tying another rider. "You're holdin' my woman an' kids against their will, Marshal. There's laws against that."

Abe beckonned for the third cowboy to lie face down. As he was being obeyed, he gazed at Jeff. "No one is holding Mary Ellen against her will. She was worried about the kids, so Perc Hudson took them back to town. You're a damned fool, Jeff, in a lot of ways—but mostly for hittin' her in the stomach."

Jeff straightened up. "Now, by gawd, you're goin' to mind my business for me, are you?"

Abe did not look up from his work on the prone man. "It's too late for that, Jeff. Someone should have done that long ago." Abe shoved up to his feet, looking steadily at the cowman. He had one length of the butchered catch-rope dangling from his left hand. "I'll tell you what I'd like to do—hit you in the gut the way you hit her. But instead, I'm going over to the house to smoke out your gunfighter."

Jeff blinked. Joe stepped up, took the length of rope from Abe, and pointed toward the ground with his Winchester barrel. Jeff went down, but stiffly, sullenly, with his jaw muscles rippling.

Abe waited until he too was tied, then he told Joe to go out front and signal for the distant town riders to come down to the yard. Joe grounded his Winchester and leaned on it, looking at the lawman. He began to wag his head. "Wait until they get here, then we'll both go over there."

Abe smiled slightly. "Joe, that son of a bitch made me look like a fool back in town. He owes me one for that."

Joe protested. "You're crazy. He's got guns over there. And he'll see you coming. Abe, it isn't necessary to do it this way. Let the riders from town get into the yard, then—"

The marshal jutted his jaw downward at the prone men, who were listening to every word. "If one of 'em gets raunchy, bust him over the head with your carbine."

Joe was still leaning on his rifle as Abe Sutherland hitched up his britches and walked toward the rear of the barn. He disappeared from sight back there, turning left in the direction of the bunkhouse, beyond which was the well house. Those two structures concealed him from the view of anyone watching at the main house. But after he passed the well house, there was an open area of about sixty or seventy feet. Beyond that was the Demis ranch house.

A horse whinnied from the open country behind the barn. He was the only one who had returned. It would have been a safe bet to wager that he belonged to one of Demis's children, was a pet.

Abe reached the rear of the bunkhouse, where there was a small overhang above a washstand and towel rack. He paused there, studying the well house. It was no larger than an outhouse. He walked across to it, and leaned against the warm rear wall. From this point to the northwest corner of the long, shaded porch of the main house there was nothing. Not even a shade tree.

He pulled out a blue bandanna and mopped his face and neck, stuffed it back into his hip pocket, and glanced back in the direction of the barn. Joe Holden was standing there like a statue. Abe raised an arm in a casual wave, then moved to the southernmost corner of the well house, took off his hat, sank to one knee, and eased half his face around with just one eye showing.

The main house looked deserted. If it was empty, Abe was going to look like a fool twice in the same day. He leaned back and dropped the hat back atop his head.

He could have called to the gunfighter as he had done with Jeff Demis. But if he had, and if the gunfighter was in there, a yell would not only warn the gunfighter, it would also tell him where Abe was.

He had nothing to say to the gunfighter, anyway. He settled his back against the warm wood and gazed westward in the direction of the stand of pines where he had met Joe. There were some loose saddle animals out there in the middle distance. They were picking grass and grazing along as they did it, like a band of old cows.

If he sprinted, he might make it. And he might not. Tom Grant was not likely to miss a target. Even if he zigzagged, Grant would probably nail him. Moreover, he wanted to get up alongside the house without Grant knowing he was being stalked, but Abe had no illusions. His chance of walking away from a stand-up, face-to-face meeting with Grant was one out of a bucketful. A big bucketful. Abe was good enough with six-guns to qualify as perhaps a shade better than average, but a professional gunfighter was a lot more than average.

That would not come close to making Abe a match for the gunfighter. He would need every trick in the book just to be able to crawl away from what he was going to do. He knew the tricks, but that kind of information would be satisfactory only if he survived. Dead lawmen couldn't exult.

He heard the sound of riders around in front of the well house—Joe's friends from Buckhorn. Abe stood up and flexed his knees as it occurred to him that the riders might provide the diversion he badly needed.

If Grant was watching the town riders enter the yard, maybe to count them, maybe for some other reason, Abe might be able to make his dash.

He got his diversion but when it came, he nearly jumped out of his boots. Someone behind him fired a carbine. The noise was so abrupt and unexpected, Abe swung around looking for the shooter, and wasted five seconds. He saw him: the shadowy figure of Joe Holden out behind the barn, lowering a smoking Winchester from his shoulder.

Abe heard window glass shatter as he lunged forward and ran harder than he had run in years.

No one shot at him. He flattened against the house, looking back. Joe was standing in sunlight behind the barn, grinning like an idiot. He waved, and Abe shook his head as he turned to go down the side of the house.

Out back, there was only half a covered porch. It sheltered the back door and a yard or two on both sides of it, otherwise there was no shelter and only two windows, both small, both well above the reach of the average man.

There was a tangle of vegetable rows and flourishing weeds inside a stake fence. Whoever had planted the vegetables had not weeded them lately, if at all, and because the ground had been properly prepared before seeding with wheelbarrow-loads of corral dust and more solid matter from the barn, the weeds formed a very dense thicket of interlaced stalks and limbs which were more than waist-high.

Otherwise, there was little of interest back there. Someone had stretched an old lariat for a clothesline: the bathhouse formed one anchor for the rope while the southeast corner of the main house formed the other anchor.

Abe was interested first in the door, then the high little windows. He was not sure that he would be able to squeeze through the windows, even if he could find something to stand on while he was trying to open them.

That left the door. It was handmade of very rough slab-wood, and was probably three inches thick. It was certainly barred from the inside. He edged along the back of the house from the west, where there were no windows. Once he was close enough to examine the door, he was not sure he could shoot it off its hinges. They too were handmade; someone had fashioned them over an anvil. Abe guessed they had been formed out of two thick steel straps, the kind used on the running gear of wagons.

He had no intention of trying to shoot that door loose from the wall, and getting inside through one of those little windows would be next to impossible. It would also be very risky. If the gunfighter heard him and came out, or even poked his head past the other little window, Abe would be balancing on something like a box with both hands raised to the sill. It would be hard to imagine a better target.

He considered the farthest corner of the rear wall, and edged toward it. He was very careful not to make any noise. When he reached the little windows, he discovered that he hardly had to bend down at all to pass beneath them.

There was an occasional sound from the yard, probably down by the barn, and if Abe could hear it, so could the man inside the house. Hopefully, he would be watching in that direction. He had reason to, after Joe Holden had shot out the big front window.

After reaching the southeast corner of the house, Abe paused to look back. He had made no noise, but there was always the possibility that the gunfighter might become uneasy and want to look out the back door.

Abe eased around the corner to avoid being caught like that. The front porch and overhang continued on the east side of the house. There were two old chairs near the door leading from the kitchen to the porch, and a wall washrack, complete with roller towel and chunk of lye soap.

Abe concentrated on the door. Getting to it across the porch planking required him to move one step at a time and to stay as close to the house wall as he could, because there was less chance of a plank squeaking at the wall than away from it.

This wall had no windows. He flattened against the house, approaching the door very carefully. His concentration was broken by two men calling back and forth from around front, probably down by the barn. He halted, drew his weapon, cocked it, and held it high. With his left hand, he gripped the door latch and slowly squeezed. Barred doors had a scantling bolted to them on the inside. At the opposite end, the scantling had a bent nail or a screw eye, imbedded to which was attached a length of cotton rope. Squeezing the latch raised the rope which in turn raised the piece of wood which was resting in a U-shaped piece of steel. A hard squeeze would yank the scantling high and make a noise. Abe increased his pressure on the latch until he felt the weight of wood on the cotton rope. He only wanted to raise the scantling high enough to clear its hanger.

He squeezed gently, felt the *tranca* rise, and squeezed a little harder, holding his breath because he expected it to stop moving when it reached the bolt—but it did not stop. Whoever should have dropped the locking bolt into place had not done so.

He had discovered how to enter the house.

He squeezed until he knew the door-bar was well above the hanger, then pushed very gently to make the door swing inward. As it swung, he very gradually let the scantling down. It required more time to do this than it had taken to raise it, and Abe was sweating like a stud wood tick before there was slack in the cotton rope as the scantling went as low as it would go.

His heart was hammering as he pushed the door farther inward. If Tom Grant was in the kitchen and had seen what was happening at the doorway, he would be waiting with a cocked gun.

Abe paused when the door was open enough for him to squeeze through sideways, got belly-down on the porch and eased his head and gun hand around the base of the door.

The kitchen was empty. It smelled faintly of greasy cooking. He got back upright, took two very careful steps inside and halted, cocked gun poised. He could see into the parlor where the torn blanket which had been hanging over the shot-out window kept full daylight from entering.

There was not a sound inside the house or out in the yard. For a fleeting moment, Abe thought Grant had made him look bad again; there was nothing to indicate that he was in the house. Possibly Jeff Demis had told the truth. But that was nothing a man would bet his life on.

In the yard there was the abrupt sound of a stalled horse kicking wood, followed almost immediately by someone's profanity and someone else's irritable shout for the swearing man to take his damned horse out back and put him in a corral where it could kick to its heart's satisfaction.

Abe used the corner of this ruckus to cross the kitchen soundlessly and hover just inside the doorway leading to the parlor. Then he saw Grant. The episode with the horse had drawn the gunfighter from over by the barred front door to a torn place in the window-blanket. He moved on the balls of his feet. Something had caught and held his attention, and it had not been the kicking horse, because he had been tense, crouched and waiting before that.

In his right hand, he was holding one of the guns a Demis rider had left behind when he had walked out of the house. It was a typical rangeman's weapon—all the bluing had been worn off long ago. As the gunfighter inched toward the torn blanket and raised the gun, Abe could see bruised steel on the butt plate where someone had used the gun for a hammer.

Winchesters were placed strategically around the room, and Grant had another six-gun, as old and scarred as the first one, shoved into his elegantly hand-carved holster. That old gun looked ludicrously out of place in the handsome holster made for the gunfighter's superior weapon—which was on Sutherland's desk down in Buckhorn.

The gunfighter leaned to peer out through a rip in the blanket. His thick, powerful body was exposed in back to Abe Sutherland and the lawman knew what most lawmen, in fact most men of any kind who had reason to, would do. They would not risk their lives, they would shoot the gunfighter in the back.

CHAPTER 22

An Afternoon to Remember

GRANT was motionless and tense, watching something beyond the torn blanket, or at least trying to locate something. He moved only his head, his gun hand poised to flash downward. He was totally engrossed in what he was doing. Abe loosened a little and lowered his gun hand.

The gunfighter remained in his coiled-spring crouch as he began to maneuver his handgun to the left, in the direction of the door. Abe had thought Grant was watching something farther away, perhaps down by the barn. He wasn't, he was straining to see something to his left that had his full attention, perhaps down at the same northwest corner of the house Abe had reached in his spring from the well house.

Instead of feeling annoyed, Abe felt resigned; he was sure he knew who the gunfighter had caught a glimpse of: that darned fool, Joe Holden.

Abe could have easily been mistaken. There were a number of men in the yard down by the barn or inside it, and there was always one damned fool—or hero, depending on how things turned out—in any crowd.

The marshal's heart was beating normally, most of his tightness had dissolved. He thought he had an edge because no matter how fast the gunfighter might whirl, Abe already had his weapon aimed and cocked. He took down a shallow breath and without raising his voice, said, *"Grant!"*

He expected a second of astonishment to root the gunfighter to the floor before he whirled. But Tom Grant did not recoil in surprise or whirl, he folded both knees and hit the floor rolling. Abe fired. The slug made the torn blanket whirl and writhe as the bullet passed through it. Grant was not there.

Abe's breath choked in his throat as he hunched his shoulders and swung the gun toward the big man, who was as agile as a cat the way he rolled and twisted. Grant fired in the direction of the kitchen doorway while he was twisting to get both legs beneath him. The bullet missed Abe's body by no more than an inch; it tore through his clothing, making him shift one foot to maintain his balance.

While he was staggering to the left, Grant dropped the hammer over his second shot. This time, the bullet went to the right and splintered the distant rear door, slamming it resoundingly closed under the impact.

Abe hauled back the dog for his next shot, but the gunfighter was already lurching to his knees. He was motionless, correcting his aim as Abe tried frantically to beat him to the shot.

A thunderously loud handgun explosion coming from the direction of the shattered front window distracted Abe for a second. He saw the gun and the man behind it where the ragged blanket had been savagely torn aside.

The gunfighter was hit while he was still on his knees. If he had not been as thick and massive as he was, and if he had been off balance, the impact would have punched him sideways. Instead of sagging or falling, he swung his weapon so quickly Abe never afterwards was able to recall seeing it move. Grant fired twice very fast, so fast, in fact, the explosions appeared as one prolonged detonation.

Joe Holden was already lunging desperately sideways. Niether bullet hit him; they went speeding in the direction of the barn, instead.

Abe had his finger inside the guard, retracting, when Tom Grant dropped his gun, put a hand to his side and fell.

Abe's reflex was not up to it. He could not free his finger from around the trigger in time, but he could tilt the gun barrel so that when he fired the slug tore into the wall behind the gunfighter, about eighteen inches above him.

Abe's ears were ringing. Black-powder smoke made visibility difficult in the parlor, which had already been gloomy. He let the gun hang at his side as he gazed at Tom Grant. There was a thin streak of blood seeping from beneath him.

Abe shuddered, put up his weapon, and walked forward to kick Grant's gun skiddingly across the room. He stood gazing at the large, inert man whose shirt and trousers were torn, soiled and rumpled, and whose elegant, handmade boots were scuffed and lusterless.

Men were yelling down at the barn, but when Abe Sutherland walked over to tear down the remnants of the blanket, there was not a soul in sight. He assumed that at the first gunshot they had all fled deep into the barn.

As he leaned to look past the glassless window frame a dry voice said, "I couldn't have, Abe. I couldn't have beat him."

Abe looked out where Joe Holden was sitting, legs pushed straight out. "Are you hurt?" he asked.

"Yeah. But not by a bullet. I twisted the hell out of my ankle."

"Can you stand up?"

Joe levered his body around until he could use both hands to hoist himself upright while leaning on the front wall of the house. He was in bad pain, so when he spoke the words came through clenched teeth.

"Is he dead?"

Abe glanced over his shoulder before answering, then turned back toward the room. "I don't know. But he got hit. There's blood under him."

"Unbar the door, will you? I can't climb through that busted window."

Abe opened the door and stood aside as the range boss hobbled into the parlor, caught hold of the back of a chair, and pushed it ahead as he approached the gunfighter. He squinted, then wagged his head. "He ain't dead, Abe. Look, his blood's still pumping out."

Joe could not release his grip on the chair, but he was able to use one hand to help the marshal roll Tom Grant over and straighten his limbs. The bullet had not penetrated, it had been diverted by a rib and had gone around beneath the skin to emerge in back, leaving a ragged hole where it had exited. The two men scanned the nearest wall. There was a large, jagged hole in the wood.

Abe pulled down a big breath and let it out noisily. He stood gazing at the large man lying in blood at his feet. After a moment he said, "I don't think anyone could have beat him. Hell, Joe, I was aiming straight at him from no more'n fifteen feet for my first shot—and I missed."

Joe leaned on his chair eyeing the gunfighter. "You want to save the son of a bitch, Abe? He's goin' to bleed to death." He raised smoldering eyes to the lawman's face. "As far as I'm concerned, I'd just as soon turn my back and walk out of here."

Abe made no comment as he sank to one knee and lifted away the expensive, torn, blood-soaked shirt to examine the wound. "Get a rag or a towel or something, Joe."

Pushing the chair ahead of him for support, Joe found two greasy dishtowels in the kitchen and tossed them to Abe, who wadded one up as a compress and wrapped the second one around the wound. He cinched it so tightly, the unconscious man started having difficulty pulling in air.

Joe said sourly, 'He'll never make it to town."

Abe stood up, wiping blood on his trousers. "I'll go down to the barn and have 'em hitch a team to a wagon. He'll make it, Joe."

"What's the sense of this? They'll hang him anyway for what he did to Jack Waite and Mr. Burke. Probably McElroy too."

Abe turned toward the range boss, his face ashen but resolute. "Maybe. But you an' I aren't goin' to just walk away."

Joe was looking down again as he said, "I'll go tell them to hitch up a wagon."

"You can't do it on one leg. I'll go."

"The hell I can't," growled the range boss. He pushed the chair to the door and beyond it out onto the porch.

Abe picked up the gun he had kicked away from Grant. It had been shot out. He hefted it in his right palm while inspecting it—and the truth of what had happened hit him hard. The old gun, which had been used as a hammer, had also been used as a pry-bar at some time in its rough life. Abe raised it high and squinted down toward the front sight. The barrel was crooked.

This accounted for the gunfighter's faulty aim, twice, when he had fired at Abe in the kitchen doorway. He shoved the gun into his waistband and went back to the kitchen to the water bucket, drank deeply from the dipper, and returned to the parlor with a wet cloth to wipe dirt off the unconscious man's face. Grant did not move nor make a sound, except to struggle weakly as he pulled in breath.

One of the town riders came to the door looking in, his expression dour. It was the town blacksmith, English. Two more townsmen pushed up to stare at the overturned furniture, the large, inert man lying in blood, and at the marshal, who ignored them as he arose to toss the wet cloth aside.

English said, "Well, that was the dumbest damned thing you'll ever do, Marshal, stalkin' him until you two was face to face. He's dead ain't he?"

"No," Abe replied, still without facing the doorway.

"Too bad," the cantankerous blacksmith growled, and moved away so the other men crowding up onto the porch could look inside.

Buster Munzer shouldered his way into the room, looked long at the gunfighter, at the wreckage, and finally at Marshal Sutherland as he said, "Abe, which one of you shot a couple of times out the window?"

Abe jutted his jaw downward. "Him. Why?"

Buster looked enormously relieved. "Because one of those shots splintered the north log of the barn doorway—and the other one went through Demis's head from front to rear."

Abe turned. The bar owner returned the steady stare he was getting without adding another word.

Someone down at the barn was yelling irritably for the men on the porch to come back down and help hitch a team to the wagon. The horses had had to be caught first, then led back to be harnessed. It took time, and the men who had done it were annoyed by the lack of help they got from the men whose curiosity had made them remain in the doorway, staring at the downed gunfighter.

Abe called three men by name. They waited until Abe had found a blanket in a bedroom, then they helped him lift the gunfighter onto the blanket. Each one grasped a corner of the blanket and carried the unconscious man out of the house. His bandage was soaked through. When they placed him on some straw in the bed of the wagon, Marshal Sutherland climbed up to twist the towels as hard as he could before rebandaging the gunfighter. Up front, there were now too many hands helping with the team, and that caused more acrimonious profanity.

Finally, the men returned to the barn to bring out the dead man. Abe remained on his knees in the wagon straw, watching as Jeff Demis was placed beside his hired gunman. Death for Jeff had been instantaneous. There was very little blood, even in the back of his head where the exiting slug had taken some bone with it.

Buster found an old, stained wagon canvas in the barn and brought it out to throw over the dead man. The sun was departing, but both the heat and the visibility remained strong.

George Dunhill, whom Abe had not noticed before among the riders from town, came from the house with a blanket. When his eyes met those of Abe Sutherland, Dunhill did not say a word. He simply leaned over the wagon side to help arrange the blanket over Tom Grant.

It would be some time before Dunhill would be talkative again. He would never again join a posse with the exuberance and adventuresome spirit he had shown the first time he had ridden out.

The riders swung up and headed southward from the yard, past the Demis house with its bloody floor, riddled walls and broken furniture, riding loosely, and in the same disorder they had exhibited when they had ridden out of town.

There was some conversation, but there were also long periods of silence. Marshal Sutherland and Joe Holden rode on either side of the wagon. Later, with dusk on the way and the rooftops of Buckhorn in sight, Joe reined over to Abe's side and leaned slightly as he quietly said. "Who tells Miz' Demis and her kids?"

Abe had already considered that. "I expect Perc will. We'll pull up there, out back in the alley and unload. . . . Unless you got a better idea."

Joe did not have a better idea. In fact, he'd had no idea at all—which was why he had asked the question. He had removed the boot from his badly swollen ankle. It was bouncing along, tied on the right side of his saddle.

Every step his horse took caused pain, but Joe had a stoic streak, which was just as well because unless he'd wanted to ride in the wagon with its corpse and its bloody straw, he would have to sit the saddle and grit his teeth.

By the time they reached town, there were lights showing from windows, and darkness settling everywhere else. As Abe had said, they went down the west alley and halted beyond Doctor Hudson's rickety old picket fence with its long-gone gate, leaving a hole for Abe to pass through on his way toward the rear of the house.

The town riders drifted away. Joe bleakly watched them

go. Within an hour, Buster's saloon would be a beehive of shouting men offering to recite instances of their valor out at the Demis ranch.

Doctor Hudson returned with Marshal Sutherland. He was pulling a napkin from his collar as he walked through the gate hole and leaned on the side of the wagon.

No one said a word. Hudson lowered the tailgate with a noisy rattling of chain, climbed in and lifted the canvas briefly to look at Jeff Demis, dropped it, and turned his back as he leaned down to roll back the blanket over the gunfighter. He had to lean very close in the gathering night, and finally straightened back as he said, "I can't see anything out here. Carry him into the shed and put him on the table."

Joe's brows shot up. "Where's Mr. Burke? He didn't—"

"No, he didn't die," snapped Hudson, who was helping to hold the gunfighter's blanket—Tom Grant weighed over two hundred pounds. "Mary Ellen and I got him into a bed in the house. . . . Joe, lend a hand."

Abe moved in to assist. "He can't. He's got a sprained ankle."

They had to leave the shed door open for light enough to see the table by, and if it had not been painted white they would have had to light a lamp, which was done anyway, after the gunfighter was stretched out.

Hudson hung the light directly above the table and frowned. "He hasn't regained consciousness since he was shot?"

Joe shook his head. "Nope. Does that mean he won't make it?"

Abe bumped the range boss to catch his attention. "Come with me. You can drive the wagon down to the livery barn. We got some horses to look after."

As the two of them passed through the gateless opening, Joe stopped limping long enough to say, "You hungry? It's been a hell of a time since breakfast. I hope the café man's still got his store open."

Abe was not hungry, but he certainly could use a long pull off that bottle he kept in a bottom drawer of his desk at the jailhouse.

CHAPTER 23

Perc Hudson's Secret

THE following morning, several people came by the jail-house. Every man who walked in had been at the Demis place the previous day. They wanted to talk, so Abe listened. The only thing he had no knowledge of was what the town riders had been doing once they reached the Demis's yard. All but Joe had wanted to remain inside the barn, except for an occasional peek southward after Joe told them where the marshal had gone.

Each man said the same thing about Jeff Demis: He took a position up near the front barn opening where he could see the house, and he did not budge, not even after the gunfire erupted. The wild shot that had killed him had frozen the men deeper in the barn. They saw him fall, saw the back of his head, and would not go up there to see if he should be dragged deeper into the barn or not.

It was the consensus that the reason Jeff had refused to leave the front barn opening after he knew Marshal Suther-land was heading for the house was because he knew his gunfighter was in there and he did not want to miss anything when Abe Sutherland met Tom Grant.

When the traffic through his doorway thinned out along toward noon, then stopped altogether, Abe got a cup of hot java from the stove and took it back with him to the desk. He had Jeff's riders in his cells. They had been herded back to town like genuine outlaws by the townsmen.

Abe leaned back, holding his coffee cup. There was no charge he could use to hold those rangemen, nor was he

195

inclined to hold them. They had done nothing; had not been able to do anything. Working for Jeff Demis was not a crime. As far as Abe knew, none of those men had been involved in Jeff's underhanded schemes.

Bob Cheney and Joe Holden came in out of the sunshine. Joe had his foot and ankle bandaged. Because it looked to Abe like a professional job, he asked if Perc Hudson had done it. Joe hitched his crutch around to sit down as he nodded his head. "Yeah."

Bob Cheney went to the wall bunk to sit. He sat gazing at the large bandage as he said, "He's got a little busted bone in there. Otherwise it's swollen ligiments an' muscles and all." Bob paused to raise his head. "Mr. Burke teased him, said Joe's the first man he ever heard of who went up against a gunfighter and come away with a sprained ankle."

Abe nodded. "He's got a point. How is the old devil?"

Bob looked at Joe, who answered. "I've worked for him a long time, Abe. He's smelled of sweat and manure and hoof parings. Sometimes of burnt food and whiskey, but so help me Hannah, he never smelled pretty before."

Abe waited for more and when Joe did not offer it, Bob Cheney did. "It's Miz' Demis. She figured to give Mr. Burke a bath."

Abe's brows climbed. "An all-over bath?"

"Yeah. That was what she was fixing to do."

Abe's brows were still raised. "And Henry . . .?"

"She had to call the doctor in. Henry was goin' to get out of that bed, find his pants and leave."

Joe Holden nodded while gazing at his outstretched leg with the huge bandage on it. "Perc had to give him something to make him sleepy. He was fit to be tied, an' you know Mr. Burke when he gets his dander up. Scairt that poor woman half to death."

Abe leaned on the desk. "Did he hurt himself going through all that?"

Joe looked at Abe. "Naw. You can't hurt one of those old

rawhide and sinew mossbacks. But I guess it scairt hell out of Perc, too. He wouldn't let Miz' Demis go back in there until Mr. Burke rang his little bell and asked Perc to let her come back."

Abe nodded. "And he apologized."

Both Bob and Joe nodded their heads. "He said it was havin' to lie there while you'n the rest of us was smoking out Demis and his gunfighter—and—lettin' the ranch work go to hell—and a few other upsetting things. I guess Miz' Demis understood." Joe stopped speaking to regard his foot again for a few moments.

Abe guessed he knew what the range boss was thinking about and said, "What about her and her husband?"

Joe replied without looking away from the bandaged foot. "She took her little girl and the boy for a long ride in Perc's buggy. They haven't come back yet." Joe leaned to position his crutch for arising from the chair. "Perc'd like to talk to you when you get a little time." Joe stood, hunched around his crutch, and followed Bob out of the jailhouse office. At the door, he looked back and said, "I got to find about four men to go to work at the ranch. You got any ideas?"

"Try Buster and maybe down at the livery barn."

Those were places the range boss had already intended to visit. He nodded and walked out, leaving Bob to close the door after him.

Abe gazed at the door. He never had been told why they had said Henry smelled pretty. But he did not have to guess that Henry had needed an all-over bath.

He went to the café for some buckets of grub for his prisoners, listened to their angry clamoring, and left the jailhouse on his way up the opposite side of the road.

At the café he got a number of candid stares, but since all he did was nod back, no one started asking questions about what was uppermost in folks' mind: How had he known Tom Grant was in the house, and what would the outcome have been if Joe Holden hadn't sneaked over to the porch in time to fire through the broken window? The answers were simple enough. He hadn't *known* the gunfighter was in the house, he had *thought* he was in there. As for the other question, if Joe hadn't shot Tom Grant, either Grant would have missed again with that crooked-barreled gun, or he wouldn't have, and that was something people could speculate about until the cows came home.

Abe ate like a horse, left the café feeling ten pounds heavier and went up the road to see what the gunsmith had to say about that gun Abe had given him, the one Tom Grant had tried to kill him with.

The gunsmith had been one of the town riders. He and Sutherland had ridden together on the way back to town for a couple of miles, talking about the gunfighter. Abe had given him the gun at that time and the gunsmith had promised to vice-fire it this morning.

When the marshal entered the shop, the gunsmith was wearing his old, stained, oily apron again. He looked up from a cup of coffee, and smiled. " 'Morning, Marshal. Care for some hot java?"

Abe accepted, as he usually did, even though he'd already had enough coffee this morning to float a battleship.

The gunsmith wiped his oily hands on a cloth already saturated, and finished the drying process by running both hands down the front of his apron, as he regarded a six-gun lying on the counter. "He should have nailed you with that first shot, Marshal. The one that tore your shirt. He would have if he'd had his own gun, or at least almost any gun but that one. I'd guess after he saw the gun fired to the left he would have corrected his aim. But in a mess like that, things happen awful fast. A man don't have time to think much, he acts by instinct."

The gunsmith picked up the weapon and shook his head over it. "I get 'em like this all the time. Darned rangemen forget a hammer when they're patchin' a gate or something, and the first thing they think of is their gun. Look here on the butt; whoever owned this gun used it to pound nails and to break ice off troughs. They all do those things, but this here gun's been used to prize something. Maybe a stuck gate latch, or the wood off the top of a keg of horseshoes. Not once, Marshal." He handed Abe the old gun, wiped his hands down the front of his apron again, and went after the blueware coffeepot to refill both their cups. As he was putting the pot aside, he said, "Only way you could kill anything with that weapon would be by shoving the barrel right up against it." The gunsmith raised his cup, sipped, looked steadily at the marshal, then set the cup down. "Where was his personal gun?"

"In my desk drawer."

"Well, about all I can tell you is that you were awful damned lucky yesterday."

Abe finished his coffee, left the old gun on the counter to be picked up some other time, and walked back out into the dazzling sunlight. for a fact, luck had a lot to do with it, but that worked both ways. He should have killed Grant with his first shot, so Grant'd had a little luck too. The difference was that Grant's luck ran out too soon.

Over at Perc Hudson's place he visited Henry Burke in the small, immaculate room where he had been put up. Henry had been shaved. He looked clean too, but as Abe pulled up a chair to the bedside and sat down, he caught the aroma of lilacs. He knew Henry was watching him, so he kept a straight face as he said, "I guess by now Joe's told you everything."

Henry answered dryly. "Yeah. Him an' everyone else who's come prancin' through that door this morning. Have you talked to Perc?"

"No. That's why I came up here. Is he out on a call?"

"He's out back in the shed," Henry said, adding nothing to it as he looked steadily at the law officer. "There's somethin' I'd like to know, Abe."

"All right. If I got the answer."

"I'd like to know exactly where my range boss was when Jeff got shot through the head."

Abe met the older man's keen stare without difficulty. "I can tell you exactly where he was an' what he was doing—and Henry, Joe did not shoot Jeff in the head. He was trading bullets with Jeff's gunfighter. . . . Henry, the bullet that downed Jeff was supposed to hit Joe. Joe jumped sideways right after Grant shot through the window. He wasn't even facing in the direction of the barn. Grant fired twice, real fast. It was his second slug that angled past the south jamb of the barn opening and caught Jeff through the head." Abe paused, gazing at the old cowman. "Joe made a lot of war talk. I know that. But sometimes fate pulls strange tricks—like having the gunfighter Jeff hired kill his employer unintentionally." Abe arose, holding his hat at his side. "Joe didn't do it, the gunfighter did. But as far as Jeff's concerned, it don't matter who did it. Whether a man gets killed accidentally or on purpose, he's just as dead, isn't he?"

Henry made a very slight head-nod. "Just wanted to hear it from you, is all. . . . I guess Mary Ellen took it hard about Jeff."

Abe had not seen Mary Ellen, so he shrugged thick shoulders. "She's the kind that would, Henry. Even a miserable bastard like Jeff was. Anything I can do for you?"

"No. No, thanks. I'd just like to go home, but I expect it'll be a while yet. There's an awful lot of work waitin' at the ranch."

Abe went to the door before speaking again. He showed no expression at all as he said, "Henry, I got to tell you—you're the prettiest smellin' cowman I've ever come across."

Abe stepped out quickly and closed the door after himself. As he was turning toward the rear of the house, he could hear Henry's profanity.

When he reached the shed behind the house, he knocked lightly. Doctor Hudson opened the door looking irritable, motioned for Abe to enter, and shook his head.

Abe gazed at the large man on the white table. He was naked from the waist up and was either unconscious or had been put to sleep. He had been scrubbed and rebandaged. His color was faintly pink.

"He looks pretty good for what he's been through," the marshal said, and got a rueful, sidelong glance from the medical practitioner.

"Does he? Well, Abe, I'll bet good money I'm going to lose this one."

Abe continued to gaze at the man on the table. From what he had seen of Grant's wound yesterday, it had not looked genuinely serious. "The bullet didn't go in, Perc. But he lost a lot of blood."

Hudson approached the table. He looked tired. "The bullet didn't have to go in," he said quietly. "There is a broken rib and a pretty bad wound where it went around under the skin through the muscles before going out near his spine. . . . I don't think he lost too much blood, and as for the rest of it, he could be patched up. He wouldn't be able to go to any dances for a couple of months, or do any horseback riding."

"He's got good color, Perc."

Hudson nodded solemnly, looking at the gunfighter's slack features. "He does for a fact, doesn't he? Well, he wasn't as lucky as Henry was." Before continuing to speak, Doctor Hudson's gaze drifted to a corner of the room where someone had thrown some bloody towels. He brought his gaze back to the man on the table. "You think his color is good? That goes with blood poisoning, Abe. They look fine then they get redder. They sweat and shake and go out of their heads." He checked himself. "It's my lifelong enemy, Abe. Gangrene. Before I die I hope to gawd someone comes up with a way to halt it. Right now all we do is recognize the symptoms, and wait. Make it as easy for them as possible, and wait."

"Hell, Perc, he only got hurt yesterday."

Again Doctor Hudson's glance went to the filthy, bloody rags in the corner. "Once it takes hold," he said, "it can move pretty darned fast. In some cases. I've seen other cases where it took a lot longer to kill people. But not this time."

"Does he know?"

Hudson shook his head. "He comes and goes. When he's conscious for very long and feels the pain, I put him out again. There's damned little else I can do."

"How long will he last?"

Hudson raised his shoulders and let them drop. "I can't tell you, Abe, except to say that he'll be dead within a week."

Marshal Sutherland went to perch on the room's tall stool as he studied the gunfighter. "The Taurus Gun," he murmured.

Hudson nodded again. "Did you shoot him?"

". . . well, Joe Holden and I were both shooting at him. Joe hit him."

"Who bandaged him?"

"I did."

Hudson's gaze drifted back to the filthy red rags again, but he did not mention them. Maybe Joe had shot the gunfighter, but the person who had used old, greasy dishtowels to bandage him was the one who really killed him.

Doctor Hudson went to a table, groped behind a large formaldehyde bottle and brought forth a pony of brandy. He took a long pull and handed the bottle to Abe. While Abe was swallowing, Hudson gazed at the flushed face of the man on his white table, and wondered how many more secrets he was going to have to be the custodian of before he died or retired. If Abe Sutherland knew what he had done up there in the Demis parlor when he was actually trying to save a life, it would probably haunt him for as long as he lived.

Hudson took back the bottle, had another swallow, and returned it to its hiding place.

After Marshal Sutherland had left, Doctor Hudson gathered up the dirty, blood-soaked towels and took them to the stove, dropped them in it atop some kindling wood, and struck a match. With the fire went the evidence of what had put an end to the life of the Taurus Gun.

CHAPTER 24

Charges

ABE didn't see Joe Holden again for several days, but Bob Cheney was in town three days later and stopped by to say Joe'd only been able to find one rangeman who wanted to hire out. He also said Joe, with his wrecked ankle shoved through a blanket looped from the saddle horn, and the man he had hired in town, were starting to make a gather.

Abe was curious about Bob being in town if they were that shorthanded at the ranch but he said nothing. Bob cleared that up offhandedly.

"Mr. Burke told Joe to wait four days and send in a wagon full of straw for him." Bob smiled. "Joe knocked a day off, an' sent me in."

Abe wondered about the wisdom of this. "What does Perc say?"

"I don't know. I haven't been up there yet. Had some supplies to get and a few errands to run in town. I'll get up there directly."

After Bob had gone across to the emporium, Abe took his key ring down to the cells and herded the Demis riders up to his office where he stoically gave them back their belongings and stood gazing at them. He knew them, not very well, but he'd seen them to nod to.

A tall, bronzed man with sunburned, light brown hair finished filling his pockets and buckling his gun belt, then smiled at Marshal Sutherland. "No hard feelings. It was a damned mess right from the start when Jeff put me up yonder with his cattle in the foothills."

Abe nodded, still silent, and opened the door as he said, "Good luck."

They trooped out, hesitated in the dazzling sunlight, then headed for the café. Abe left the jailhouse about an hour later. He went around back and walked up the alley in the direction of Doctor Hudson's shed.

The Taurus Gun was dead. He had died night before last. There was no mourning, and until Abe could return to the Demis place and get the man's war bag, he would not know whether Grant had kin or not. And he might not even know then.

That tall, sun-darkened rangeman Abe had released with the other Demis riders was sitting on an upended round of red fir from someone's woodpile, and at first Abe did not see anyone else.

Jason Demis was sitting on the cowboy's far side. He did not see Marshal Sutherland right away. His head was low, both hands were draped on his knees, slack and limp. The boy's entire demeanor was one of listless indifference.

The rangeman pushed up off the round of fir as Abe Sutherland approached, dusted his seat, and waited. Jason Demis did not raise his head.

Abe nodded to the cowboy, studied the lanky lad, and threw a quizzical gaze at the cowboy, who said, "It's pretty hard on young fellers, Marshal."

Abe considered the youth. "How is your mother?" he asked, and got a husky reply without the youth even looking up. "She's all right. Betsy isn't, but maw's all right."

Abe was at a loss for words, so he addressed the cowboy. "Thought you'd be out of town by now."

"Naw. Not yet. Y'see, Jase and I been sort of partners. I been advisin' him on breakin' horses. He's goin' to make a tophand one of these days."

Abe considered the tall man. "Your name is Levi?"

The cowboy nodded. "An' that was my rope you cut up."

Abe remembered and nodded. "Come by the jailhouse before you leave. I got a fund for things like that."

Levi rubbed his stubbly chin. "Naw. That's all right. It was gettin' old anyway, would have busted one of these days."

Jason Demis was looking solemnly at Marshal Sutherland. He said, "I was sayin' to Levi—because we been partners—I can't figure out what I'd ought to feel. He was my paw."

The older men said nothing.

Jason lowered his head again. "I've seen him hit maw. One time when I yelled at him, he worked me over pretty good too. . . ."

Abe could feel for the lad. "But he was still your paw, eh?"

"Yes. . . . Marshal, I didn't even hurt when Doctor Hudson told us paw was dead. Shot through the head someway. Levi was just tellin' me how it happened."

Abe knew something about this sort of thing. "Jason, sometimes it never comes, and sometimes it hits folks while they're in bed at night, maybe, or riding out, or just sittin' somewhere. All at once. I heard a man once call it 'the pain of loss.' "

The boy raised his head. "You ever had it, Marshal?"

Abe felt the rangeman's tan eyes on him, and shifted his stance a little when he answered. "Yes. I was younger than you are. When my maw died was the first time. I was just comin' to grips with that a year or so later, and my paw died. Took me a while, Jason." Abe held a hand down, pulled the lad to his feet, and smiled at him. "There's nothin' anyone can tell you. Not the wisest man on earth. You got to weather this one yourself. Just let it happen, whatever it is, tears or something else. Don't bottle it up." He gave the lad a light clap on the shoulder and turned toward Levi. "Are you leaving?"

Levi saw Jason's eyes spring instantly to his face. He regarded Marshal Sutherland wryly and stroked his stubbly chin again. "I kind of had a notion to go back to Texas an' visit some kin I got down there for a while."

Now, finally, Jason Demis's eyes swam. "You never told me," he said in a tightly controlled voice.

"Well, Jase, I been on the Demis place two seasons now . . ."

"Levi, I was countin' on you. Maw'll make you range boss. We'll hire a new crew. . . . Gosh, Levi, this here is right in the middle of the workin' season."

Abe was watching them. He could see the cowboy's discomfort. He said, "They'll sure need someone to help them get those cattle back across the road an' out of the foothills."

Levi cocked an eye at the lawman. "Jeff homesteaded that land."

Abe nodded; this was not the time to start an argument. "Maybe. Even so, those cattle can't stay over there after the grass is gone, and who's goin' to help Jason here and maybe his maw get the animals back onto good feed?"

Levi fidgeted. He looked from Abe to Jason, then at the wood pile.

"Range boss on an outfit as big as the Demis place is a good job, Levi," Abe stated, looking steadily at the tall man. "And there's somethin' else. Men don't just up and run out on their partners."

Levi brought his wandering gaze back to Marshal Sutherland, and gazed steadily with his head barely cocked to one side, as though he thought there was something behind what the lawman was doing. There was.

The rider finally faced the gangling youth. "There's too much for you'n me to do, Jason. And the work'll commence piling up."

The marshal interrupted. "Hire more men." He hoped Levi would not ask him where to find them, because Joe Holden had been trying the same thing with absolutely minimal success. But the cowboy did not ask a question, he made a statement.

"All right, Jase, but it's goin' to be a darned hard pull unless we can find more riders."

Abe saw Levi watching him, and kept his face expressionless as he said, "You two better get to circulating around town if you're goin' to hire more men." He left them, and headed inside Perc Hudson's rickety back-alley fence, to the shed.

If it came down to real hardship, he could leave someone in charge of the jailhouse for a few days and help drive cattle himself. It'd been a while since Abe Sutherland'd done anything like that, but he knew how.

Come to think about it, he could dragoon three or four local men to lend a hand, also. They might even like the idea of getting away for a few days. The gunsmith, for one, and maybe old man English's son for another.

Perc Hudson was having coffee in the kitchen and opened the rear door when he heard someone out near the shed. He said, "Over here." Abe trooped to the door and into the kitchen, which was still too warm from a cooking fire. He dumped his hat on the floor beside the chair, and Doctor Hudson motioned toward the kitchen table as he went for a cup and the coffeepot.

"Mary Ellen and her girl back yet?"

"No." Hudson said no more until he had filled the cup at the stove and returned to the table with it. He made a rueful little smile as he shoved the cup in front of the lawman. "I'm a coffee drinker. Have been for years. The trouble is, I can't make a decent cup of the stuff. I've tried more in the pot, less in the pot, and it still don't come out very good. Then Mary Ellen showed me something."

Abe was gazing at the pot on the stove when he said, "Yeah. She taught you to wash the pot out real good after you emptied it."

Hudson's eyebrows humped in the middle like caterpillars. "She told you too?"

"No. I've been drinking java in your kitchen for quite a few years. Today's the first time I ever saw the pot sparkling clean."

Hudson placed both elbows on the table and studied his guest. Whatever his thoughts, he kept them private, and returned to their earlier topic. "She's always had a rough row to hoe. We've talked after supper when the kids was bedded down. . . . That mystic stuff—she's convinced about some of it."

Abe was looking into his cup as he said, "But you aren't." He was thinking of what she had said about the gunfighter refusing to eat poor food and about some other things about the Taurus Gun . . .

Hudson got cautious. "Well, no, I never really put a lot of faith in that stuff, Abe. In my profession, we're taught to deal only in observable facts."

Abe smiled to take some of the sting out of what he said. "Perc, I've been around doctors all my life. One thing I've noticed the good ones and bad ones got in common: if folks work up some different way of treating sickness, they call it quackery. I've seen some pretty impressive cures by non-doctors. I think what bothers doctors is that what they mean by quackery is in their view heresy, departure from what they hold to be absolutely right. Only *they* can be right."

Hudson cleared his throat. "More coffee?" he asked, to get clear of this subject, which was beginning to raise his blood pressure.

Abe laughed at him. "No thanks. I still got half a cup. How is Henry?"

Hudson leaned back down on the table. "When Mary Ellen's around, he's fine. When she's not around, he's grumpy, ornery, suspicious, and pig-headed."

"They're figuring on taking him back to the ranch. Bob Cheney's in town with a straw-filled wagon. He'll be here directly."

Doctor Hudson looked steadily across the table, his color rising. "Whose idea is this?"

Abe was not sure. "Henry's, I'd guess. No one who works for him would make a decision like that without his approval."

Hudson's fierce stare did not waver. "Abe, tell me something. Do you run across folks who know more about your job than you do?"

"All the time."

"Then you know how I feel right now. If someone moves Henry Burke, especially takes him on a long drive over bumpy ground in the back of a damned ranch wagon, they could very well cause him to bleed to death before he gets out there."

Abe nodded thoughtfully. He believed Perc Hudson. He also knew that convincing Henry Burke he should change his mind would be like convincing a big rock it shouldn't be where it was.

Abe had a sudden inspiration. "All right. Then they won't move him."

Hudson's brows shot up again. "Is that so? You know what Henry will say if you butt in and try to make him stay where he is for another week or two?"

"Yeah, I know. He'll tell me to go to hell."

Doctor Hudson bobbed his head. "Exactly."

"I've been told that so many times, I lost count long ago, and for the same reason. . . . I'm goin' to arrest Henry, and since he can't be moved to the jailhouse, I'll legally quarantine him to that room where he's lying right now."

Perc Hudson leaned back looking across the table. After a moment he laughed. "What charge?"

"I haven't thought of one yet. I got four law books on a shelf at my office. You never saw so many downright silly laws in your life. Some are good laws, but there are one hell of a lot that are not only unenforceable, but ridiculous. Don't worry. I'll find one."

"Then you better go arrest him right now," stated the medical practitioner, whose hearing was exemplary. He had heard boots clump across his front porch and was arising before Bob Cheney's gloved fist rattled the door.

Abe held up a hand, preceded the doctor from the kitchen

to the parlor, then to his right and into the room where Henry Burke was lying—fast asleep.

Hudson waited until the bedroom door closed before opening the one leading to his porch. Bob Cheney smiled at him, entered, and waited until the door had been closed, then said why he was there. Bob did not look very confident, nor did Doctor Hudson do anything to put him at ease. He jutted his jaw in the direction of the closed door and said, "I think he's sleeping. Whose idea is it to take him home in the back of a wagon?"

Bob Cheney's smile was beginning to look forced. "I expect it was his. Joe Holden sent me in for some supplies, and with a big bed of straw in the back of the rig to haul Mr. Burke home on. Doctor, I work for wages, an' do what I'm told."

Hudson nodded, and led the way to the closed door. When he opened it, Marshal Sutherland was standing at bedside. He had not yet awakened the old cowman, but now he did by leaning slightly and tapping Henry's cheek several times.

As Henry snuffled and moved slightly beneath the blanket, Abe and Bob exchanged a nod. Henry Burke's puffy eyes moved around, from man to man. Bob smiled at him. "Come to take you home, Mr. Burke. Joe'n I piled enough straw in the back of the wagon to—"

Abe interrupted. "I don't think so, Bob. He's got to stay in town."

Bob looked at the lawman, but old Henry's eyes were wide open and testy. "What d'you mean I got to stay in town?" he demanded. "I'm feelin' fine, and Bob'll drive careful."

Abe looked at the man in the bed. "Henry . . . you're under arrest."

It became so quiet in the little shadowy room when someone drove past who used chain harness instead of leather, it sounded almost as though the horses were in the room.

Henry reddened and moved both elbows to hoist himself upward. Perc Hudson, a large, heavy man, used gentle and unyielding pressure to make him lie flat.

Abe was gravely returning the older man's stare, and when Henry sputtered and swore as he asked the charge, Abe said, "For shooting up some stringers across the alley on the livery man's corral."

"What!"

". . . and for firing a firearm in the town's limits. There's an old ordinance against that. And—I got several more, Henry, but you heard enough. I can hold you."

Understanding came to Henry Burke, finally. His color remained high, but the look of baffled anger left his eyes. ". . . you can't do this, Abe. You're trumpin' those things up to keep me flat on my back here in—"

"Henry," exclaimed the big lawman. "I can do it. I just did it." He turned toward Bob Cheney and jerked his head in the direction of the door. As they left Doctor Hudson with his patient, and stood in the middle of the parlor's old threadbare carpet, Bob looked amused. "All right. He stays here. I didn't think it was a good idea, straw or no straw. But about those charges against him . . ."

"They'll be in force until Perc Hudson says you can come back for him. Maybe ten days."

"All right. And what'll I tell Joe?"

"Tell him I'm doing this to keep Henry alive. That's the only reason."

They went out to the front porch together where Bob eyed the patient-standing animals on the wagon, reset his hat to protect his eyes, turned and looked with twinkling eyes at Marshal Sutherland and said, "There's one other charge you could lay against him."

"What?"

"Moping with intent to grope."

Abe threw back his head and laughed. Bob joined him briefly, then struck out for the wagon. As he was driving away, he raised a gloved hand, still smiling.

CHAPTER 25

The Bad Ending to a Long Day

ABE was in his office after sundown. He had just completed arrangements with the town carpenter, who also sold coffins, to make a pine box Tom Grant's size, and to tell the local Baptist preacher to make arrangements for the burial. He was reaching for his hat when the door opened and Mary Ellen Demis walked in. Abe sighed under his breath, motioned toward a chair and reseated himself at his desk. If there was one damned fact a man learned early, once he'd made up his mind to be a lawman, it was that not even the best-intentioned folks on earth seemed to believe lawmen got empty stomachs like everyone else.

Mary Ellen was wearing black, and it occured to Abe that he probably had ought to be ashamed of himself for thinking this, her husband freshly dead and all, but she was a stunning woman, handsome enough to turn mens' heads, even in black.

He tried to make it easier for her, as he smiled gently and said, "How did Jase and Levi make out? Did they find any riders to hire?"

She did not know. She had just returned to town and put her daughter to bed at Perc Hudson's place before walking down to the jailhouse.

He told her what they had decided to do, and she nodded approval. It was a fact that the Demis outfit could not manage without riders. But she had not come down here to talk about that. She considered the untidy desk and only raised her eyes to Abe's face as she began to speak.

"There are so many things to do. Henry knows about Jeff's deceit in gaining title to the foothill range."

Abe nodded and clasped both his hands atop the desk.

"I just never did the letter-writing and bookkeeping. Jeff took care of those things. He used to say a woman's place was minding her children and her house. He took care of everything else."

Abe had an abrupt thought. "I'll tell you who can help you."

"Who?"

"Henry Burke. He's been doing his own work like that most of his life."

Mary Ellen smoothed her skirt and afterward gazed at the old iron wood stove. "Yes. He's offered to. He's offered to help us with all of it—the cattle, the managing . . ."

"Something wrong with that, Mary Ellen?"

". . . I don't know, Marshal. Maybe not, except that I've lived in this area a long time. I know how people talk . . ."

Abe was gazing out front at the fogged-over window of the café as he replied. "They'll always talk. Mary Ellen. If it's not about me, or you, or Henry, or Perc Hudson, it's someone else. There's nothing anyone can do about that." He brought his eyes back to her face, paused for the length of a couple of heartbeats to observe again what a handsome woman she was, then got back to the topic. "Mary Ellen, Henry's been single a long time." He paused to frame the rest of it the way he wanted it to sound. "You got a big ranch and two kids to look after, and no one to help you do any of it. I don't see much grounds for gossip, and I sure don't want to hear any about you an' Henry."

She smiled in his direction. "He is very fond of you."

Abe considered his large clasped hands. "An' I'm fond of him, but he's a lot more fond of you than he is of me—and to be downright truthful, I don't blame him."

"That," she said, "is the problem."

"Why?"

"I am very fond of Henry, Marshal. But I have two children to think about. Do you understand? I can't have him riding over and spending time with me—so soon."

Abe returned to eyeing his clasped hands. "He's not goin' to be able to ride over, or even drive over, and spend time with you for a while. He's goin' to stay right here in town. . . . Have you talked to him since you got back to town?"

"No. He was sleeping when I looked in on him. Why? Is there a complication—is he ailing, Marshal?"

'No. Nothing like that. I put him under arrest today so's he can't leave town until Perc says he can. He was madder than a hornet. I kind of doubt he's very fond of me right now. Anyway, I don't know about your little girl, but I listened to Jason today. He's confused and upset, but I don't think you'll have any trouble about him acceptin' Henry. Mary Ellen, I don't know a blamed thing about children, especially half-grown ones, but I'll take a chance and tell you I think Henry'll make about as good a paw to your kids as there is around."

When he looked at her, she was staring at him with color in her face. "Did he tell you that?"

"No ma'am. We didn't discuss you or the kids."

"But those are almost the exact words he said to me last night."

Abe was momentarily at a loss. "Well . . . I believe them. And I know Henry Burke pretty well. He's an honest, sincere man—maybe with a little age on him—an' maybe on rare occasions likely to get mad, like when you figured he needed an all-over bath, but otherwise . . . well, you can always look at it like it's strictly a business arrangement, him helpin' you run your ranch, and let the rest of it take care of itself."

She sat for a time in thoughtful silence, then arose as she spoke. "I'm sorry you were put to so much trouble and danger and all, Marshal."

He arose behind the desk. Over her shoulder he saw the light blink out over at the café.

"Marshal?"

". . . yes'm."

"I hope it works out the way we've been saying. I think it would be good for me, for the children, and I'm perfectly willing to see that it works out well for Henry. . . . I'm sorry I took up so much of your time tonight."

He smiled all the way around the desk to the roadside door, which he held open for her to pass through. When they faced each other from the roadway, she smiled at him and walked northward in the direction of the Hudson place.

Abe stood for a moment in his doorway, gazing over at the dark café window. Maybe, if he hurried, the landlady up at the rooming house might have something left over from supper. He rarely ate up there, and the landlady made it a particular point to let her roomers know that she did not run a boardinghouse, just a rooming house.

But on occasion she had fed Marshal Sutherland. If she too had retired, it was going to be a long haul until the café opened again.

He went back inside, checked everything, set the damper in its closed position on the stove, blew out the lamp, and was returning toward the roadway when a tall, graying, older man appeared. Without heeding the obvious fact that the jailhouse was being closed for the night, the graying man said, "Marshal, that feller who got hisself killed out at the Demis place . . ."

Abe blocked the darkened office by filling the doorway. "What about him?"

"It was my horse he stole. I'd like to know where it is and how I get it back."

"It's up at the Demis place. In a few days I'll bring it back to town to you. Right now, I'm in kind of a hurry."

The graying man watched Marshal Sutherland padlock his door from the roadside, and spoke again in the same unhurried tone of voice. "I got that horse from Henry Burke. Give eleven dollars hard cash for him. I'm right fond of him."

Abe was pocketing the big brass key and already moving away when he said, "Like I told you, I'll bring him back first chance I get. An' don't worry, he's up to his hocks in good feed at the Demis place. . . . I got to hurry along."

He widened his stride, set as his beacon the yellowing light showing alongside the rooming house from the rear, where the kitchen was. He was covering a lot of ground when the kitchen light, like the café man's light earlier, simply blinked out.

If he had been able to get across the road to the café before its proprietor finished locking up for the night, he probably could have cajoled him into unlocking the door for the town marshal. But he had not been able to put that to a test, and now the rooming house kitchen was also dark, and up there, he knew as surely as he knew his own name, that if he rattled the landlady's door to plead for something to take the pleats out of his stomach, she would turn the air blue. She was the widow of a teamster, the daughter of an overland freighter. If there were a cuss word she did not know, it was in Chinese. No one in Sutherland's experience could string together profanity like she could.

He reached the porch and halted to turn, looking for a light. All the buildings along Main Street were dark. The only lighted lamps were down at the livery barn, one on each side of the front opening.

He was going to go to bed hungry.

If you have enjoyed this book and would like to receive details of other Walker Western titles, please write to:

Western Editor
Walker and Company
720 Fifth Avenue
New York, NY 10019